CRIMSON STORM

ALSO BY DAVID DELEE

Brice Bannon Seacoast Adventures
Crimson Storm
Siege at Tiamat Bluff
The Yakuza Gambit
Strike of the Stingray
The Oceanic Princess
Facing the Storm

Nick Lafferty Crime Thrillers
Cold Cases
Out of the Game
Crystal White

Flynn & Levy Police Thrillers
Between Truth and Lies
While the City Burns
Moral Misconduct

Grace deHaviland Bounty Hunter Series
Too Far
Stare at the Moon
Takedown
With Intent to Deceive
Pin Money
Fatal Destiny
Runners

CRIMSON STORM

A BRICE BANNON
SEACOAST ADVENTURE

DAVID DELEE

COPYRIGHT

For more information about new releases, special events, and exclusive content only available to subscribers, sign up to get David DeLee's newsletter.

https://www.subscribepage.com/daviddelee

Thank you for purchasing this book.
We hope you enjoy it.

Semper Paratus
"Always Ready"

CRIMSON STORM

"Red sky at night, sailor's delight.
Red sky in morning, sailor's warning."
— Old mariner's adage

CHAPTER ONE

Gulf of Maine - North Atlantic Ocean
43°8'0.942" N - 68°19'35.904" W

PAINTED COAST GUARD RED with a white stripe around the tail, the Sikorsky MH-65c Dolphin helicopter sped through the night sky. The rotors beat the air with a deep, thrumming intensity. They flew low over the surface of the Atlantic Ocean. Below, four-foot waves formed ominous troughs in the black water between surging white caps. The chopper's searchlight lanced the dark sky, racing across the ocean, stirred violently by the early summer storm packing intense sixty-mile-an-hour winds. Slashing rain glowed like a meteor shower in the light's powerful beam.

A bolt of lightning illuminated the sky with a flash of blinding light, followed by a booming thunderclap.

Holding the Dolphin with a steady grip against the inclement weather was a walrus of a man with red hair and ruddy skin. CWO John "Skyjack" McMurphy. A Coast Guard legend, according to some. Beside him, wearing a stern expression, his face awash in the glow of the instrument panel, Commander Brice Bannon scanned the dark waters ahead.

The low ceiling of swollen, black clouds hid the moon from sight. Seeing anything on the churning water was difficult at best. The pelting rain dribbling down the windshield glass made it damn near impossible. Wind gusts blasted the chopper, banging against the cockpit doors like a relenting monster trying to get in.

Bannon pointed. "There she is."

"I see it."

McMurphy banked the eight million dollar, twin-engine, search-and-rescue chopper into a starboard turn, altering course toward the silhouette of a ship bobbing through the rough waters a quarter mile ahead. Barely visible against the gray horizon, the cargo container ship pitched in the storm-swollen seas, listing at nearly a forty-five-degree angle. Its bow rode low in the dark water. Lights dotted the ship's superstructure, which swung like a pendulum, dipping perilously close to the water's surface. Should the superstructure get swamped by a wave, it would capsize the ship. And within minutes, drag it to a watery grave.

Bannon spotted more lights bobbing in the deep troughs of water. As they flew closer, he saw what they were: blinking emergency beacons from two enclosed lifeboats drifting away from the sinking behemoth. The crew had abandoned ship.

"What do ya want to do about them?" McMurphy asked.

The distress call had come into the Coast Guard Rescue Coordination Center less than an hour earlier, identifying the ship in trouble as the *CS Marken*. According to records, the *Marken* was a Panamax container ship sailing from Namibia, South Africa. Nine-hundred-fifty feet long, it had a beam of one-hundred-six feet and an overall height of one-ninety. Typically, a ship that size crewed with thirteen.

Its EPIRB, electronic position indicating radio beacon, had specified a location off the coast of Massachusetts, thirty miles out in the Gulf of Maine. Bannon and McMurphy had been dispatched from Coast Guard Station Boston, out of Boston Harbor. The closest surface vessel in the area was the *USCGC Lightfoot*, an eighty-seven-foot Protector-class cutter. One of sixty-seven in the fleet. It sailed with a crew complement of ten.

"The *Lightfoot's* not far behind us," Bannon said. "They'll round them up."

"We're not gonna wait for them," McMurphy asked. "Are we?"

"We've got to make sure no one's been left behind."

"Thought you'd say that."

The chopper raced through the lightning-filled sky toward the keeling ship.

Arriving on-site, McMurphy banked the Dolphin in a tight circle over the dark ship. Hovering, he spun the chopper's tail, panning the searchlight over the deck. The powerful light revealed that a number of containers had broken free and were jumbled to the port side of the ship.

"Explains the heavy listing," Bannon commented.

After a complete pass, McMurphy said, "Don't see anyone topside. Guess it's time for you to get wet."

"Right." Bannon clasped his old friend on the shoulder with a smile. He left the cockpit.

In the crew cabin, he joined the three rescue-swimmer operators assigned to him. Members of a Direct Action Section of an MSRT, Maritime Security Response Team, posted out of Air Station Cape Cod. They were aviation survival technician rated and trained in close-quarters combat and boarding techniques. The best of the best. Led by Lieutenant Charlotte Ng, with her were Ensign Doug Ellis and Ensign Terrance Connell. Connell was their most recent addition.

Bannon and McMurphy had worked with them before. Not surprisingly, they were already geared up and ready to go, waiting to receive orders.

He had to shout over the engine and rotor noise. "Lifeboats are already in the water. The *Lightfoot* will deal with them. Standard search-and-rescue scenario. Hit the deck. Spread out and look for anyone left behind. You find someone, get 'em back to the upper deck, aft of the superstructure."

Connell would remain on the Dolphin and operate the hoist, lowering the others to the *Marken* below them. If they found survivors, he'd drop a rescue basket and haul them up.

Bannon turned to Ellis and Ng.

"Doug, you make your way through the superstructure. I'll go below deck and work my way up, fore to aft. Charlotte, Skyjack and I cleared the deck from above but double-check we didn't miss anyone. If it's still clear, proceed below deck and work your way down and forward. Stay in radio contact.

It's just the three of us and a lot of ship to search. Be thorough, but be quick. There's no telling how long the *Marken* will remain afloat."

Serious faces stared back at him. They nodded.

They were young but well-trained and experienced rescuers. Bannon had the utmost trust in the three of them.

He threw open the cabin door.

Howling wind and lashing rain whipped through the space, making it impossible to be heard. He tapped his radio mic. All communications would need to be through comms.

Bannon leaned out. The cargo ship was directly below them. Fifteen feet down. The water around it churned into violent swells under the chopper's rotors. Bannon marveled at McMurphy's ability to hold the Dolphin steady. As pilots went, there were none better.

Bannon hooked up his line and pointed downward.

Connell spooled out the line.

Bannon stepped out.

As he repelled down, the cold rain hit Bannon's face like sharp knives. His jumpsuit rippled and snapped wetly in the wind, made worse by the wash of the powerful rotor blades overhead.

He landed softly a few feet from the base of the superstructure at the stern of the ship. Buffeted by the strong wind, he took a couple of stumbling steps to balance himself on the angled deck. He hooked an arm around the rung of an accommodation ladder. There, he released the line from his harness and waved overhead.

The line was pulled back up. Ng and Ellis quickly descended. They leaned against the superstructure's bulkhead and crowded around the ladder Bannon held tight. The ship pitched forward. Waves crashed over the bow, flooding the deck.

They had their assignments. Bannon shouted, "Go!"

Between the *Marken's* steep pitch, riding the swells, and the rain-slick deck, it was impossible to walk without holding onto something. The ship wasn't long for this world.

Bannon wondered at that. The distress call had given no indication of how the ship got into trouble. As storms went, closing in on a category one event, it was navigable by a decent crew. Also troubling was that the ship's AIS, automatic identification system, hadn't been activated—which is required of ships of its size—until the EPIRB turned on. To his cynical way of thinking, there was only one reason for that.

They were trying to hide.

Why and from what, he had no idea, but there was more going on than just bad weather.

A mystery for another time, he told himself.

He watched Ng move out. A quick sweep of the deck wouldn't take her long. Most of the deck space was filled by single-stacked, twenty-foot metal containers. If anyone was still on board, chances were good they wouldn't be on deck.

When she was out of sight, Bannon and Ellis pushed their way to a hatch at the base of the aft superstructure.

Together, they pulled the heavy door open and stepped inside.

The passageway, or p-way, beyond was bathed blood-red from flickering emergency lights. The dry quiet inside was a welcome relief, even if the hollow metal enclosure felt tomb-like.

He clasped a hand on Ellis' shoulder. "Good luck, and don't dawdle."

Ellis said, "You, too, sir."

The young ensign charged up a flight of metal stairs. His footfalls echoed in the hollow metal chamber. Once he was out of sight, Bannon descended into the bowels of the old, rusty ship.

He reached the engine room.

Lights flickered. Sparks arced from exposed wires. Steam hissed from somewhere in the chamber. The cloying scent of diesel fuel hung heavy in the air. Water sloshed around his ankles. The further forward he went, the oily film-coated water rose to waist level. Bannon had to maintain contact with the bulkheads to steady himself, riding the unpredictable fall and surge of the deck.

He plunged ahead, wading through the cold Atlantic Ocean water.

Along the way, he was sure he smelled the faint lingering odor of smoke. Of something burning.

Bannon frowned.

Another mystery. But questions could wait until later. They had two priorities. Ensure no one was trapped and left behind. And get everyone off the sinking ship before it was too late.

Bannon called out for survivors. "Anyone here? Coast Guard. Call out!"

CHAPTER TWO

McMURPHY SAT IN THE cockpit of the Dolphin. Once his swimmers had been released and he'd gotten an all-clear from Connell, he moved the chopper off to a higher altitude, seeking a smoother ride while they made long, sweeping loops around the doomed cargo ship. Waiting to hear from the search party, he and Connell spent the time searching the waters around the *Marken.*, Looking for any poor souls who might have fallen overboard or been left behind by the lifeboats. Holding the mic close to his mouth, McMurphy said, "Connell. Anything?"

Connell came back quickly. "No, Chief. Looks good so far."

"Copy that," McMurphy said. "Keep your eyes peeled."

"Yes, sir."

McMurphy switched channels and radioed the cutter racing toward them. "*Lightfoot,* flying fish here. Come back, big trout."

Captain Isaac Coram's voice crackled in McMurphy's ears. "*Lightfoot* here, Skyjack. What's with the CB talk?"

McMurphy grinned. Throughout his long career in the Coast Guard, he'd always been a non-conformist. Challenging authority and bending the rules. Always pushing the envelope—sometimes just to see what he could get away with. Even back in the day, his value as a pilot, among other talents, often—but not always—spared him the worst possible punishments for his frowned-upon behavior.

Now, the special arrangement he and Bannon had with the Secretary of Homeland Security, working directly for Elizabeth Grayson, brought with it increased opportunities for him to thumb his nose at all the dumb procedures and bothersome protocols. He kept looking for that line he couldn't cross, that step too far.

He hadn't found it yet.

Well, there was that time in Hawaii when he stole Marine One. Except for that, he'd remained pretty much unscathed by his behavior.

"We've located the target, Captain crusty-pants." McMurphy rattled off the coordinates. "Swim team's onboard the *Marken* now. You've got two fish to haul in."

Coram radioed back. "Copy that, Chief. We'll scoop up the lifeboats and rendezvous with you at the *Marken* forthwith." He added, "Unless you need us sooner."

"Sooner rather than later would be good, Captain," McMurphy said. "But do what you've gotta do first. The *Marken*'s got a date with Davey Jones' locker, but she's holding her own for now."

"Understood. *Lightfoot* out."

Circling the *Marken*, McMurphy leaned to the side and glanced out the windshield. The ship was getting tossed around like a toy in a bathtub. Waves crashed across the bow as the ship surged through the white caps before crashing down into the next trough.

Of great concern to McMurphy, besides everything else, was how nose-deep the *Marken* rode. That didn't make much sense to him unless...

"They're taking on water from below," he mused. A worried expression on his face. "Sooner rather than later," he said again, referring to Bannon's rescue efforts as well as the *Lightfoot*.

BANNON MADE HIS WAY from the engine room to the lowest level of the cavernous cargo holds, making his way forward. The pitch of the floor was severe, leaning to port and nose-heavy. That was when the ship wasn't getting tossed back into a thirty-degree climb over a wave.

He climbed along the angled wall, crawling across the bins and wooden crates that had broken free and tumbled across the cargo space. In the far corner, a half dozen brand-new school buses had skidded across the deck. Jumbled together like discarded Matchbox cars in a kid's toy chest.

Bannon pulled himself around uprights and hopscotched from crate to crate.

His progress was slow and laborious.

"Coast Guard! Call out!" His voice echoed. He waited a beat, listening. "Anyone down here?"

A loud, creaking, metallic sound answered him. The ship shifted underfoot. He lurched toward the next bulkhead. Bannon checked his dive watch. They'd been onboard for six minutes. He worried they didn't have much time left.

At the next hatchway, Bannon keyed his radio. "Report. Ng?"

Charlotte Ng radioed back. "Top deck's secure. I've cleared most of the first two below decks. Nothing to report, sir."

"Bridge and officers and crew quarters are clear," Doug Ellis reported. "Ghost town in here, sir. The mess hall and common areas are next."

"Copy," Bannon said. "Rendezvous at the pickup point in nine minutes. Skyjack, what's the word on the *Lightfoot*?"

"They're fishing. About a half mile out. They can divert to us if necessary."

"No. Keep them on task." Bannon pushed through to the second cargo hold. The front half of it was completely submerged. "I'm midship in the lowest hold. Everything ahead of me is underwater."

"It's taking on water much faster than it should be," McMurphy said.

"My thought exactly." Bannon climbed up a set of metal stairs to the next level. He managed to get another ten feet forward before he was waist-deep in water again. "Make sure Coram gets us an accurate headcount from the crew once he's got 'em. I've gone as far as I can go down here."

Bannon broke contact with McMurphy. He found the conditions on the next two decks the same. Flooded clear up to the ceilings. Any search forward would require scuba and tanks. And shift the operation from rescue to recovery.

McMurphy called back. "Any chance you're ready to wrap it up down there? I don't like the way things are looking from up here."

Bannon could hear the tightness in his friend's voice. Never one to rattle easily, if McMurphy was worried, there was good reason.

"Thought I'd wait for happy hour to start," Bannon said. "But the accommodations leave a little to be desired."

"Sounds like a certain seaside gin joint I could mention."

Bannon ran a small bar on the strip at Hampton Beach on the side. He smiled at his friend's dig. "Very funny."

He called out, searching as much of the last two holds as he could physically access. He returned to the aft end. There, he climbed an accommodation ladder leading to the top deck. Above him, he pushed at the closed hatch, barely able to open it against the ferocious winds. At last report, they were gusting at fifty-to-sixty miles per hour—not quite category one levels but getting close.

A set of gloved hands grabbed the hatch above him and pulled it open.

Doug Ellis extended a hand down and helped pull Bannon into the howling wind and lashing rain. The rain stung his cheeks. "Thanks."

They made their way across the listing deck to the ladder they'd first clung to when they arrived.

Ng stepped out of the superstructure. Her search complete. Their flashlights bobbed in the darkness while they tried to maintain their footing. Ng wiped rain from her face. "We waiting for the *Lightfoot* to pick us up?"

From her sour expression, Bannon could see she didn't relish that option. A loud metallic creak answered her before Bannon could. The deck shifted under their feet. He joined her in her assessment.

"I think we've overstayed our welcome as it is." He clicked his radio. "Time to call an Uber. Skyjack, that's your cue."

"Coasties transport," McMurphy wisecracked. "Pick-ups and drop-offs are our specialty."

The Dolphin made a wide turn around the bow of the ship. The search party shielded their eyes from the rain and the wind. Squinting, they tracked the Dolphin's searchlight, watching its approach. The light cutting through the driving sheets of rain made it look like tinsel shimmering on a Christmas tree. The Dolphin settled into a position overhead. The rotors chuffed at the wind.

McMurphy expertly lowered the craft, bringing it to within fifteen feet of the *Marken's* deck.

Bannon and his team glanced upward, mindful of the lines Connell dropped from the crew bay. They whipped around like live, angry snakes. Heavy metal hooks snapped and clanged against the superstructure and the deck until Ng and Ellis grabbed them.

"All aboard who's coming aboard," McMurphy said in his best train conductor voice.

Ellis hooked up first.

Bannon paused. He looked toward the forward section of the ship.

Dozens of containers covered the deck. Some had broken loose and shifted to the port side, like the crates in the cargo hold below. Many rested against the gunwale. Some had even shot up over the gunwale, teetering on the brink of going over. Many others had probably already been lost to the sea. The added weight of the shifted containers contributed to the ship's heavy port listing.

Through all the noise, he heard a metal-on-metal banging sound.

Bannon called out, "You hear that?"

"Hear what, sir?"

Between the waves splashing across the deck, the howling wind, and the downdraft from the Dolphin's main rotor, Bannon could barely hear Ng through his comms, much less the clanking sound he thought he'd heard.

"A banging sound," Bannon insisted.

Ellis secured his line to his harness. "We're good to go, sir."

21

Bannon stepped away from them, moving toward the cargo containers jumbled across the port gunwale.

Ellis called out, "Sir?"

Bannon held up a hand to silence him. He thought he'd heard the noise again.

Ng came up behind him.

"There. There it is again," Bannon said.

"I don't hear anything," Ng said.

"Sir?" Ellis called out.

Bannon waved his hand. "Head topside, Ellis."

While Ellis ascended, Bannon pushed himself further along the angled wall of the superstructure, moving closer to a container that had slid across the deck. At an angle, propped up. It stuck out over the gunwale.

"Metal-on-metal," he shouted to be heard over the wind, spitting rainwater. "Banging."

"Probably a tie-down that broke free," Ng said. "A metal buckle whipping around."

Common sense told him she was probably right, but he needed to know for sure.

Again. There it was.

The sound was weak. Distinct. And repetitive.

"No," he said, "There's a pattern."

Gripping the gunwale, he shimmied toward the container protruding over the side.

Tap. Tap. Tap.

Bannon knew he wasn't hearing things now. "It's coming from inside this container."

He grabbed for the metal locking bars. They wouldn't budge. It was easy to see why. Both bars were locked with big, heavy padlocks.

Ng joined him.

He banged on the side of the container with the back of his metal flashlight.

From inside, the tapping got louder and faster—almost frantic. And voices. He heard voices—low, muffled, and desperate.

22

"There's someone inside."

"How does someone get locked inside a cargo container?" Ng asked.

"The bigger questions are who locked them in," Bannon said. "And, how the hell do we get them out?"

CHAPTER THREE

McMURPHY'S VOICE BOOMED IN Bannon's ear. "What's the hold-up, kids?"

The *Marken* crested a rough wave, then rode the downward trough. Cold ocean water washed over the ship, sending a deluge of water cascading across the deck. It slammed into Bannon and Ng. It was like getting hit with the force of a dozen firehoses.

Ng lost her footing. She tumbled toward Bannon. He reached out an arm and ensnared her waist like a tango dancer, sweeping her off her feet. They spun. He pulled her down to the deck. They rolled across the inclined metal plating and crashed into the gunwale. He held his arms around her. In a tight bear hug, taking the brunt of the blow to his back. More water slammed into them. Cold and bracing. It took Bannon's breath away. The deck rolled. Metal groaned. Somewhere, a strap snapped. A container slid across the deck and smashed into the gunwale. It upended like a train car derailing, hung up in the air, then slammed down, hitting the deck.

When the water receded, Bannon grabbed the top of the gunwale and pulled himself to his feet. He held out a hand for Ng, pulling her up, too.

"You okay?" he asked.

"Because of you. I thought I was a goner."

Bannon shouted to McMurphy, "We've got an unexpected development down here."

"We don't have time for any developments, buddy. Unexpected or otherwise. That rust bucket's about to go under."

The Marken groaned and shifted under them again as if to underscore McMurphy's concerns. Pitched forward, it rolled farther to port. The big ship plowed through the next wave. More water crashed over the bow.

Bannon spun Ng around him so she could grab hold of the container's locking bar. The deck's pitch had steepened. He shook another bracing spray of water from his face. Another swell or two like that would likely swamp the ship.

"We've got to find something to cut open those locks," he said.

Ng frowned. "I think I left my bolt cutters in my other outfit, sir."

Bannon smiled, appreciating the woman's humor in such a dicey situation.

"That's unfortunate," Bannon said. "Because I did, too."

"There's sure to be something in the machinist's shop."

The ship groaned and pitched. Bannon's stomach rolled with it. "No time for that."

Ng frowned again.

"Even if we can get it open, Commander, the *Lightfoot* won't get here in time. There's no time to airlift survivors up. We don't even know how many people are inside. It's hopeless, sir."

Bannon refused to accept hopeless. He never would. He rapped his flashlight on the side of the container and shouted, "We're still here!"

His efforts were rewarded by more banging, even more frenzied. If that were possible.

Bannon shielded his eyes and looked skyward. The belly of the Dolphin was close. It rolled and pitched, buffeted by the wind. Keeping the chopper steady overhead was no easy task.

"Hey, Skyjack," he shouted into the comms. "How do you feel about turning that bird of yours into a cargo hauler?"

"Are you insane?"

"I've been accused of that before, yes."

"What's so important down there we've gotta take it with us?"

"A container. With people locked inside. Can you do it or not?"

McMurphy didn't answer right away. Bannon knew he was calculating the problem in his head.

"How big we talking?" McMurphy asked.

"Twenty-footer."

An empty twenty-foot container weighed in at fifty-five hundred pounds. Bannon knew the Dolphin had a max take-off weight of ninety-five hundred pounds, less the chopper's empty weight. But they weren't taking off. All McMurphy needed to do was to keep the damn thing in the air. Fly thirty miles back to Boston. Through a tropical storm. In the dead of night. Piece of cake. In his mind, he could hear his friend scoff.

"Skyjack. Can you do it or not?"

"With who knows how many people are inside? And who knows what else? No."

"But you'll try," Bannon shouted.

McMurphy sighed. "Sure. But no one better complain when we *all* end up in the drink."

He kept the commlink open.

Bannon heard him barking orders to Connell and Ellis. Seconds later, a thick canvas strap was tossed down. McMurphy lowered the Dolphin another five feet. It hung nearly on top of them. The downdraft alone almost blew Bannon and Ng overboard.

The strap had plenty of slack, the end weighted down by a heavy hook and buckles, and a come-a-long device. They'd use that to tighten the strap once he and Ng got it looped around the container and reattached it.

Bannon and Ng worked efficiently. She scrambled under the crawl space between the gunwale and the bottom of the propped-up container. Bannon used the ribs of the container's doors and the locking mechanisms as hand and foot holds to scramble up to the top of the container. There, prone against the hard, wet roof of the container, he reached down for the hook end Ng tossed up to him. He connected the hook, completed the loop, and ratcheted the come-a-long device until the strap was tight around the rear portion of the container.

"That's one," Bannon said. The next part was going to be a little trickier. "Skyjack, you ever rope a steer?"

"I look like I'm from Montana? Hell, no."

Bannon issued quick instructions to his team.

A minute passed.

Then, a second strap was thrown down from the open crew cabin. This one was already looped. Equipped with a second come-a-long device, the hook and buckles formed a giant lasso.

The container stuck out over the side a bit more than halfway. They needed to get the loop around the end of the container jutting out over the gunwale. The strap dangled along the left side of the container.

"Time for you to get topside, Lieutenant," Bannon shouted, lying on the low end of the container's roof.

"With all due respect, sir," Ng said. "No way."

"No time to argue, Charlotte. Skyjack! One to beam up."

"One?" McMurphy said.

"For now." Bannon glanced over the edge back down at Ng. "That's an order, Lieutenant."

Still on his stomach, Bannon pulled himself across the container to the left side. Before he started the arduous climb up the slanted incline to the top end of the container, he glanced up at the Dolphin's belly looming dangerously overhead. Ng had hooked up to her line. With a worried look back at Bannon, she signaled for Ellis and Connell to haul her back into the chopper.

When she reached the cabin door, her teammates pulled her inside.

Grateful they were all safely aboard, Bannon moved forward.

Over comms, McMurphy said, "We're into overtime, Brice."

"You're telling me."

As if to emphasize the point, the *Marken* pitched downward.

Bannon slipped across the rain-slick roof. He held tight to the container's edge. His fingers ached in protest. As strategies went, Bannon knew this one was a dog. But nothing better had come to mind. Not with the limited time they had.

The looped strap dangled just six feet away. The top edge of the container, where he'd have to loop it, was less than eight feet away. Rain coursed down his face. He blinked the water from his eyes.

An eight-foot climb on the smooth, rain-slicked roof. It might as well be eighty feet away.

Still, he started the tedious crawl upward.

He pulled himself up until he reached the dangling strap. He seized it in one hand and continued his climb, dragging the strap along with him. His muscles ached. He could feel the strap tug and pull as McMurphy fought the biting, gusting wind to keep the Dolphin steady and not yank the strap from Bannon's grasp.

The *Marken* entered a trough and pitched forward under him. The ship yawed to port at the same time. Bannon began to slide along the suddenly downward-sloping decline toward the container's edge. A good thing, except he had no way to stop his trajectory. No way to prevent himself from sliding right off the edge into the Atlantic Ocean.

Bannon cursed.

Sliding headfirst, about to be swept off the container, he scrambled frantically, fighting gravity and the elements. His boots squeaked against the smooth metal, with nothing to catch. It was like being on a giant slip-and-slide. He started to pick up speed. Bannon wrapped his arm around the strap. The container bucked and slammed back down on the gunwale under him, sending him sailing over the edge.

Bannon swung out over the turbulent water.

His momentum launched him a dozen feet out before he began to swing back.

He slammed into the side of the container. Hard.

The jarring impact threatened to loosen his grip. The strap slipped through his fists. He squeezed harder. Tighter. Desperate. His efforts arrested his drop, leaving him banging against the side of the container, five feet below the roof.

Exhausted, Bannon planted his feet against the container. He climbed hand over hand up the strap, step after step, scaling the side of the container.

His shoulders throbbed. His muscles ached.

Reaching the roof, he rolled onto the container, breathing heavily.

Over the comms, McMurphy said, "If you were to hurry this along, Brice, that would be great, buddy."

"You know," Bannon said, panting. "There's those of us in the arena, and then there are critics."

"That may be," McMurphy retorted. "But unless you wanna end up sleeping with the fishes, I suggest you lasso your bucking bronco and get your butt up here."

Maintaining his grip on the strap, Bannon scrambled as quickly as he could to the top of the container, once more angled upward. There, he grabbed the edge. The ship dropped, rose again, tilted, and then righted itself.

The container slammed against the gunwale, jarring Bannon's teeth while he looped the strap over the end. He wiped the relenting rain from his face. Once he shimmied the loop down about five feet, he could tighten it with the come-a-long, securing the container in their makeshift cradle.

"Almost there."

With the strap looped and in place, Bannon sighed.

"You know," McMurphy said. "There's still a better than even chance that box drags us all down to the bottom of the briny blue sea."

On hands and knees, Bannon held the strap and the grip of the come-a-long. He started to ratchet it. Through the ordeal, the occupants inside the container had fallen silent. Had the last jarring slip of the container injured them? Rendered them unable to continue banging and shouting? Or had they simply given up? He didn't waste time trying to reestablish communications. There'd be time for that later. He hoped.

The *Marken* let loose a great, shuddering groan and rolled farther to port. The container shifted under Bannon, teetering on the gunwale. It started to tip toward the ocean.

Bannon cursed. "Not again."

But this time was worse. This time, the container slid across the gunwale. The metal screeched. The container was going over.

He frantically ratcheted the come-a-long. He needed to get the strap, the loop, as tight as possible before....

McMurphy shouted, "Hang on!"

Bannon clutched the straps, holding on for dear life.

The Dolphin dipped.

Bannon heard the engines straining. With his feet planted on the container, he used his free hand, and the last of his strength, to hold onto the bright red handle of the come-a-long device and ratchet it tighter and tighter. His forearms screamed in agony, bulging from the effort.

The Dolphin had the full weight of the container now. A weight now dragging the chopper out of the sky. It plunged toward the black, angry sea.

Bannon wrapped his arm around the canvas strap.

The Dolphin nosedived toward the roiling ocean below.

Bannon's heart skipped a beat.

Had he condemned them all to a violent, watery death?

He held on and planted his feet on the pitched container roof. From inside the container, he heard screams. They're still with us, he thought. Until he gets them all drowned, trapped inside a steel box.

Six feet below him, the ship yawed and gasped its final breath. It slipped under the turbulent sea.

And the Dolphin continued its downward plunge toward the ocean.

Bannon resisted the urge to close his eyes as impact with the black sea seemed inevitable.

Overhead, the engines surged. A loud whine. McMurphy swung the Dolphin in an upward arc, away from the sea. The container whipped around and skimmed the ocean surface, sending a thick, frothy wake of white water high into the air. A surfer's plume before the Dolphin rose, flying a dozen feet above the water, leaving the sinking *Marken* behind, swallowed by the angry sea.

Bannon let out a held breath.

McMurphy let out an ear-splitting whoop. "That's it, baby. I love this machine."

CHAPTER FOUR

U.S. Coast Guard Station
Boston Harbor

THEY KNEW FROM THE jump, flying the container to the *Lightfoot* wasn't an option. The cutter was too small to accommodate either the container or the Dolphin. That left them just one choice. Fly the container the thirty miles back to Boston Harbor, dragging the payload under them the whole way.

McMurphy radioed Captain Coram, relaying their situation. He, in turn, alerted the Boston Harbor authorities to expect their arrival.

A blood-red sun rose beyond the horizon. As night gave way to day behind them, the swollen storm clouds began to dissipate. Dawn broke, painting the sky with crimson, scarlet, and red streaks. Tinting the gray clouds with burgundy outlines.

For the time being, the storm was over.

And it had born a spectacular sunrise.

Yet, Bannon couldn't shake the old sailor's adage: red sky in the morning, sailors take warning.

The Dolphin flew into Boston Harbor. The weight of the container caused them to fly slow and low. Deemed too dangerous to try and haul Bannon back into the helicopter while on the move, he'd been forced to ride out the trip on top of the container. His grip tight on the canvas straps.

McMurphy angled the chopper upward as they came across solid ground at the docks.

There, he hovered over the helipad he'd been directed to. He gently lowered the container down to the ground. All the while, Bannon stood on top of the thing, like a mariner on the bow of a ship, returning from victorious battle. All he needed to complete the image was a triton.

A half dozen emergency vehicles lined the helipad. Police cars, fire trucks, and several ambulances. Their lights pulsated electric blue and white in the pre-dawn gloom while the emerging sun painted the glass facades of the Boston skyline red.

Once the container landed on solid ground, McMurphy hovered low, releasing the slack on the straps. Bannon unhooked the canvas straps, then waved at McMurphy with cramped, aching fingers. Grateful to the best damn pilot he'd ever known for saving his life. Again.

Bannon opened comms to McMurphy and Ng's team. "Drinks at the Keel Haul are on me."

"Drinks are always on the house for me," McMurphy said.

"I meant for the others. Yours? They're going on your tab."

McMurphy barked a laugh. "Ha. Ha. Like I have a tab. Wait. I don't have a tab. Do I? Brice. Brice?"

Bannon smiled without saying.

"Oh, sure. Now you stop yapping," McMurphy said. "Let me go park this baby. We'll catch up with you in a minute."

No longer burdened by the weight of the container, the Dolphin rose smoothly into the air. The sound of its rotors faded. It turned, veered west, and headed toward a nearby helipad.

Bannon climbed off the side of the container and dropped the three remaining feet to the ground. He stumbled. His muscles quivered like gelatin in an earthquake. Soaked to the skin, he shivered.

Uniformed police officers and other emergency workers moved in on him.

Bannon pointed at the lock. "We need to get that open."

A firefighter in full turnout gear stepped forward. He carried a handheld disk grinder. He knelt by the lock. With sparks flying and a loud whine, he made quick work of cutting through the shackles.

A second firefighter pulled the locking bars up and opened the heavy doors. They squealed on rusty hinges. A cop with them shined his light inside. The powerful white beam panned the interior.

What it revealed chilled Bannon to the bone more than the cold, wet rain had.

The first to step inside, he was nearly knocked off his feet by the stench. Urine and feces. Other bodily odors and fear. He pressed the back of his hand against his nose.

Crowded in the rear of the container, shrouded in shadowy darkness, were six women. He estimated them to be between fifteen and thirty-five years old. They huddled together, clinging to one another. Disheveled, some of them were wearing little more than rags. They stepped back in mass. Most of the women were dark-skinned. African or Middle-Eastern.

Apprehensive. Fear in their wide, gleaming eyes.

Scattered across the floor were torn, thin, soiled blankets. Pails used as toilets had upended and spilled their contents during the turbulent ride on the *Marken* and afterward. Plastic cups, sporks and tin plates littered the floor. It had been the plates they'd used to bang on the walls.

Bannon held his hands in the air. "It's okay. I'm with the United States Coast Guard. You're safe now." He indicated the uniformed cop next to him. He pointed the light down to the floor, out of their faces. "This is the police. We're here to help. You're going to be okay now."

The women murmured. Bannon couldn't make out what they were saying. A foreign language he couldn't readily place.

Behind him, other responders gathered at the open door.

To the women, Bannon said, "Does anyone speak English?"

No one responded.

Keeping his tone low and nonthreatening, he asked again in Arabic. "*'Iinjilizi. niema?*"

He'd learned only a few essential words and phrases during his time in the sandbox. Being able to say *everything's going to be okay* had been an important one. *"Kulu shay' ealaa ma yuram."*

The cop beside him tried Spanish, *"Hablar Inglés?"*

"The ship's from Namibia, South Africa," Bannon said. "They're probably speaking Afrikaans or a dialect. Maybe another local, lesser-known language."

"We'll get someone," the cop said.

"Thanks."

Fearful his trembling legs would finally give out, Bannon exited the container, leaving the cops and the EMTs to do their jobs.

Back in the fresh air, he took a deep, cleansing breath as he leaned heavily against the front grille of an ambulance. A paramedic approached him with a blanket. Shivering, Bannon let him toss it over his shoulders. The young man tried to tend to a small cut on his forehead he'd sustained sometime during the search-and-rescue operation. Bannon pushed the man's hands away.

He pointed at the container. "Help them. They need you more than I do."

McMurphy pushed through the crowd of first responders, cops, firefighters, and a handful of dockworkers who'd come around to see what the commotion was all about.

He crossed his arms and settled in beside his friend. "How you doing?"

"Alive. Thanks to you."

One at a time, the women were led out of the container and into the pre-dawn morning. They squinted against the flashing lights. Cringed at the loud sounds of crackling police radios. They winced, hearing the sirens as more emergency vehicles arrived. They were skinny. Malnourished. Their hair was matted and dirty. They shivered, clutching the filthy rags around their shoulders and shuffled along with nothing on their feet. The women had hollowed eyes, like zombies.

The EMTs and cops were calm and gentle, going about their work.

Skittish, the women jerked away from even the gentlest touches by the first responders who carefully guided them toward the backs of open ambulances.

"Jesus," McMurphy said.

Bannon ground his back teeth. "Yeah. Come on. Let's get out of the way."

As they started to move away, a man in a plaid shirt and brown sportscoat called out to them. He had thick brown hair and a cleft chin, strong features, in his mid-thirties. He wore a tie pulled down around an open collar. A gold police badge hung on a chain strung around his neck.

"You," he said. "Hey, you two."

McMurphy knotted his thick, bushy eyebrows. "That joker talking to us?"

"Seems like it," Bannon said.

"You Bannon? Brice Bannon?"

"Who wants to know?"

"Detective Curtis Martin. Boston PD. Family Justice Division." He held out his shield.

He shook Bannon's hand. And then, McMurphy's.

"What's the Family Justice Division do?" McMurphy asked.

"We investigate crimes against children, domestic violence, sexual assault." Martin paused. "And human trafficking."

Bannon pointed at the women. Many were now sitting at the open doors of ambulances, being tended to by EMTs. Some were talking to cops, but it was clear nothing of value was getting interpreted between the language barrier. The women looked scared and apprehensive.

"You're here about this?" Bannon asked.

"That's right."

"How'd you hear about it so quickly?"

"We have a mutual friend," Martin said.

"Do we?"

"Tarakesh Sardana."

McMurphy said, "Blades."

Martin smiled. "Blades. Yes. She called me when she heard what you'd discovered. I'll need a full rundown on what happened out there—everything you can tell me."

"Of course."

The uniform cop who'd first entered the container with Bannon stuck his head out from inside the container. He'd donned a facemask and blue rubber gloves. "Detective. You need to see this."

Martin moved toward the container. He hesitated as Bannon and McMurphy fell in lockstep beside him. "You two need to stay out here."

"If Blades told you anything at all about us," Bannon said, "you know that's not going to happen."

Martin frowned. "Yeah. Said you two were more stubborn than she is. I can't imagine what that even looks like."

"Try and stop us," McMurphy said, "and you'll find out."

Martin sighed. "Fine. Stay behind me. Don't touch anything."

He pulled out a heavy Maglite flashlight and turned it on. Several cops crowded around the open container. A uniform cop led Bannon, Martin, and McMurphy inside and to the back.

Bannon's eyes watered.

In the far corner, the cop aimed his flashlight beam at what Bannon first took to be a lump of dirty, discarded blankets and soiled mattresses. But once Martin added his light to those of the other cops, Bannon saw what they were looking at.

A woman. Curled up in the corner. Her head craned to the side at a strange angle. Blood stained the back wall of the container and had pooled in the corner where sodden rags had been used in a vain attempt to stop the bleeding from a severe head wound.

A paramedic squatted beside her glanced up. He squinted in the harsh light. "I checked. Impossible to say how without an autopsy. Either a broken neck or blood loss. But, she's dead."

CHAPTER FIVE

The *USCGC Lightfoot*
Gulf of Maine

LIEUTENANT KAYLA CLARKE STOOD on the stern deck of the eighty-seven-foot Protector-class Coast Guard cutter. With a beam of nineteen feet and a draft of almost six, the multi-mission class vessel serviced a wide range of functions, such as search-and-rescue, law enforcement, fishery patrol, drug and immigration interdiction, and homeland security operations. Powered by two MTU diesel engines, the cutter had a max speed of twenty-six knots and a range of nine hundred nautical miles. It crewed with a complement of ten.

The *Lightfoot,* like all Protector-class cutters, was equipped with two fifty-caliber M2 Browning machine guns. But what set this class of cutter apart from the fleet was the stern launching ramp. The point-class cutters, which the Protector-class replaced, had to stop for five minutes or more to retrieve or deploy their RHIBs, rigid-hull inflatable boats, using a crane. With the launching ramp, which could be operated by a single crewman, RHIBs were launched and retrieved 'at speed', meaning while the cutter was underway.

Dawn broke over the horizon. The sun looked like an angry, burning red ball in the sky, parting the storm clouds and brightening the world as it rose. Its warmth chased away the bone-penetrating chill from the overnight storms.

Dressed in the standard dark blue operational dress uniform, Kayla wore her auburn hair tied in a ponytail snaked through the back of her standard-issued blue baseball cap. Her lieutenant's bar center under the yellow embroidered U.S. Coast Guard.

Assigned to the First Coast Guard District Staff Judge Advocate Office out of Boston, Kayla participated in field operations at regular intervals. Ten years in the Guard, her first five had been spent on ships, then later assigned to a DOG, Deployable Operations Group, in the Middle East. Back in the day, DOG units were the Coast Guard's special operations element, similar to the Navy's SEALs, with whom they received Naval Special Warfare training and often worked in joint operations. They were deployed on high-risk, high-profile assignments involving counter-terrorism and intelligence-gathering operations. They also combated piracy operations in Afghanistan, Iraq, and other areas with Navy and DoD groups.

Her unit had been commanded by Brice Bannon. That was where and how they first met.

When the DOG program was decommissioned, Bannon and McMurphy retired from the Guard full-time but retained their reservist status. Kayla remained active and transferred to the Staff Judge Advocate Office, 1st District, stationed out of Boston. She tried to have her field rotations coincide with Bannon and Skyjack's required reserve assignments.

The two lifeboats recovered from the *Marken* were tied alongside the cutter's starboard hull. They had dropped Jacob's ladders over the side and brought the crew on board.

Captain Coram emerged from the pilothouse with two cups of coffee in hand. He handed her one. A tall, reed-thin man with white, close-cropped hair. In his early fifties, Coram had over thirty years in. He'd refused numerous promotions over the decades, preferring to remain right where he was, commanding a ship out at sea. His face was deeply tanned from a lifetime on the water. His hands were chapped and lined from years of hard, physical work.

Kayla accepted the cup. "Thank you. I must say, I could get used to all this pampering."

Coram sipped his coffee. "Today's Coast Guard. The kinder, gentler service."

Kayla laughed. "That should be the new recruitment pitch."

They looked over the motley crew they'd pulled from the lifeboats. Exhausted, frightened men sitting on the deck. Most of them soaked to the skin. Some suffered from superficial cuts and bruises.

Kayla frowned. "Only twelve. There should be thirteen, no?"

"Maybe they crewed a man short. Happens."

Kayla felt the muscles in her jawline pulse. "I've talked with Brice. There were seven women locked up and left to die inside that container. One of them is dead."

"As if trafficking those poor women isn't bad enough." Coram shook his head. "How do we want to proceed?"

"Just like any other rescue operation," Kayla said. "No need to let on what we know. When we reach port, we turn them over to the authorities. Boston police. FBI. And DHS are all waiting for them."

"It'll take all I've got to act ignorant," Coram said, "when all I want to do is rip them apart."

Kayla felt the same way. "Have we identified the captain yet?"

"It's a guy named Bakari Gumede. I don't know which one he is."

"Let's find out. We can start by collecting IDs."

They stepped out from the shadows of the pilothouse. The rising sun had chased the last of the clouds away. The air was thick. Sticky and muggy. A stiff sea breeze cut across the ship. They approached a man sitting on the deck, sipping from a bottle of water given to him by an ensign.

"Your captain?" Coram asked. "Which one is he?"

The crewman glanced over to a disheveled man kneeling beside a crewman in a basket stretcher. Kayla had been told the man in the stretcher had broken his ankle leaping to the lifeboat.

"Captain Gumede," Coram called out. "A word if we might."

He and Kayla crossed the deck. Gumede snapped his head around. Kayla saw apprehension in the man's eyes as they approached.

Gumede rose to his feet. His eyes darted around the deck like a trapped animal looking for a means of escape. "About what?" he asked in heavily accented English.

"We need to gather some information," Coram said. "Make sure everyone is present and accounted for."

Gumede pressed his lips into a frown and narrowed his eyes. "Everyone's here."

"We count twelve, including yourself," Kayla said. "Don't Panamax vessels typically crew with thirteen?"

Anger flared in the sea captain's weathered face. "There's just twelve of us. I just told you. Or are you Americans calling me a liar?"

"Not at all, sir. We just want to make sure we haven't missed anyone." Kayla reached her hand out. "I'm Lieutenant Clarke. I'm with the Coast Guard JAG unit."

Gumede took a step back. "We've done nothing wrong."

"Of course not." Kayla forced a smile. "I didn't mean to imply otherwise. I'm here as part of my annual field rotation. Re-certification, if you will. But, in my capacity with the JAG unit, I can certainly help smooth the way for you and your men through the investigation process."

"What investigation? My men, I... have done nothing wrong," Gumede insisted.

"No one is saying you did. But your ship's gone down. The Coast Guard's required to investigate—"

"It was the storm. The *Marken*. She is an old, decrepit boat."

"That's the kind of thing we need to know." Coram reached out his hand to lead him toward the pilothouse. "We can talk in the mess hall. Grab a hot coffee."

Gumede snapped, "No!"

He backed away from Coram and Kayla. Panic in his wide eyes. He backpedaled into a young ensign behind him. They sidestepped each other.

"You're accusing me of doing something wrong," Gumede said. "Something bad."

"I assure you," Coram said. "We're not."

41

Gumede pushed the ensign to one side. He pulled an old revolver from under his jacket.

Coram shouted, "Gumede! What is this?"

"Captain Gumede," Kayla said. "Put the gun down. There's no need—"

"No," Gumede shouted. "Stay back."

He waved the gun, stepping from the others gathered around his injured crewman. The three ensigns who'd brought the crewmen on board drew their weapons. All of them trained on the captain of the *Marken*.

"Gumede," Coram said. "What do you hope to accomplish here?"

"Captain," Kayla said. "You don't want to do this."

Gumede had moved to the starboard side. He glanced down at the two lifeboats secured to the hull.

"There's nowhere for you to go," Coram said. "You can't escape in a lifeboat."

Gumede glanced at the launch system. He eyed the two RHIBs docked in the inverted ramp. He nodded toward them. "Release an inflatable. Then no one will get hurt."

The inflatable boats could reach forty knots, fast enough to outrun the *Lightfoot*.

"We'll track you, Captain," Kayla said. "Law enforcement will be waiting for you on shore. There's nowhere for you to go."

Gumede grew increasingly agitated. "Release the boat! Now."

Coram stood his ground. "No."

"Release a boat, or I start shooting." He aimed the gun at Kayla. "Her first."

"Don't be a fool, Gumede. You've got three guns trained on you," Coram said. "You're dead before you pull the trigger."

Gumede's eyes narrowed. The gun in his hand shook. He strained to steady his grip. The muscles in his arm tensed.

An ensign named Peterson stood to Coram's left. He fired first. His bullet hit Gumede in the shoulder. The captain gasped and staggered back. He fired his weapon.

Kayla ducked.

The shot was off the mark. Gumede had missed.

He leaned against the gunwale. Blood leaked from his wounded shoulder, staining his shirt. With pleading, watery eyes, Gumede said, "I did nothing wrong. Only what they told me to do."

He glanced up into the sky and squinted at the blood-red sun. "I had no choice. Please forgive me."

Peterson took a step toward him. "Drop the gun."

Gumede looked at him and put the gun to his temple.

Kayla and Coram rushed forward.

She shouted, "No! Don't!"

Gumede gave her a final sad glance and pulled the trigger. Blood sprayed out from the contact wound. Gumede's head snapped to the left. He dropped the gun and slumped to the stern deck.

Dead.

CHAPTER SIX

Keel Haul Tavern
Hampton Beach, N.H.

DETECTIVE CURTIS MARTIN STOOD across the street from the Keel Haul Tavern. Dinnertime, but the early summer sun still burned hot overhead. A refreshing ocean breeze swept across the beach. He'd parked in the lot next to the bandstand.

Traffic on Ocean Boulevard was at a standstill. Cars honked, and bass-heavy music blared while teenagers hung out of car windows, cat-calling and wolf-whistling the girls, and families strolled past the boardwalk-style surf shops, eateries, and novelty stores, stopping traffic while they crossed the street going to or from the beach. The scent of pizza, grilling hot dogs, seafood, and fried dough wafted on the salt-filled air.

Martin crossed the street, not sure why he'd come. Curious, he guessed.

He pulled open the heavy oak door to the Keel Haul and stepped inside.

A blast of cold air-conditioned air struck him while the Beach Boys sang about endless summers from a jukebox in the corner. The joint packed to capacity. The crowd was mostly young and boisterous. The men wore tank tops and Bermuda shorts or baggy swim trunks. It was bikini tops, cutoffs, and sundresses for the girls. The tables were filled with pitchers of beer, glass mugs, and fruity summertime drinks with little umbrellas in them, and the typical bar food fare: wings, burgers, fried seafood platters. A young man wearing an apron served the tables. Several surfboards leaned against a back wall. The bar, which ran along the opposite wall, was dark teak wood polished to a glossy shine.

While he'd never stepped foot below deck on an eighteenth-century sailing ship, he imagined it probably would've looked a lot like this. The walls were horizontal knotty wood planks. Booths lined the wall under the front windows, shuttered against the bright sunlight outside. Thick timbers ribbed the ceiling. Lighted lanterns hung from the beams. Candle-like sconces glowed over the booths. They had electric bulbs but flickered like flames.

Next to the jukebox were wooden barrels lashed together. Beside the door was an old wooden sea chest. Ropes, anchors, pulleys, fishing nets, and period-appropriate coastal maps hung on the walls. The smell of teak oil filled the air.

The tables and booths were all occupied except for one in the far back corner. It had a reserve plaque on it. The holder was a tiny replica of a brass wheel from an old ship.

Martin spotted Tara Sardana behind the bar. She was drying glasses with a bar rag. Bannon stood beside her, counting cash from the till of an old-fashioned cash register. Seated at the corner was the imposing redheaded Irishman named McMurphy. His large, ruddy hands wrapped around a heavy glass mug full of beer. Bannon had called him Skyjack.

Must be a nickname. Martin wondered if there was a story behind it.

Tara noticed him and nodded.

He crossed the room and sat at the one open spot at the bar. "Hey."

Tara laid down a paper napkin. "Drink?"

Bannon finished counting the cash and pushed the cash register drawer closed. "That 'I'm on duty, so I can't' excuse doesn't work here. Don't even try it."

He offered Martin his hand. They shook. Martin said, "Wouldn't dream of it. Beer. Whatever's cold and on tap."

"Good luck, sonny," said an old timer sitting farther down the bar wearing an old captain's hat. "You'll die of thirst before toots there will get around to serving you."

Martin still didn't know Tara all that well, but he braced for her volatile reaction.

She surprised him with her—for her—low-key response. She pointed the paring knife she'd been using to slice up limes at the old man. "You know what I can do with this, you old geezer."

"I'll tell you what to do with it," he thumped his glass mug on the bar, "you don't get me filled up."

"Keep it up, Floyd," she warned. "I'll cut your eye out."

"That's Captain Floyd to you, missy."

Tara waved the knife. "It'll be one-eyed Jack; you don't watch it."

Floyd cackled. "I always wanted to be a pirate. Argh."

Tara couldn't keep from laughing. She poured another beer and slid it down the bar to him.

"Don't mind him," Tara said to Martin. "He's nobody."

"He kind of came with the joint when I bought it," Bannon explained. "Thanks for coming, Detective."

Tara filled a frosted glass mug with a Sam Addams seasonal. She put it on Martin's napkin.

McMurphy downed the last of his beer. "I'm ready, too, Blades."

"When aren't you?" Tara shook her head. Her dark eyes sparkled with a mirth Martin had never seen before. She poured the big man a drink. The cop enjoyed seeing her this way.

He'd met her, stopped her from doing a very bad thing for an admirable reason, about a year ago. Since then, she'd insinuated herself in a few of his investigations. Had even saved his life a time or two. He liked her. And respected her. But he'd never known her to have a playful side.

At that moment, he realized how little he actually knew about her.

Martin sipped his beer and looked around. "Nice joint. Looks like you do pretty well, no?"

Bannon shrugged. "Summers are good. Out of season—"

"It's deader than a Louisiana crypt." McMurphy got up and walked over to Martin.

He shook Martin's hand. To Bannon, the pilot said, "Booth?"

"Yeah. We'll be right over."

McMurphy landed a heavy paw of a hand on Martin's shoulder. "Come on, copper. Over here."

He led Martin to the reserved booth. McMurphy slid in one side. Martin took the seat opposite. McMurphy pushed the reserved sign out of the way.

"Skyjack?" Martin said. "There a story behind that?"

"Yup."

"Care to share?"

"Nope. How long you known Blades? How'd you two… hook up."

Martin coughed, feeling like he was getting grilled by Becky Stuhlbarg's dad when he picked her up for their first date in high school.

"We've not…hooked up. We—"

"Aren't doing this," Tara said.

She put a tray on the table. It held five drinks. She slid in beside the cop.

Bannon joined them, pulling a vacant chair from a nearby table to sit at the end, leaving a space open next to McMurphy.

"We're waiting for one more."

Martin surveyed the three of them. "While we wait, how about you tell me why I'm here."

"We're just looking for a follow-up," Bannon said.

"To what?" Martin asked. "You're Coasties. Reservists, at that. You rescued those girls, and that's great work. Really, it was. But your job's done."

Bannon sipped his beer. An IPA from the 603 Brewery out of Londonderry. His mug was heavy glass with a Coast Guard cutter painted in black. Under the picture, it read: PATFORSWA.

Martin knew that stood for Patrol Forces Southwest Asia.

Tara had mentioned she'd met the two men while they were in Afghanistan, working for the Guard. He also knew she was an Egyptian national. Now in the U.S. on a government visa. She never talked about the circumstances of how she met the two men.

"Let's just say," Bannon set down his mug, "we don't leave in the middle of a movie."

Martin nodded. "You're curious. About the girls. I get that. They're—"

"We're more than curious," McMurphy said.

"We like to see things through to the end," Bannon added.

"What the hell's that mean?" Martin asked. "Like you want to be part of the investigation? It doesn't work that way."

"Curtis, we want to help," Tara said. "You've let me do that before."

"That...That's been different." Martin shook his head. "Thanks, fellas, but the BPDs got this. Besides, with the FBI, ICE, and Homeland Security involved, I've got too many chefs in the kitchen as it is."

Before anyone could respond, a pretty brunette approached the table. She wore blue jeans and a white sleeveless shirt, unbuttoned over a tight, black tank top shirt. She removed her sunglasses and hooked them on her shirt.

She slid into the booth next to McMurphy. The big Irishman draped an arm over her shoulders, gave her a quick squeeze, and a brotherly peck on the cheek.

Bannon made the introductions.

Among the drinks Tara had delivered, there was a tall glass filled with a pink liquid and ice, topped with a fruit slice of some kind, with what looked like mint leaves and a little red stir stick straw.

"This for me?" Kayla asked, brightening. She looked like she'd been through a tough day.

"I thought you'd need it," Tara said.

Kayla grabbed the drink and sipped.

"What is it?" Martin asked.

Kayla finished sipping and smiled. "A Urrak. Tara. It's wonderful."

McMurphy wrinkled his forehead. "What the hell's an Urrak?"

"A drink from Goa in India," Kayla explained. "It's a distilled spirit from the fermented juices of cashew apples."

McMurphy screwed up his face even worse and hoisted his mug. "I'll stick with Sam Addams. Thank you very much."

Martin returned his attention to Bannon. "What's this all about? Really?"

Bannon sipped his beer. "We're working this. We can either do that together... or you can enjoy your beer—"

"Over there." McMurphy pointed at the bar. "And watch from the sidelines."

"Curtis," Tara said, "We can help."

Martin felt backed into a corner. Tara had helped him in the past. That was true. And she'd proven to be a capable partner in the field. But if his bosses ever got wind he'd involved a team of civilians, put them in harm's way during an investigation...

"You're putting me in a tough predicament," Martin said. "You have no authority. No jurisdiction—"

"The things you're worried about, Detective," Bannon said. "Aren't the things you need to be concerned with."

"You mean my career. My pension."

"Curtis," Tara said. "Do you trust me?"

Martin looked at her. Without hesitation, he said, "Yeah. Sure."

"And I trust them," Tara said. "With my life. I have. Many times."

"Okay," Martin said. "Let's say for a hot second I could entertain this. What is it you want? And more importantly, what can you bring to the table?"

"Bring us up to speed on the human trafficking problem in Boston," Bannon said. "In the whole of the Northeast, I would guess."

Martin downed the last of his beer as the waiter brought over another tray of drinks. He took away the empties. "It's for prostitution and pornography, mostly. Women, girls, young boys. There's some indentured servant stuff. Migrant workers, and the like. But here in Boston, the girls are usually more homegrown. Runaways, drug addicts, homeless, they're our more typical victims."

"But you get imported girls, too?" Bannon asked.

"Sure. The cartels gotta cater to everyone's taste, I suppose. But this container thing? That's new." Martin paused. "When we find victims from overseas, they're usually not from Africa. More often, they're from Eastern Europe and Southeast Asia. And, of course, Mexico and South America."

"Our intelligence tells us the same thing," Kayla added. "Africa supplies Eastern Europe and Asia more than here."

"Who runs it?" Bannon asked. "The prostitution here. Who are the major players?"

"Funny you bring that up," Martin said. "There was a major upheaval in the criminal underground here a few months back. The major players, as you put it, are the Italians, the Irish, and the Asians—Japanese and Chinese. They're the big three. The Russians and Serbs, blacks, and motorcycle gangs? They each get their little turfdoms to run, kicking back a hefty piece of their profits, of course. All of 'em run girls."

"And this upheaval you mentioned," Bannon said. "Tell us about that."

He glanced at the others at the table. Martin couldn't decipher the meaning behind the look, though.

"Surely you saw some of it on the news," Martin said. "The leader of the local Yakuza, Toi Kwon, was arrested on kidnapping, murder, and attempted murder charges. Jimmy 'Paddy' Flanagan, the top guy running the Irish mob. He got caught with a storage unit full of drugs. Enough to put him away for years. They're both currently incarcerated, pending their trials."

McMurphy looked down at his beer. Then he tossed it back in a single gulp.

Martin continued, "And Vinnie 'Knuckles' LaScala, the boss of bosses here in New England. He just up and vanished. Houdini-style."

"Or," McMurphy said, "Jimmy Hoffa-style."

"Yeah," Martin said, "Like that."

"That would be a good thing," Bannon asked. "Isn't it?"

"You'd think, but no," Martin said. "The world doesn't seem to work that way. With nobody in charge, everybody and their uncle are trying to grab the brass ring. We've had gang spats, and when I say spats, I mean bullets flying, bodies dropping, bloody street battles. A bunch of dead gangster wannabes. Luckily, no civilian casualties... yet."

"Where's New York in all this?" McMurphy asked. "The families down there run the show up here. At least, they used to."

Martin leveled him with a curious stare.

"I heard that," McMurphy backtracked. "Read it somewhere. A Boston Globe exposé, maybe."

"Typically, that is true," Martin said. "But the New York families, they're not what they used to be."

"Surely the violence from the lower echelon the cops can handle," Bannon said. "Can't they?"

"Usually," Martin said. "But this is unlike anything I've seen. Whenever there's been a power shift, a few knuckleheads try to step up to the plate. It gets ugly but stays relatively self-contained. But the intel we're getting, including from my contacts in the NYPD Organized Crime Bureau, is there's a new player in the game."

"Who?" Bannon asked.

"No clue. Intel we're getting is that these spats we've had aren't the typical turf battles like we originally thought," Martin said. "They could be the open salvo of a widespread takeover. My NYPD guy says the New York families are being uncharacteristically cagey about it all."

"Laying low to see who's strong enough to win the throne?" McMurphy asked.

Martin shook his head. "That's the way it used to play out. And if no one stood out, they'd step in and anoint a new king. This? The fear is, they're worried about this new... player."

"Because they don't know who it is?" Bannon asked.

"That," Martin said. "Or, they're afraid because they do."

After a few moments, as that thought sunk in and they drank, Martin said, "Okay, my turn to ask the questions. What have you got for me?"

"The crew of the *Marken*," Bannon said, "the ship carrying the girls, they're in custody, being detained and questioned by DHS. We've got an inside source there. When we know something, you'll know it."

"Not exactly how the alphabet agencies usually work with us locals, so thanks for that."

Kayla cleared her throat. "One person they won't be interrogating is the captain."

"Why not the captain?" Martin asked.

Kayla filled the table in on what had occurred on the *Lightfoot*. "Captain Gumede took his own life rather than be captured. His final words were, 'I did nothing wrong. Only what they told me to do. I had no choice. Please forgive me.'

"Whoever they are," she said, "had him scared to death."

CHAPTER **SEVEN**

Chinatown
Boston, M.A.

THE NEXT DAY, MARTIN PULLED his detective ride
to the curb opposite a dry cleaners' establishment. A three-
story brick building. The storefront had a large shop window
covered with vertical blinds inside. From the looks of it, office
space occupied the second floor. Each had large windows and
sleeve air-conditioning units embedded in the wall. On the
opposite side of the street where Martin parked was a row of
residential apartment buildings. Green space and thick trees
shrouded the building, casting full, cooling shadows over the
green lawn and sidewalk.

Tara leaned over to get a better look at the dry cleaners
through the windshield. The name and services provided were
painted across the plate glass along with a rising sun over
a horizon line.

Golden Fresh Dry Cleaners & Laundry Services
Same-day drop-off & pickup
Lowest prices in Greater Boston

"A dry cleaner?" she asked Martin. "Really?"

"A surprisingly lucrative cash business," he said. "Great
for laundering. Money. That is. Wang's got an office on
the second floor."

Tara had had a previous run-in with Yang Wang a few
months earlier. As criminal masterminds went, the young
Asian man was a joke. Incredulously, she asked, "Wang's in
position to take over the Yakuza?"

Toi Kwon, the former Yakuza leader was Wang's father-in-law.

"Yes and no. Prison doesn't stop the old man from running things," Martin said. "But he needs a proxy. Wang's an idiot, but he's easy to control. And he's family."

"You think he'll know something?"

Martin shrugged. "The criminal underbelly in Boston has imploded. Impossible to know who knows what anymore. Not til the dust settles." He stared at her from behind his dark Ray Bans. "After our little sit-down yesterday, I can't help but ask. You and your friends."

"What about them?"

"I get the sense there's more going on there than some old service buddies hanging out, reminiscing about your time in the sandbox?"

Tara dodged the question. "Let's go see what Wang's got to say."

She reached for the door handle, but Martin put a hand on her arm. "Blades, be straight with me. You asked me if I trust you. And I do. But this only works if we're honest with each other."

"There's nothing I can say."

Martin didn't drop it. "I know McMurphy is Paddy Flanagan's kid. I know Kwon was arrested and brought in by a police chief operating way out of his jurisdiction in Portsmouth. Where a couple of his henchmen were found dead from multiple stab wounds. All that, after you had your own run-in with Wang, Blades."

Tara remained silent.

"Because it was Kwon, nobody asked too many questions," Martin said. "But that police chief's from Hampton Beach. Where the Keel Haul is. Owned by Bannon. Where you tend bar. Where McMurphy hangs out and day drinks all day. All of that is not a coincidence."

That he'd learned all this since the night before didn't surprise Tara. She knew how good a detective he was.

"I also know McMurphy's father's in jail on a barrage of charges. A man who hadn't so much as had a parking ticket in years. Suddenly he's sloppy enough to get caught with enough product to put him away for two lifetimes. Then there's LaScala's disappearance. Happen to know anything about that?"

Tara did know the man's fate. It wasn't a promising one. And yes, the three of them had played a part in the city's crime lords getting the justice they all richly deserved. But she couldn't tell Martin that.

"There are things I can't tell you," Tara said. "It's a need-to-know thing."

"That sounds like government-speak to me."

Tara shrugged. Her silent 'I can neither confirm nor deny response' spoke volumes, too.

"Who are you people?"

She gave him a hapless smile. "You just have to trust us. We won't lie to you."

"You just won't tell me the whole truth."

"It's the best I can give you, Curtis," Tara said. "Now, please...."

"I guess that'll have to do." Martin snapped up the car door handle and got out. She could feel his anger. "Come on. Let's see if we can get more information out of Wang than I can from my own so-called partners."

Tara got out of the unmarked car, feeling trapped and frustrated. Her anger surged inside her. She stormed across the street, stopping traffic.

Martin raced after her. "Blades, wait."

She didn't.

Tara pushed through the dry cleaners' front door. The overhead bell jangled. There was a small, middle-aged Asian woman behind the counter. Tara was relieved to see there were no customers around. That would make what happened next easier.

"Can I help you?" the woman asked.

"Where's Wang?"

"Who? There is no Wang here."

As she spoke, the woman took a step back. Her eyes flittered to the underside of the counter.

Tara noticed.

Quicker than her age would have indicated, from under the counter, the old woman whipped out a sawed-off, double-barrel shotgun. She pumped the slide.

Tara lunged over the counter and grabbed the weapon's stock. Stronger than the older woman, Tara yanked her forward. The woman stumbled but held the weapon in a death grip. Tara grabbed her by the throat with her free hand.

The woman gasped.

Tara tightened her grip around the woman's throat. "Drop it."

The bell over the door jingled again. It was Martin coming inside.

"Jesus! That didn't take long."

He rushed forward and helped wrestle the gun from the woman's hands.

"Got it," he said.

Tara held the woman's throat. "Wang. Where is he?"

She worked her way around the counter without loosening her grip. The older woman gasped. Tara pressed her against the counter, arching her back. Tara leaned in. She lowered her voice to a threatening whisper. "Last chance. Where is Wang?"

She waited for a response. She didn't get one. Squeezing harder, she said, "I'll squeeze until your head pops off. Where. Is. Wang?"

Fear filled the older woman's eyes. Her voice a horse whisper. "Upstairs. He's upstairs."

Tara shoved the woman toward Martin as he came through the swing gate. He caught the woman. Tara headed for the back, pushing through the forest of plastic-wrapped clothes hanging from mechanical racks.

"Blades."

She turned.

He pointed at a camera aimed down at the counter. It's little red light on. If Wang was upstairs, he had eyes on them.

That meant a welcoming committee waiting for them. Tara's lips twisted into a menacing smile. She pulled her haladie knife from its sheath at the small of her back.

Martin frowned. "Here we go."

He pushed the woman to the wall and secured her to a thin metal pole that supported the overhead rack with flexicuffs from his jacket pocket. He darted back to the front door, flipped the thumb lock, and turned the store closed sign facing out. Then he closed the Venetian blinds. The last thing they needed was for civilians to wander in.

Martin unloaded the shotgun, pocketed the shells, and pulled his Glock. "Blades. Wait for me."

Again, she didn't.

At the archway in the back of the store, Tara came to a door with a red emergency exit sign. Beside it, there was a black railed staircase leading up to the second floor. She'd just stepped on the first tread when a door upstairs banged open.

That would be the welcoming committee.

Three young Asian men rushed to the top of the stairs, crowded around the small landing. They all wore leather jackets and oversized pants too large for their hips. One carried a switchblade. Another armed with a sword. They looked down at her with dark, menacing eyes.

She looked up at them.

In their pursuit of Toi Kwon, Tara had been forced to face off against two actual ninja-trained assassins. Their skill had been formidable. It had been a tough fight, but in the end, she'd come out victorious.

They were the dead bodies Martin had referenced earlier.

She watched these three rush down the stairs. They were chaotic and amateurish, undisciplined. Like a pack of wild animals stomping and yelling.

Under her breath, she said, "Stupid kids who watch too many kung fu movies."

Still, every opponent, no matter how unskilled, can be dangerous.

The one with the switchblade was in the lead.

Tara stepped back as he leaped the final three steps. He whooped and landed on the floor, squatted, with the knife over his head. A crouching tiger pose.

Tara fisted the handle of her haladie, with its curved blades on either side. With her other hand, she waved at the young man. *Come on.*

He charged with another yell.

He brought the knife down. A striking motion.

Tara easily sidestepped his advance. She moved to the side, avoiding his downward swinging arm. She swiped the haladie up. The left blade cut through the man's upper arm before she twisted her wrist, slicing the right blade through his cheek. Neither cut was deep enough to seriously harm. But they bled. And they would hurt. A lot.

Her attacker grabbed his arm, covering the wound.

Tara shouldered him into the wall, then pushed him back. He tripped over the step behind him and fell, dropping his knife. Clutching his arm with one hand and cupping his face with the other, he rolled away from her, moaning.

She turned to face her next attacker. The man with the sword.

A terrible weapon choice for the confined space they were in.

Tara advanced up the stairs.

The swordsman raised the long blade over his head and swung it in a downward arc without finesse.

Tara easily avoided the attack. Her attacker swung the sword to his left, catching the blade between the spindles of the railing. He cursed. Tara rushed up the stairs before the young man could withdraw the blade from between the railing.

She grabbed his arm and pressed it across his body. Her momentum forced him back. He fell onto the steps behind them. She sliced her blade across the back of his wrist. Not cutting deep but enough to cause serious pain. Her control over the haladie was that precise.

He screamed and released his grip on the sword. It clattered to the stairs.

Tara swung her bent elbow. Struck the man in the nose, breaking it. Her attacker howled and covered his bloody nose.

Martin shouted, "Tara!"

He tossed her a set of steel handcuffs. She cuffed the man to the railing and kicked the sword the rest of the way down the steps as she stood up. Martin had secured her first attacker to a thick waterpipe with flexicuffs.

Seeing his friends quickly dispatched, wide-eyed, the third would-be assailant ran back up the stairs and disappeared into the room they'd come out of.

Martin joined her, stepping over the downed wannabe swordsman.

"Nicely done," he said.

Tara headed up the stairs. At the door, she tried the knob. Locked.

Martin joined her. She stepped back and kicked in the door with her booted foot.

The old wooden frame splintered. The door slammed against the back wall. In it, the frosted glass panel shattered. She stepped through the open doorway.

Their third attacker stood cowering in the far corner.

Wang stood behind a desk. Framed by the picture window and bright sunlight behind him. He had his hand inside a top desk drawer.

Tara twirled the haladie in her hand. Despite being a dozen feet away from him, she said, "You pull a gun out, I'll slice your hand off. And that's just where I start."

Wang pulled his hand out very slowly, holding his hands in the air. His fingers spread wide.

"You. Again. What did I do to deserve this."

Martin stepped into the room behind Tara. To the man in the corner, he said, "You. Out."

The young man didn't even look to Wang for permission. He bolted.

Martin moved farther into the room. "Sit down, Wang. We need to talk."

Wang sat. "I've done nothing wrong."

Martin circled to Wang's side of the desk. "That's a lie. We both know it."

"I want my lawyer."

Martin pushed Wang out of the way and opened the top desk drawer. He retrieved a small, silver-plated revolver. He admired it before stuffing it in his belt at the small of his back.

"That's a family heirloom."

"I'll treasure it as if it's my very own," Martin said.

"What do you want?"

Tara let Martin ask the questions. She stood to one side of the door, where she could listen and keep an eye on any incoming reinforcements. She didn't expect any.

"A cargo container came into port yesterday. Inside it were seven women. Trafficked women. One of them is dead."

Wang tried to look defiant but only pulled off frightened. "I don't know anything about that."

"You sure?" Martin pressed.

"I'm sure. I didn't have anything to do with it."

"Oh, that we know," Martin said. "You're not capable of anything on that scale. Don't have the connections to do anything that ambitious."

Tara moved closer to the desk. She twirled the haladie through her fingers like a baton.

Wang watched her advance. He licked his lips nervously. "Then why are you here? Other than to harass me. Insult me."

"We want to know who does have those connections," Martin said. "Who has that kind of ambition?"

"What about your father-in-law?" Tara said.

"What about him? He's in jail," Wang said. "You put him there."

Martin gave her an accusatory look but said, "He's still running things."

Wang's shoulders sagged. "Not that. The girls. I read in the papers they're from Africa. What do the Yakuza know about African women?" Wang hesitated, clearly gauging how much to say to get clear of this situation without getting him in deeper trouble with the cop. Or worse, the woman.

"Trafficking like that?" He shook his head. "Too much trouble. Too expensive. Why do that? When there's so many...."

"Vulnerable girls here in Boston you can exploit," Martin said.

"There's someone else," Wang said.

"Who?" Martin asked.

"How do I know."

Tara pressed. "Who?"

"I don't know."

Tara twirled the haladie faster in her hand. "We're not leaving without an answer."

Wang sighed. "I don't know. I don't. Things are… messed up lately. Turmoil everywhere since…."

"LaScala disappeared," Martin guessed.

Wang nodded. "And the Irish got neutered. And Kwon."

"There's someone new," Tara said.

"That is the word," Wang admitted.

"It's got to be more than just word on the street," Martin said. "They've had to have reached out by now. Talked to you. To the Irish and the Italians. They can't just take over without anyone knowing who they are. How big is their operation? Their reach? How much muscle do they have?"

"I told you. I don't know. Only that my people, Flannagan, and the Italians, too, they're getting slaughtered out on the streets. Ambushed. Executed. It's not like it's ever been before."

"Who's behind it?" Martin asked. "Who?"

"All I can give you is a name," Wang said.

"What is it?" Tara asked.

"*Skaduwee*," Wang said. "He—they go by *Skaduwee*."

CHAPTER EIGHT

THE STORE CLOSED SIGN on the dry cleaners' door worried Jade van Wyk.

She stopped her companion from crossing the street. A large man with a bald head and dark skin, Arno Mzobe, paused at Jade's touch on his arm. Dressed in loose white trousers and a beige safari shirt that stretched at the seams to contain his broad chest and tree-limb-sized arms. With a 9mm Vektor SP1 tucked in his waistband at the small of his back, he had a billao sheathed on his hip. The untucked safari shirt concealed both.

They stepped back into the shadows under the trees. Behind them were the apartment buildings across the street from the Golden Fresh Dry Cleaners.

"What is it?" Mzobe asked. His voice was deep and rumbling.

"I don't know," she said. "We wait."

Jade wore a yellow, halter tank top blouse and white shorts with stylish sandals. The bright colors accentuated her almost ink-black dark skin, which gleamed in the bright summer sun. She wore large gold earrings. Her hair shaved to a number two buzzcut. She boasted a sinewy muscular frame with less than five percent body fat.

They didn't have to wait long.

Minutes later, the door to the dry cleaners opened.

Two people emerged. Neither was Asian.

Customers perhaps, Jade wondered, but then why the closed sign? She studied the two people. The man was in his late twenties. He had brown hair and alert eyes. Handsome, with a cleft in his chin. He immediately struck Jade as police.

His companion was another story.

Strikingly beautiful. Her skin was deeply tanned. She had a full-flowing mane of raven black hair. She walked with a determined gait. Confidence radiated from her. Fully attentive to her surroundings. Alert. The woman had dressed for functional comfort. Thick dark boots. Gray denim jeans, a scoop-neck t-shirt under a men's style dress shirt, unbuttoned, with the sleeves rolled up her forearms.

Jade didn't know why, but this one intrigued her. There was something about her that made Jade uneasy. As they crossed the street, she pulled Mzobe into an embrace and kissed his mouth. Hard. She watched the woman and the cop over his shoulder as they got into an unmarked police car—he took the wheel—and they drove away.

Mzobe was neither surprised nor put off by Jade's sudden action. They were lovers, after all.

When the car was gone, she took him by the hand and led him across the street without explanation. They hurried, looking like lovers darting across traffic.

The dry cleaners' door wasn't locked. Mzobe pulled it open. Once inside, he closed and locked it behind them, leaving the store closed sign in place.

Jade arched an eyebrow, spotting the middle-aged woman secured to a pole with flexicuffs. A young Asian man used a switchblade knife to see through her plastic binds. Hearing the bell jangle, he backed away from the woman. He pointed the blade at them. His hand shook. He had a fresh cut across his cheek. His sleeve soaked with blood.

Jade wondered at what had happened here.

"You're back," he said. "Stay away."

Was he mistaking her for the dark-skinned woman who'd just left? There was a passing resemblance, maybe. Perhaps the shock of his injuries confused him. His fear was undoubtedly real enough.

"Put the knife away," she said. "We are not the people who just left."

The man's features softened, realizing his mistake. But he remained cautious.

"What do you want?"

"To talk to your boss. Yang Wang," she said. "Is he here?"

The man nodded quickly. "Yes. Upstairs."

Jade strolled through the counter swing gate with Mzobe close behind her.

As she passed through the archway in the back, she heard the young man's soft grunt as Mzobe gutted him with his billao. Then, he did the same to the woman. Killing them both.

He used a freshly laundered and pressed dress shirt to wipe the blood off the magnificent double-edged, leaf-shaped blade. The hilt was made of buffalo horn. The weapon had historical significance. It dated back to the Dervish Resistance of 1869 to 1920.

Jade gave it to him as a gift from her father's collection after the first time they made love.

Finished cleaning the blade, Mzobe frowned when he saw another man sitting on the stairs, cuffed to the railing. He shook his head, slit the young man's throat, then went about wiping down the blade. Again. He followed Jade up the stairs.

In the office, they found Wang with yet another young Asian. Both men alerted like frightened possums in the wild when she and Mzobe entered the office.

Behind the desk, Wang jumped to his feet, spilling a bottle of Hibiki Japanese whisky across the desk. Two tumblers rolled off the desk and hit the floor.

"What do you want now? I told you everything—"

He cut himself off, quickly realizing his mistake.

"What did you tell, Mr. Wang?" Jade asked. "And to whom?"

"I didn't say nothing. I swear. Not a word."

Jade made a tsk, tsk sound. "I do not believe you, Mr. Wang. Arno, do you believe him?"

"No," Mzobe said. The single syllable sounded like a thunder boom.

"I just meant...."

Jade glanced from Wang to his last remaining henchmen.

"You. Step outside with Arno so Mr. Wang and I might speak. In private."

Mzobe walked with the man to the door. He pulled the door closed, its window in pieces on the floor. Glass crunched under their feet.

When they were gone, Jade said, "Your visitors, Mr. Wang. Who were they?"

"Cops. A detective named Martin."

"And the woman?"

Wang dropped down into his chair. "A psychopath. Off her rocker, looney tunes."

"A name, Mr. Wang."

"I don't know." He held out a hand, motioning, "I swear I don't know. The cop. He called her Blades. That's crazy, right? All I know is," he stammered, "she's crazy. You saw what she did to my guys, right? With some kind of double-bladed knife. And this isn't the first time she's attacked my people. A couple of months back. She… she needs to be put down, like a wild animal."

"Detective Martin. Boston police?"

"Yes."

"What did they want?"

"They were talking about girls, women, coming in from overseas. On cargo ships. How one's dead. They're trying to pin it on me. I told them. I didn't have anything to do with that. Nothing. That's all I said."

Jade didn't like it, nor did she believe the little man. "That was all?"

"That's it. Everything. I told them to get out. That I didn't have anything to do with those trafficked girls."

"I know you didn't. But, Arno. Do you believe that's all Mr. Wang told them?"

Mzobe had silently appeared at the door again. He was again wiping blood from his billao. "No."

"Oh, come on. I swear."

"You know who I am, don't you?"

"Specifically, no. But you're the one I was told about. The one wants to take over."

"Not exactly, Mr. Wang."

65

"That's fine, lady," Wang said. "Whatever. I don't want no part of this anymore. All this, the criminal stuff, that's all my father-in-law. Kwon. I just married his daughter, is all. I went to school to be an architect, not for any of… this. You want to take it all over. Be my guest. Have it. Run everything."

Wang swallowed hard. "I just want out."

Jade smiled. "Do you hear that, Arno? Mr. Wang just wants out."

"You offer no resistance?" Mzobe asked.

"No. I can read the writing on the wall."

"Or in a fortune cookie?" Mzobe said with a tight smile.

"Yeah. Sure. Whatever. You want me gone. I'm gone."

"We're glad to hear that," Jade said. "It makes things much simpler."

"Then I'm free to go?" Wang stepped out from behind the desk.

"In a minute," Jade said. "There's just a few minor things we need to work out. Final details."

"Happy to. Anything."

"I'll leave you to work them out with Mr. Mzobe here." She patted her lover's arm, stretched up on her tiptoes, and kissed his cheek. "I'll meet you outside, my love."

Jade left the room.

She glanced down at the third henchman slumped dead in the hallway outside the office. Bright red blood pooled in his lap. She stepped over the body. Going down the stairs, she heard Wang cry out. His body thumped to the floor before she reached the bottom step.

Five minutes later, Mzobe came out of the dry cleaners. He used a key to lock the front door and crossed the street. He held a computer hard drive in his hand. A smear of blood on the outer casing.

Joining her, Jade took his hand. They strolled down the street as lovers do in Boston in the summertime.

"I'm worried about this woman," Jade said. "This Blade person."

"Do not," Mzobe said. "If she's a problem, we'll eliminate her."

She kissed his hand. "What shall we do with the rest of the afternoon?"

"The Boston Ballet is playing at the Opera House."

"Oh," Jade shivered with delight. "I do love the ballet."

CHAPTER NINE

The USCGC Lightfoot
Gulf of Maine

INSIDE A CRAMPED ROOM on the *Lightfoot*, McMurphy sat at a table wearing headphones, staring at a monitor awash in a watery purplish glow. Tiny bubbles rose across the screen.

He gingerly manipulated a joystick control.

Bannon stood behind him, leaning over his shoulder. The video signal being sent back to them came from an ROV underwater drone McMurphy maneuvered through the dark bowels of the *CS Marken*. Now resting on the rocky ocean floor of Wilkinson Basin, two-hundred-ninety-one feet below them.

Tethered back to the *Lightfoot* by a thin yellow cable, the M2 drone was constructed of compact aluminum alloy, painted bright yellow. It had eight vectored thrusters, giving it the ability to move in all directions. Equipped with a robotic claw, a 4K UHD camera with a f/2.5 aperture, and two 2000-lumen LED lights. The remotely operated vehicle had a 155Wh lithium battery, giving them six hours to complete their search.

There was a knock on the door.

Bannon straightened up. He arched his back with a groan, welcoming the interruption. "Come in."

Captain Coram stepped inside carrying a tray with a silver coffee pot and three white coffee cups and saucers. The cups had the Coast Guard emblem on them. "Thought you could use this."

Bannon smiled. "Kayla said you were a gracious host."

"Maybe I'll open a seaside bed and breakfast when I retire."

"An old seadog like you retiring? Fat chance."

McMurphy set the drone's one-touch depth-lock mode and tossed his headphones onto the table. "I don't suppose you doctored any of 'em with a little Irish whiskey?"

"Sorry, Chief. We operate a dry ship. Regulations and all."

McMurphy accepted the offered coffee cup. "No worries."

He set the cup and saucer down next to his joystick. He dug around inside a duffle by his feet. Came out with a silver flask. He unscrewed the top and poured a healthy dollop of booze into his cup. He raised the flask. "*Semper Paratus*."

The Coast Guard's motto. "Always ready."

Coram shook his head. "I'm not seeing this."

McMurphy offered the flask around.

Coram shook his head, filling cups for Bannon and himself. He indicated the computer monitor. "Any luck?"

Bannon and McMurphy had returned to the *Lightfoot* with questions about why the *Marken* went down so quickly. Beyond the turbulent seas, the cargo ship had taken on water below deck, a lot of it. Bannon had seen that while he was below deck searching for survivors. Barely a category one, the storm's severity couldn't account for the amount of flooding he saw, for the loss of the ship. Any halfway-seasoned skipper should've been able to sail through it safely.

Something more had happened onboard the *Marken*. Bannon was sure of it. Something sinister.

And they found it.

"Show him," Bannon said. McMurphy tapped a few keys on the keypad.

The image on the screen scrambled and then cleared. Now, it showed the small ROV making its initial descent through the purple-black water of the Atlantic Ocean. Its powerful lights passed across the superstructure before dropping down along the hull.

"This is a recording of what we found," Bannon said.

The *Marken* laid at a severe angle on its port side but, lucky for them, hung up on a shallow rock formation that kept the port bow section from settling into the sandy bottom, which would have covered up what McMurphy and Bannon had discovered.

The drone moved along the hull. Coram leaned closer to the screen. He saw what they'd found. An irregular, blackish shape in the forward nose of the ship. "Is that a hole?"

"Yup," McMurphy said.

The drone moved closer. The opening jutted out in an asymmetrical starburst pattern. If one could call it a pattern. The outer edges peeled back, like the top of a metal can that had...

"An explosion," Coram said. "From inside."

"A good size one, too," McMurphy said. "Considering the damage."

"What could have caused it?"

"Not a what?" Bannon said. "I suspect a who."

McMurphy let the recording play for a few minutes more, displaying the drone's earlier examination of the hole before shutting off the playback.

"We just moved the drone inside when you arrived," Bannon said.

"Then, by all means," Coram said. "Continue."

McMurphy sipped his doctored coffee, then set his cup down, put his headphones on, and unlocked the drone's depth-lock mode.

The drone moved deeper into the dark interior. Its powerful LED light gave them a clear view of the p-ways it traversed. The deeper McMurphy sent the drone in, the slower he worked it, careful not to tangle the tethering cord.

"See anything that tells you what caused the explosion?"

"Not yet," Bannon said. "For a more detailed inspection, we'll probably need to make several runs at it. We've brought four more batteries with us. That'll give us a total of twenty-four hours. Time enough to recharge the batteries and cycle through them again if necessary. For now, we're just trying to get a cursory look around."

"Well, here's something I didn't expect to find," McMurphy said.

Bannon and Coram crowded around, leaning in over his shoulders. If he minded, the big Irishman didn't say.

On the screen, the drone had moved along a darkened corridor. A school of fish darted across the screen, then away.

Bannon frowned, noticing the water in the bright white beams of light had clouded significantly. Bits of large particles drifted around the drone like falling cottonwood. He braced for what he suspected McMurphy had figured out.

Coram leaned in closer and squinted. "Is that…a body?"

McMurphy panned the drone to the left, then moved it closer to a metal ladder at the end of a passageway. What Coram had seen came into focus. A human body sat on the floor. Their legs splayed out. The trousers and loose shirt floated in the gently stirring water.

McMurphy moved the drone in tighter.

A man. He had dark skin. His longish, dark hair swished in the water. Fish and other sea creatures had nibbled at his exposed skin, leaving flaps waving. The flecks of skin and blood accounted for the floating cloudy particles. His eyes were wide open. One had been pecked clean.

Coram turned away from the screen. "Before Gumede killed himself, we questioned him about there only being twelve crewmates onboard."

"A life for a life," Bannon said. "Look."

He pointed at the screen.

The dead man's arms were clasped around the rung of the ladder. Around his wrists were a pair of silver handcuffs. They winked like sparkling diamond bracelets in the drone's powerful lights.

The man was bound to the ladder.

Left to die as the cargo ship went down.

CHAPTER TEN

Suffolk County House of Corrections
Boston, M.A.

WHILE BANNON AND McMURPHY were on the *Lightfoot* discovering the body of the murdered crewmate, Kayla Clarke was cooling her heels in the waiting area of the ICE Detection Center, housed in the same building as the Suffolk County House of Corrections. Given that Immigration and Customs Enforcement and the Coast Guard both fell under the purview of Homeland Security and that she was assigned to the Staff Judge Advocate's Office, it wasn't Kayla's first visit to the facility.

She wore her service dress blues and checked the gold watch on her left wrist. A gift from her dad. She'd been waiting for ten minutes.

Deciding to give those in charge five more minutes, she was relieved to hear the inner door buzz. She glanced up. A middle-aged African-American man with dark skin and graying hair at his temples stood at the open door. He wore khaki pants and a dark blue t-shirt. An ICE badge embroidered on his shirt. He wore his actual badge clipped to his belt.

He held the door open. "This way, Lieutenant."

Once she'd passed through, the steel door closed behind her.

They had entered a large room the size of a high school gymnasium. With a cavernous ceiling, the space was sectioned off into large, twenty-by-twenty-foot cells. Eight-foot-high chain link fencing. Each cell had a single bench inside along one fence. Each cell was crowded with dozens of people.

Many clung to fences, watching her and the ICE agent walk by.

"I'm Ernest Abioye," the agent said. His accent was deep and rich. "Ernie's fine."

He held out his hand. They shook, continuing past the rows of cages.

"Kayla."

"I'm from the Philadelphia office. Came up this morning. There's not many of us who speak Afrikaans."

"I would imagine not."

He caught her looking at him.

"I'm a U.S. citizen," Abioye said. "If that's what you want to know."

"I didn't say—"

"People always have questions. Son of an immigrant. Why ICE?"

"I didn't question—"

Seems like an odd choice, doesn't it?" Abioye smiled broadly. "My mother's American. An officer in the Navy. My father was Namibian. It's how she and Dad met. She believed in service to her country. But that doesn't answer your question. Because my father was foreign-born, you think I should support open borders and widespread immigration. Illegal or otherwise."

"I didn't say that."

"In my opinion," Abioye said, "this is the greatest country on Earth. There's a reason so many people want to come here. And I think everyone should be welcome. But just like your home, we lock our doors. Control who we let in and when. That's how we grant the greatest access to the most people. Without depleting our resources. And keep our country safe. ICE wasn't my first choice, but I believe in their mission."

He left it at that. "Here we are."

They stopped at a cage.

Inside were the six women who'd been rescued from the *Marken*. They wore ICE sweatshirts and non-descript gray slacks. They'd had an opportunity to shower and clean up. And to eat. Several of them sat huddled on the bench. There was a table in the corner. Snack foods and drinks on it. One woman held an apple in her hand.

Abioye unlocked the gate.

The women watched them with sideways glances. Suspicion in their eyes.

Stepping inside, Kayla said, "Hi. I'm Lieutenant Clarke. Kayla. I am with the United States Coast Guard."

She paused as Abioye translated in Afrikaans.

It was a little thing, but watching their expressions, particularly their eyes, Kayla read continued confusion. Did they not understand what Agent Abioye was telling them?

She turned to him. "They don't seem to understand you."

Abioye frowned. He spoke again.

What he said sounded close to what he'd said earlier. Just slightly different to her ear. But several of the women brightened, clearly understanding him now.

Abioye smiled. "It's not Afrikaans they speak. It's Oshiwambo."

"I've never heard of it," Kayla said.

"It is a Bantu language. A dialect cluster mostly spoken in southern Angola and northern Namibia. There are only about one million Oshiwambo speakers, but it is widely spoken by the migrant workers there."

"How do you know—"

"My father," Abioye said. "A migrant worker before he immigrated here and married. He worked in the uranium mines in the Erongo region of Namibia."

"Can you tell them I'm here to help? That we want to make sure they're okay."

She waited for Abioye to translate. Then she went on.

"While you are here, nothing bad will happen to you. You are safe. But we need your help. We know you were brought here against your will. We know you were abused. That you almost died. We want to bring the men responsible for this, for hurting you, to justice."

A small woman, barely over five feet tall, stepped forward. She was young, in her early twenties, and Caucasian, though with rich, tanned skin. She stood in front of Kayla. Planted her feet. She stared up at Kayla with hard, defiant eyes.

In English, she said, "What do you want from us? And how do you plan on caring for these women?"

Kayla blinked. "You speak English?"

"I just did," the woman said. "And I'd like an answer to my question."

"I'd like to know who I'm speaking with," Kayla said. "Your name, please."

"Aletta. Aletta Kamati. The men who did this to us, the crew of the *Marken*. Are they arrested?"

"They are being detained."

"Detained is not arrested."

"They will be held while we conduct our investigation."

"Are we detained?"

"No. We understand you were brought here against your wishes. No charges are pending against any of you. But we would ask for your patience. And your cooperation. While law enforcement and legal authorities investigate, build a case against the crew of the *Marken?*"

"Or?" Aletta challenged.

Before Kayla could reply, a woman came up behind Aletta and whispered in her ear. It was not in English.

"She wants to know what is to become of them," Abioye said.

"Can you tell her?" Aletta asked. "Tell them all?"

"It's complicated," Kayla said. "You were forcibly brought here. We understand, but our laws. We need to sort out your... their statuses."

"They do not wish to go back," Aletta said. "They demand asylum. Can you give them that?"

Kayla hesitated, framing her response as carefully as possible. "We can make that case. Hire attorneys to represent you. But, I," she paused, "I can't promise you that. I don't have that authority."

"I do," a firm voice behind Kayla said.

She spun. From his expression, Abioye was as surprised as she at who they faced.

The Secretary and Director of Homeland Security, General Elizabeth Grayson, stood with a stern look on her face. With her was a stoic-looking black man in a dark suit, wearing sunglasses. Kayla knew him. Franklin Gregg, SAIC of Grayson's Secret Service detail.

With an intense, no-nonsense stare, Grayson said, "I am—"

"I know who you are, Madam Secretary," Aletta said. "I'm representing these women. They are victims of a human trafficking ring. I expect them to be treated accordingly."

"And they will," Grayson said. "But we expect their cooperation in turn. Can we count on that?"

"Before we discuss that, ma'am. There is something you need to know. I have a friend, Simon Angula. I believe you know who he is."

"Agent Abioye," Grayson said. "Can you arrange somewhere quiet so that I might speak with Ms. Kamati and Lieutenant Clarke in private? I suspect we have much to talk about."

CHAPTER ELEVEN

ABIOYA HAD CLEARED OUT a breakroom used by the ICE agents and other staff personnel of the correctional facility. Grayson's Secret Service protection detail cleared the room. When they were done, Agent Gregg stood at the door. He nodded.

Aletta and Kayla filed inside.

Gregg handed Grayson a TV remote. "The feed's been set up. It is secure."

"Thank you, Franklin."

"I'll be right on the other side of this door, ma'am."

Grayson smiled. "I know you will."

The tiniest tic of a smile played across his lips. He nodded and closed the door.

Grayson strolled over to the service counter at the far end of the room. On it was a coffee pot, a toaster oven, a microwave, a sink, and, next to that, a full-size refrigerator. The counter was littered with sugar and discarded sugar packs and teabag wrappers. Grayson swept the trash into a wastepaper basket with a tsk, tsk. She pulled three mugs from the overhead cabinet. Each was embossed with an ICE badge.

She said, "Coffee? Ms. Kamati? Lieutenant?"

Kayla approached her. "Ma'am, I can get that."

Grayson held up her hand. "I can handle pouring a few cups of coffee, Lieutenant. Yes, or no?"

"Yes, ma'am. Thank you."

Aletta settled into a worn sofa. She sank into the cushions with a sigh. The woman had to be exhausted. She didn't seem to have a problem with the older woman serving her. One of the most powerful women in the current administration.

"Ms. Kamati?"

"Yes, please," Aletta said. "And call me Letty."

Grayson handed the hot mugs around. After returning with hers, she motioned for Kayla to take a seat as well. Kayla chose a hard plastic chair. She pulled up to one of the many square tables around the room. She put a napkin down and rested her cup on it.

Grayson pointed the remote at a flatscreen that hung from the ceiling. On it had been a promotional slideshow used to recruit people to the Immigration and Customs Enforcement Services. The scrolling images disappeared.

Replaced with a wide-screen view of Bannon and McMurphy.

"Good to see you, Commander."

"You as well, General," Bannon said.

Grayson smiled warmly. "John." She was the only one who called him John.

McMurphy grinned. "Hiya, Lizzie."

And he was definitely the only one who could get away with calling her Lizzie.

McMurphy lifted a can and took a deep pull from it.

Grayson recognized the silver logo of a can of Coors Light.

"That's not what I think it is. Is it Chief Warrant Officer McMurphy?"

When she called him by his full title and name, that was like a mother calling their child by their first, middle, and last names. He knew he was in trouble.

"What, ma'am?"

"You know the regulations against having alcohol on a Coast Guard ship."

McMurphy dragged the back of his hand across his mouth. Sheepishly, he said, "Yes, ma'am. I do."

Bannon surreptitiously slid what looked suspiciously like another can of beer across the desktop, out of view of the camera.

Grayson frowned, exasperated by the two of them. She introduced Aletta Kamati.

"Why don't you start by telling us how you ended up on the *Marken*, Ms.… Letty."

Aletta cleared her throat. "You'll take care of the girls? You promise?"

"If any of them wish to return home. Or go anywhere else. We'll make that happen as quickly as we can. If they want to remain here in the States, we'll arrange asylum and get the immigration process started. You have my word."

Letty nodded, accepting that. "I am what you call here a social worker. I work with girls, women, that society has cast aside. Prostitutes, homeless women, girls abused or abandoned by their husbands, their families. Transients. The type of women who disappear easily and whom no one looks for. About a year ago, colleagues and I began to notice a large number, a larger than usual number, of girls going missing in my country."

"Namibia," Grayson confirmed.

"What's larger than usual?" Bannon asked.

"A few in a month, at first. That soon grew to become dozens."

"What did you think was happening to them?" Kayla asked.

"At first, we did not know. We spoke with local law enforcement, to the communities. It appeared these women had vanished without a trace. The locals said they'd been lost to *Skaduwee*. The shadow. The more we looked into it, the more stories we heard of women being abducted, rounded up in the middle of the night, spirited away. Never to be seen or heard from again."

"Scooped up by human traffickers," Bannon guessed.

"Yes. But at alarming rates. International trafficking has always been a problem, but this—"

"South Africa is a major supplier of trafficked women worldwide," Grayson said. "But the typical international routes for them are to Europe, Russia, and India. Much more so than the U.S."

With Customs and Border Protection, ICE, and Homeland Security her responsibility, Grayson was well aware of the trafficking problem. "We're working with nations throughout the world. Making progress."

"Not enough. In our small country alone—"

"How did *you* come to be on the *Marken,* Ms. Kamati?" Bannon asked.

"A few months ago," she said. "A man approached me. He said he was working with the Namibian Police Force."

"NAMPOL," Bannon said.

"A U.S. agent."

"Simon Angula," Grayson said.

Letty nodded. "My inquiries into the missing women were being noticed. By some rather bad people. Simon tried to warn me."

Bannon interrupted her. "Wait a minute. Who is this Simon Angula?"

"He's an ICE agent, Brice," Grayson said. "He's working undercover and in conjunction with the Namibia authorities. A joint operation, if you will."

Bannon frowned.

Letty continued. "I'd learned of a group of women being held at the docks. Told they were bound to depart. Shortly."

"This came from Agent Angula?" Grayson asked.

"Yes. He meant to warn me about the danger I was putting myself in. He assured me the authorities were looking into the problem, but… I didn't listen. I thought I knew better. I went down to the docks to get proof. Take pictures or videos with my phone. Get the evidence authorities would need to prevent the girls from being taken away."

Letty seemed near to tears. "I know now how foolish I was."

"What happened?" Grayson asked gently.

"I was careless. I got caught."

"They took you aboard," Bannon said. "Held you prisoner. With the others."

"Yes."

"You were kept in that cargo container the whole time?" Kayla asked.

"No. We were kept in cabins. Fed. Well-treated, considering."

"Kidnapped and held against your wills," McMurphy said. "Not exactly Carnival Cruises, you ask me."

80

"When were you put in the container?" Bannon asked. His steely eyes narrowed.

"After the explosion."

Almost as one, Kayla and Grayson asked, "What explosion?"

"It was why I contacted you, General," Bannon said. "The *Marken's* hull sustained a massive rupture."

"A hole in the side of that old tub," McMurphy said, "you could drive a Volkswagen through."

"It could only have been an explosion."

"What caused it?" Grayson asked.

"Simon," Letty said.

"Agent Angula?" Grayson said. "What's he to do with this?"

"I did not know it at the time," Letty said. "But the information he gave me, he gathered by working, how do you say it, undercover, on the docks."

"He planted a bomb on the boat?" Kayla said.

"No," Letty said. "Not initially. It wasn't until after our second day at sea I learned Simon didn't just work the docks. He was part of the *Marken* crew. He was on board."

Bannon frowned.

"We only had a chance to talk once. The captain. Simon said he was paranoid. Irrational, short-tempered. Extremely fearful. They'd taken everyone's phones away from them. All their IDs. Searched their cabins regularly."

"None of the crew had IDs when we picked them up," Kayla said. "Nothing whatsoever to identify them."

"Do you think they were on to Agent Angula?"

"I do not know. But he told me the radio room was off-limits. Guarded day and night. He feared he would not be able to contact his—how do you call them—his handler. Alert them that the women, that we, were onboard. He was afraid if he could not once we reached port. The women, we'd be taken away too quickly for him to stop it.

"He told me he had a plan to do something to stop the ship. Something drastic, he said. Something that would get the attention of the U.S. authorities. I did not know what he planned... until the explosion."

"That got everyone's attention," McMurphy said.

Grayson glanced at Bannon and McMurphy. "Afraid the ship was sinking, Gumede ordered the women locked into the container."

"Send all the evidence to the bottom of the ocean," Bannon said.

"Where is this agent now?" Kayla asked. "If he's part of the crew, why hasn't he come forward yet?"

"There's something you all need to see. I'm sorry, Ms. Kamati. This will be a bit graphic, but we need to know."

Bannon and McMurphy's images on the screen disappeared. They were replaced with a video of their drone weaving through a flooded p-way. It settled on the individual they found handcuffed to the ladder earlier.

Letty covered her mouth and gasped.

"That's Agent Angula, isn't it?" Bannon asked.

"Yes." Tears filled her eyes as she turned away from the image.

"It is," Grayson confirmed, having seen his photo in his agency file.

"The thirteenth crewman," Kayla concluded.

A stunned silence filled the room as Bannon and McMurphy's images returned to the screen.

"We need to find who's responsible for this, Brice. For all of it. AS high up as it goes. Find them and stop them."

"We will, General," Bannon vowed. "We will."

CHAPTER TWELVE

Versteek Island - Isles of Shoals
42° 58'24.3" N - 70°37'19.8" W

SIX MILES OFF THE COAST of Portsmouth, New Hampshire, sits an archipelago, a cluster of islands collectively known as the Isles of Shoals. Europeans first settled the islands during the early seventeen-hundreds and have since been used as a seasonal fishing camp, a summer retreat for artists and the well-to-do, a marine research facility, and a place for at least one pirate, John Quelch, to hide his stolen treasure. There'd even been a famous double murder committed on the Shoals. The subject of much speculation, books, and even a movie.

Appledore, Smuttynose, Cedar, and Star islands straddle the border between New Hampshire and Maine. On the leeward side of Star Island, surrounded by Lunging and Seavey Island, is Versteek Island. Forty-five acres and privately owned, Versteek is the only island at the Shoals occupied by a year-round resident.

A boomerang-shaped landmass of granite rock. The northeastern coast is a rugged, deeply steeped, cliff shoreline. In contrast, the southern shore, with its gentler abraded stoss face consisting of asymmetric bumps, crevices, and densely shrubbed slopes, formed around a large, natural, boulder-strewn, rocky beach and cove. A fifty-foot concrete jetty had been built two years earlier. It extended from the southernmost point of the island alongside the naturally formed cove. Old-fashion-styled lanterns dotted the jetty with yellow light.

An accompanying conical lighthouse stood over it all at sixty feet tall. Made of granite walls two feet thick, it had an automated light with a VLB-44 LED lighting unit that made a full rotation once every thirty seconds.

A sleek, twenty-five-foot Talon powerboat cut a wide arc through the dark water, leaving a thick, white frothing wake behind it. Entering the dark cove, the Mzobe throttled down the powerful eight-point-one liter, four-hundred-twenty-five horsepower Mercruiser engine.

The craft hummed quietly, maneuvering to the end of the jetty where a tall African-American man stood holding a Coleman LED lantern. A second figure, a boy, on his knees, expertly wound the bow line around a dock cleat, then scampered to the rear of the boat and did the same with the stern line, pulling the craft in against the bumpers. When the sleek craft was secured, knowing better than to offer assistance, the man holding the lantern stepped to one side.

Jade van Wyk jumped onto the dock. Her almost constant companion, Arno Mzobe followed suit.

The evening was still quite warm. Humid if she were to be honest. Jade wore a halter-neck black, open-throated, knit crochet fabric sundress over a white micro bikini. Her dark skin gleamed in the glow of the midnight moon. Mzobe wore off-white linen pants and a black, sleeveless muscle shirt. His safari jacket draped over his arm.

Jade told the man on the dock, "Leave the boat here. We shalln't be long, Dieter." She glanced up the roches moutonnées at the two-story house at the highest point of the island. "Where is he?"

"The main house. Poolside."

The glass walls of the house were awash with warm yellow light. The lighthouse light swept across the island's main plateau.

Jade walked purposefully up the dock carrying her sandals by the straps. Arno by her side. A half step behind and to her left. They traversed the serpentine series of pressure-treated cedar staircases and landings to the main house.

Jade moved quickly through the main room to the patio and the infinity pool beyond. Steam rose from the lighted water. Tiki lamps staked out the four corners of the pool. Black smoke curled from the burning flames. The acrid scent meant to drive away the mosquitos.

Jade slapped her arm, killing one of the insects.

Her father swam laps in the pool. His lean body cut across the water's surface, barely making a ripple. He propelled himself forward with smooth strokes and short, powerful kicks.

Jade stood at the pool's edge, waiting to be noticed.

A final lap and Bernardor van Wyk stood. The water reached his waist. He wore only a shiny black Speedo. Water dripped off his thin, sinewy body. His skin was darker than hers and gleamed in the overhead moonlight. He walked up the pool steps, wiping water from his face and bald head.

"Father, we need to speak."

"So you said in your text. And your voicemail messages."

"Which you did not return," she said, struggling to keep her temper in check. She was not some frivolous princess baby who ran to daddy with every meaningless little crisis in her life. "It is important."

He stepped onto the hexagon porcelain tiled patio and snapped his fingers. A young girl emerged from the shadows. She rushed over with a towel. She could not have been more than sixteen years old. He took the towel and dried his face. By the time he finished, the girl was gone.

He draped the towel over his narrow shoulders. "Which brings you here to me, daughter."

He picked up a fresh drink waiting for him on a table beside a chaise lounge. He noticed Arno standing by the doors. His hands clasped before him. His hooded eyes ever watchful. His bald head shiny in the moonlight.

Van Wyk nodded. "Arno."

"Sir."

To Jade, van Wyk said, "Now, daughter of mine. What is it that is so urgent you needed to come all the way out here in the dead of night?"

"The *Marken*. It sunk."

"I am aware."

"Are you aware—"

Van Wyk held up his hand. He stepped toward the open sliders of the house where the young girl had returned. "Yes, Belinda. What is it?"

She held out a cell phone. Specially encrypted, it was not a phone he received calls on often. And with good reason.

Belinda cast her eyes away as she handed him the phone. "It was ringing."

He took it and put it to his ear, walking away from the girl and his daughter. "Yes?"

Jade could hear the voice on the other end. A male voice. "We've got trouble."

"When do we not? Specify."

"The *Marken*."

Van Wyk glanced at his daughter. The reason she was there. He waved her to his side and put the phone on speaker, lowering the volume so only the two of them could hear.

"What of it?" van Wyk said.

"The container's been recovered. One of the girls is dead."

Van Wyk ground his back teeth. He hated having his time wasted. "I am aware of these facts. It's been on the news."

"What's not on the news is who rescued them. A Coast Guard commander named Brice Bannon and his pilot Jack McMurphy."

Van Wyk rolled his eyes. "Why do you concern me with trivialities like this? Why should I care about two nobody servicemen who got to play hero for a day? Nothing can tie back to me. To us. Tomorrow, this will be forgotten. Yesterday's news."

"You're wrong."

A muscle pulsed along van Wyk's jawline. That wasn't something he heard very often. And Jade knew he believed it could not be true. A van Wyk never makes mistakes. A mantra he told her often while growing up.

"This isn't going away," the voice on the phone said. "Not with these two."

"Explain," van Wyk demanded.

"They're not just a couple of Coasties doing their job. It's Bannon and McMurphy."

"You say that as if their names mean something to me. I assure you, they do not."

"They should," the distorted, distant voice said. "They're the two who rescued Kingsley and Grayson from Tiamat Bluff a few months back."

Jade was aware of the ill-conceived attempt to assassinate the President of the United States and the Secretary of Homeland Security. Her father had had nothing to do with the scheme but had been furious when he found out.

"These two," the voice said. "They don't back down. They don't stop coming until everyone involved is in jail or dead."

"You are neither in jail nor dead," van Wyk said.

"Because I'm careful to make sure things tie back to me, either. But with these two, I'm telling you, it might only be a matter of time. We need to do something."

"We will," van Wyk said.

"Losing that container. That's a costly mistake. We can't afford any more...."

Van Wyk clutched the phone so tightly veins bulged in his hand and along his forearms. When he spoke, his voice was tight with barely contained anger. "Mistakes made by you. Not me. You stupid *bliksem*. It was you who allowed an agent, a spy, onto my ship. Into my crew."

"How could I have stopped that?"

"That is for you to figure out. If you cannot do your job, of what use are you to me? To us?"

He threw the phone as hard as he could into the pool. It splashed and sunk. He watched it settle on the pool floor. Then he slugged down his drink, ice and all, and threw the glass into the pool, too.

"Father?"

"What?" van Wyk shouted.

Jade gave him a hard, narrow-eyed stare. "Do not speak to me in that tone, Father. No one does. Not even you."

Arno had dropped his hands to his side and took a step forward. Jade shook her head, returning him to his place by the door.

Van Wyk held up his hand. "Apologies, daughter. You are right. I lost my temper."

"What is this bad news you have to deliver?"

"It has to do with the *Marken.* And the two men who rescued the girls."

Van Wyk snapped his fingers and waved his hand in the air.

Belinda rushed out to the pool with two fresh drinks. She put them down on the small table next to the chaise and hurried back inside, where she would watch, out of sight, and wait to be of service.

"Tell me," van Wyk said, sipping his drink.

Jade recounted her visit to Yang Wang's dry cleaners. When she finished, she said. "The man is a cop. I've heard about him before. Curtis Martin, a detective with Family Justice Division. He specializes in human trafficking and special victims."

"Just a cop. Pay him off or kill him." He dismissed that as no concern. "And the woman?"

"A bartender. At a place in Hampton Beach on the seacoast."

Van Wyk frowned. "That doesn't sound right."

"As I thought as well, Father. We," she said, meaning Arno and herself, "dug deeper. Her name is Tarakesh Sardana. She is Egyptian, a nationalized citizen, and former MARCOS."

"Indian Naval Special Forces. Did you not just say she was Egyptian?"

"Records revealed she was part of an exchange program. She went by a different name at the time. She was one of only six females to be MARCOS trained. Our intelligence people discovered not long after she completed her training, she went AWOL. Became a mercenary. Operated under a number of assumed aliases and several interests."

"A bartender?" van Wyk mused. "How does this connect to our two troublesome Coast Guardsmen?"

"The bar she works at is called the Keel Haul. It's owned by Brice Bannon."

Van Wyk's mouth formed a tight smile. "That can be no coincidence."

. "No, Father. Certainly not. What do you want to do?"

"We've no time to fool around with those who would interfere with our plans. Nor our American counterpart's insufferable incompetence." Van Wyk finished his drink. "Eliminate them, daughter. Kill them all."

CHAPTER THIRTEEN

Main Channel
Boston Harbor

IT HAD BEEN DECIDED the *Lightfoot* would remain on-site over the sunken container ship. Their mission was twofold: assist the local and federal authorities tasked with recovering the dead DHS agent from the wreck and gather more information and forensic data pertaining to the explosion that brought the cargo ship down. Bannon and McMurphy debriefed and supervised the prep for the morning dive to the *Marken,* then left at daybreak.

With the Coast Guard's blessing, they borrowed a high-speed, twenty-five-foot, rigid-hulled, inflatable rapid response boat, one of two onboard the *Lightfoot.* The crafts were designed to pursue and interdict fast-moving, non-compliant vessels. For the moment, it was perfect to get them to a scheduled meeting at the Coast Guard Station in Boston.

The sun broke over the horizon behind them.

At the helm, McMurphy pushed the boat's five hundred horsepower Cummins diesel engine hard for no other reason than he could. The aluminum hull pounded hard into the whitecaps. A fat cigar held in his mouth, McMurphy grinned like a kid playing with a new toy.

Bannon sat in one of the five specially designed shock-absorbing seats and enjoyed the view of the fast-approaching Boston skyline and harbor. They passed Logan Airport on their right. McMurphy navigated them through the channel between East Boston and the North End.

Slowing, McMurphy moved to starboard, giving wide berth to an ocean-bound Legend-class Coast Guard cutter.

A lone guardsman stood on deck. Bannon waved and got a wave in return. The pilot of the cutter gave them a friendly blast on the horn.

McMurphy shouted over the wind and spray. "What do we know about these two yo-yos?"

After the conference call with Secretary Grayson the day before, in private, she told the two men she'd arranged for them to meet with the DHS case officer who'd been Simon Angula's handler.

"Nothing but a name. Darren Hornsby," Bannon said, answering McMurphy's question. "And that he's bringing another agent. Parker Quinn."

"How we supposed to know who they are?"

"The way you're coming in, I'm guessing they'll find us."

"Don't lie. This is fun."

Bannon slipped on a pair of dark sunglasses. He smiled. The sun. The wind in his hair. The smell and feel of the saltwater spray. It was more than fun. It was exhilarating.

And became even more so when the first bullet pinged off the craft's console six inches from McMurphy's hand on the wheel. At the sound, McMurphy yanked his hand back. "What the hell?"

A second round ripped into the foam collar, narrowly missing Bannon's arm. It deflated a section of the inflatable sponson. Bannon twisted out of his seat, spotting the gunman on the waterfront pier where the Tall Ship Boston docked. A two-hundred-forty-five foot, two-mast ship converted into a floating oyster bar.

"Sniper!" Bannon shouted.

The gunman had his elbow rested on the pier railing. He looked up to see where the shots had landed. The shooter wore a dark jacket and a baseball cap. He returned his eye to a high-powered scope, sighting in the rifle again.

"Get a move on!" Bannon shouted.

McMurphy had already made a sharp, deep turn. A wall of white spray shot up between them and the pier, making an accurate shot impossible. The channel was too narrow to escape the effective range of a decent sniper rifle. All McMurphy could do was duck and weave. He raced across into the shipping lane, then swerved back, zigzagging.

They bounced over the water at full throttle. McMurphy held the wheel in a death grip and glanced over his shoulder at Bannon. "What the hell was that?"

"Not the end of it." Bannon pointed.

Three sleek, red, blue, and white wave runners shot out around the pier. Two from the right side and the third from behind the Tall Ship Boston. The first pair tracked a course behind the RHIB. Giving chase. The third was on an intercept course ahead of them, aiming to cut them off.

The sniper on the pier packed up his rifle and was skedaddling.

Each wave runner had a driver and a passenger. Dressed in black neoprene wetsuits, wearing hoods and masks that revealed only their eyes. The passengers were armed with handguns.

"You've got to be kidding me?" McMurphy said. "Who'd we piss off this time?"

"We'll worry about that later," Bannon said. "For now, let's work on getting out of here alive."

"Any great ideas on how we do that?"

"Drive faster," Bannon suggested.

He recognized the watercrafts. Yamaha's FX series. Standard, they were equipped with a one-point-eight-liter engine capable of fifty knots, making them a match for the RHIB's max speed. The one ahead of them had a white cowl. The red and blue ones were behind them.

McMurphy veered to port and throttled the engine. "Hang on."

The RHIB leaped forward, skimming over the water's surface at breakneck speed.

The wave runners behind them sped up, whining loudly. They were closing fast.

The white one in front of them had reached the crisscross point of their trajectory. It turned, facing them with the throttle wide open, entering into a ridiculous game of chicken.

The passenger on the blue wave runner behind them opened fire.

"They're shooting," Bannon said.

"I noticed," McMurphy said.

He zigged the response boat, then zagged in a tight turn away from the forward craft, so tight it almost swamped them, sending a high spray of water in the air. When McMurphy straightened out, they faced the two fast-approaching wave runners.

"What are you doing?" Bannon shouted.

"Going on the offensive." He throttled the engine. "They want to play. Let's play."

Both wave runners opened fire.

"Now what?" Bannon said.

"Tell you the truth. I didn't think that far ahead."

A bullet pinged off the aluminum boat's raised hull. Another bullet deflated a second sponson section. Bannon eyed a box attached to the underside of the collar. "As far as plans go, not your best effort."

"Everybody's a critic."

Bannon snapped the latch of the box open and grabbed the flare gun inside. He loaded a cartridge. The RHIB bounced high on the water, its bow raised, providing cover as they raced toward the oncoming wave runners. Bullets pinged off the aluminum bottom.

Bannon anchored his foot under the seat and leaned far out over the side of the RHIB.

As they reached the point of no return, he hoped their assailants would peel off. He knew McMurphy wouldn't. As the RHIB bounced, gaining speed, Bannon wiped sea spray from his face.

"Come on, turn. Turn."

And, at the last minute, they did.

Both crafts turned to their left, the blue one slightly ahead of the red one. Bannon aimed the flare gun at the lead wave runner. The passenger still shooting at them.

Bannon fired.

With a corkscrew contrail of smoke, the flare sizzled like a line drive hit in baseball. The charge hit the blue wave runner's driver. It bounced and whizzed around in his lap, exploding into a starburst of white-hot light and flame. The driver screamed and leaped off the machine. The craft swerved to the left and slammed into the cowl of the second wave runner.

The impact sent the passenger headlong over the controls and into the water.

Driverless, the blue wave runner began to turn in a wide, pre-programmed circle. The cowl of the red wave runner was cracked and split. The crash had nearly swamped the craft before the driver righted it and spun it around to re-engage in the pursuit.

"Nice shot," McMurphy shouted, the stogie still lit and clamped between his teeth. "But they're still coming."

"It buys us some distance," Bannon said. "Time to figure out what to do about them."

More gunfire alerted Bannon to the pressing problem of the remaining white wave runner still in pursuit. It charged full speed ahead, opening fire.

McMurphy ducked and turned the inflatable, bringing them back on course to make a run for the Coast Guard base. McMurphy cut across the channel. "I have an idea."

"A fully thought out one this time?"

"Where's the fun in that?" He grimaced around the cigar. "You got any more flares?"

"Sure." Bannon loaded the gun. "Three more."

In the center of the channel, a tug boat was pulling a loaded deck barge. Heading out to open water.

McMurphy aimed for it. The wave runner altered course, aiming to reach the RHIB before it reached the bow of the tug boat. The passenger kept shooting but without hitting anything.

"I don't think I like this plan," Bannon said, moving next to McMurphy.

"Just shoot."

"You realize the last one," Bannon said. "That was just dumb luck, right?"

"I don't need you to hit 'em. Just brush them back."

Bannon started to see what McMurphy had planned. He lifted the flare gun and steadied his aim at the approaching craft. He fired. By following the contrail of smoke, he knew his shot was off. But it was enough to get the driver to alter course, slowing them down.

The flare flew past and hit the water with an anticlimactic sizzle.

"Again," McMurphy shouted.

In quick succession, Bannon fired off the last two flares. Both missed. The wave runner swerved farther away even as the passenger fired several more shots.

McMurphy punched the RHIB throttle forward and shot past the diverted craft, putting the tug and barge between them. McMurphy had cut it so close they plunged into the chilly shadow of the large barge. The tugboat let loose an angry blast of its horn.

Cruising alongside the hull of the barge, McMurphy slowed to almost a crawl.

The red wave runner charged after them. A section of its cowl flapped. Gray smoke poured out from the engine.

"We've still got company," Bannon said, glancing over his shoulder.

McMurphy cruised forward slowly, his concentration locked ahead of them. "I'm not worried about them."

"I am," Bannon said.

As if to validate his concerns, the pursuing wave runner opened up with more gunfire.

Over the low-speed thrum of their Cummins engine, Bannon heard the loud, high-pitched whine of an approaching engine.

"Hang on!" McMurphy goosed the throttle.

The RHIB surged up and forward, nearly tumbling Bannon out of the back of the boat. He grabbed the seat and plopped down heavily.

Over the upraised bow of their boat, Bannon saw—for a fraction of a second—the first peek of the white wave runner. They'd circled the tug and the barge, hoping to cut off Bannon and McMurphy behind the stern.

A maneuver McMurphy had anticipated.

He threw the throttle full forward. The raised aluminum hull slammed into the wave runner broadside. Bannon caught the wide-eyed expressions of the two men under their masks a split second before the inflatable slammed into them, effectively running them over. The impact jarred McMurphy and Bannon. They were thrown forward but held on as the RHIB launched in the air like it had hit a ski jump.

As they reached the apex of their jump, Bannon heard a muffled scream suddenly cut off. Behind them, a spray of red water fanned out. The propeller had hit one of the men, slicing and dicing him before the boat completed its arc and slammed down into the water, sending a thick spray of water across them and filling the RHIB's shallow deck.

"Wahoo!" McMurphy hollered.

Bannon, still with a death grip on his seat, glanced behind them. The white wave runner bobbed on the water with no rider. The engine had conked out. Blood smeared the double seats and the machine's cowl.

"What about them?" McMurphy said, nodding toward the last wave runner. They were still coming but had cut their speed.

"Maybe too scared to come after us now," Bannon said.

"I would be."

Then disaster struck.

They were about fifty yards from one of the Coast Guard piers.

But the engine clattered and smoked. Probably bent the propeller or cracked something in the engine, causing a leak. McMurphy tapped at the controls. The engine coughed and died.

"Well, crap."

"Skyjack."

Preoccupied. McMurphy fiddled and tapped at the control gauges. He turned the ignition key, which revved the engine but failed to do much more. "Yeah?"

"The last one," Bannon said. "The red one?"

"What about it?"

"We're in play again."

McMurphy spun around.

Though it spewed oily smoke in the air, the pursuing wave runner charged fast. The passenger was standing up in the rear, aiming his gun. He fired.

Seeing them dead in the water had changed the minds of their assailants. They were coming in hard and fast, bullets flying.

"Get down!" Bannon shouted, but the shooting stopped.

McMurphy blinked. "What the hell?"

The shooter twitched and fell back, falling off the wave runner.

A split second passed. Bannon heard the gunshot. But it hadn't come from the wave runner. A second shot. The wave runner driver leaned forward as if he'd suddenly gone to sleep. The craft began its pre-programmed circle. When it passed the RHIB, Bannon saw the man's forehead was smeared with blood.

Bannon and McMurphy glanced over at the pier, locating the source of the gunfire.

Two people stood there. One wore a business suit and a cowboy hat. The other was a woman. Her hair was big and full and bright red. Both held handguns aimed at the wave runner circling lazily around the channel.

In the distance, Bannon heard sirens and saw the electric blue emergency lights of approaching police cars.

"You think they're good guys or more bad guys?"

"Guess we're about to find out," Bannon said. "Here." He handed McMurphy an oar. "You're gonna need this."

CHAPTER FOURTEEN

The Barking Crab
Fort Point Channel, Seaport District

IT TOOK ALL MORNING and most of the afternoon to sort through what had happened in the channel. The local police were the first on the scene, waiting for Bannon and McMurphy as they paddled in. The staties arrived soon after, and even two agents from the local FBI office showed up. A call to Grayson got the state police to stand down, but DoJ refused to yield. A symptom of the ongoing jurisdictional feud between the two agencies. Boston PD's Harbor Patrol began the gruesome task of fishing the survivors and the bodies out of the water. The detective was less than thrilled when DHS Agent Hornsby let him know in no uncertain terms it was their case and they would take the lead. He told the cop, BPD was welcome to remain and assist, but that was all.

In a huff, the cop left.

By late afternoon, Bannon and McMurphy had been released by the FBI with a promise they remain available for follow-up questioning. Bannon took the agent's card. Asked that he be kept up to speed on whatever the Bureau learned about their assailants, both alive and dead, knowing the cooperation wouldn't go both ways.

McMurphy deposited four frosty cold mugs of beer on the pine high top.

The Barking Crab was a popular outdoor eatery under a sprawling yellow tent and strung lights. The place had become so successful in recent years the owners expanded into the adjoining Neptune Lobster and Seafood market. Bannon preferred the outdoor accommodations. Perfect for the hot summer afternoon and a chance to regroup.

He wore dark sunglasses and kept a watchful eye on their companions. Department of Homeland Security special agents Darren Hornsby and Parker Quinn. The pair that came to their rescue with their marksmanship skills at the harbor earlier.

McMurphy returned to the table carrying a tray, along with two pretty waitresses who delivered even more food. They set down bowls of New England clam chowder, Caesar salads, shrimp cocktails, littleneck clams, fried calamari, mussels, crab cakes, and ahi tuna tacos. And more beers.

The waitresses left, and McMurphy sat.

Parker said, "Lord have mercy, don't they feed you boys up here?"

"You ever eat Coast Guard chow?" McMurphy asked, slugging down a mugful of beer. He set his cell phone on the table after canceling an incoming call.

"Can't say I've had that pleasure."

Bannon smiled. "You'd understand. It's no pleasure."

Parker raised her mug of beer. "To the most exciting first date I've had in quite some time."

She was the redhead. Big hair, pale skin, bright, expressive green eyes, and a wide, pixie-like smile that lit up her whole face when she smiled. "Grayson warned me things might get interesting around you two."

Darren Hornsby was railthin. He wore a business suit, a cowboy hat, and black framed glasses.

They clicked mugs and drank.

Between bites of shrimp cocktail and white wine mussels, Bannon said, "Thanks for helping us out. That was some shooting."

"You get brought up on an Oklahoma ranch you learn how to shoot."

"You ride cattle down in them there parts, too," McMurphy asked, ribbing the redhead.

"Ride 'em, rope 'em. And eat 'em, too, Yankee." She gave him a winning smile. "But you don't get seafood like this down there. I'll tell you that."

"What about you, Hornsby?" McMurphy asked. "You from Oklahoma, too?"

"Texas. Austin. Son of a Ranger. I learned to shoot real good, too." He got down to business. "Anything you two want to share with us that you didn't share with the locals or the FBI?"

"Like what?" Bannon asked.

"Like who your attackers were. Four dead. One in a coma. And one who doesn't speak English. None of them had ID on them."

"You two killed two of them," McMurphy reminded them. His phone buzzed. He looked at it, silenced it again, and slurped down an oyster.

"And don't forget the sniper," Bannon added.

"Seven armed attackers," Parker said. "You boys must have stirred up one hell of a hornet's nest."

"It's obviously connected to the *Marken,* to the girls," Bannon said. "But beyond that, I have no idea."

McMurphy stared hard across the table at Hornsby. "You know what bothers me? How'd they know where to find us?"

"You've got an accusation to make?"

"Just saying. It bothers me." McMurphy took a bite of calamari and washed it down with a beer.

"Grayson said you were Agent Angula's handler," Bannon said. "Tell us about the op in Africa."

Hornsby leaned back heavily in his chair. "Have you ever had anyone you're responsible for die?"

"I have," Bannon said. "Too many times."

"I haven't," Hornsby said. "Not until now."

"I get it," Bannon said. "It's tough. But the best thing you can do now for Angula, the only thing you can do for him, is get the people responsible for killing him. Find them. Stop them. And make them pay."

"And the guilt?" Hornsby asked. "The second-guessing? What do I do about that?"

"Bottle it up and deal with it later," Bannon said. "And learn from it."

"Sounds like you speak from experience," Parker said.

"Too much of it."

"You're right. Of course." Hornsby cleared his throat. "Africa accounts for twenty-three percent of the human trafficking problem worldwide. They are a major region of origin for victims. Women. Girls, mostly, but young men and boys, too. Trafficked to other parts of the world. Mainly Western Europe and the Middle East, but also here to North America."

"That was what Lizzy told us, too," McMurphy said.

"You call Elizabeth Grayson Lizzy?" Parker asked around a mouthful of prawn. "Not to her face, for sure."

"Wanna bet?" Bannon said, grinning.

Parker blinked, unbelieving.

"Thirty-seven percent of all victims are trafficked for the purpose of forced labor," Hornsby said. "Migrant workers, domestics, laborers. The rest are victims of sexual exploitation. Porn, prostitution. Women and underage children as young as twelve or fourteen."

McMurphy tossed his fork onto his plate with a loud clatter. "Kids."

Bannon said, "Go on."

"The Criminal Investigations Directorate of the Namibia National Police Force contacted us about a year ago. They'd closed down a large drug and human trafficking operation earlier. A big operation. Splashy, as those things go, only to have a new operation spring up literally days later."

"We spoke with Aletta Kamati," Bannon said.

"Yes. The information she brought to light was invaluable. That, in conjunction with what NAMPOL was learning from other sources."

"What other sources?" McMurphy asked.

"On the ground police work, contacts, paid informants. The usual chatter and gossip that comes from the criminal underbelly. But they had a problem. Because of the earlier investigations, most of their usual undercover operatives had been burned, outed. They reached out to us."

"You gave them Angula?"

Hornsby nodded. "The intel from the start told us this operation was different."

"How so?"

"The trafficked girls. They were mostly bound for the U.S., not the Middle East or Europe, which is more typical for South Africa. The *Marken* wasn't the first."

"Angula got in deep?"

"Yes. Almost immediately." Hornsby got wistful. "The kid...he was good."

"If Angula got himself on the crew of the *Marken,* how come no one here knew about it?"

"You mean, why didn't I know about it?" Hornsby asked.

"Stow the recriminations," Bannon said. "That's your cross to bear later. I don't give a rip if you're good at your job or you suck, Hornsby. All I care about is knowing what happened and when. So we can put a stop to this now."

"Okay. Okay. Things were moving fast. Simon learned a group of women had been scooped up and would be moved soon. New transport was being arranged, but he didn't know when or how. He missed his last check-in. That turned out to be the day the *Marken* set sail."

"Angula did tell Letty the captain was extremely paranoid," McMurphy said. "Took all the crews' phones away, tossed their cabins repeatedly."

"He never told us he was part of a ship's crew." Hornsby frowned. "It must have happened lightning fast. In his last contact with us, Simon reported he'd met some people. At a bar. One of them talked about a girl that had gone missing. Simon knew it was someone Ms. Kamati was looking for. He said he was getting in good with these guys. That he should have more information soon."

Bannon gave it some thought. "Letty reported he was worried about no one here knowing they were coming in."

"Explains his extreme measure of blowing a hole in the ship," Parker offered.

"A good way to get someone's attention," McMurphy said, "except he overachieved."

"He'd been right," Hornsby said. "If that ship had docked as scheduled, those women would have been gone, never heard from again."

McMurphy dug into an ahi tuna taco. "What happens now?"

Hornsby frowned. "We start over. Everything we've gotten from Simon, Ms. Kamati, and the Namibia police is that this new operation is run by a new player. Someone big. Someone with a lot of pull and a lot of resources."

McMurphy's phone rested on the table. It buzzed. He glanced at the screen and frowned.

"You need to take that?" Hornsby asked.

"Naw. Ain't important." He pocketed the phone. "I'm good."

Bannon put his beer mug down. This was what he wanted to know. Who was the guy in charge? Who was the one on top? He wanted the head of the beast, and he wanted to chop it off.

"Who?" Bannon asked. "Give me a name?"

"That's the problem. We don't know. Whoever he— or she—is, they're very secretive. Simon had only been close, getting good intel for a few months. He'd made great headway but was still at the very bottom. The level where people don't really know anything except what's the job and how much does it pay."

"Compartmentalized. Terror groups operate like that. One hand doesn't know what the other is up to," Bannon said. "If things go sideways, they can't divulge what they don't know."

"You're not suggesting this is part of a terrorist organization?" Parker asked.

"I don't know," Bannon said.

"Drugs, prostitution, smuggling," McMurphy said. "They've been funding terror groups for forever."

"We saw it in the Middle East," Bannon said. "But without more information, a lead…."

"None of our intel points to any of the regular—the traditionally known—terrorists' groups."

"Just what we need," McMurphy said. "A new asshat to deal with."

"To bring down, you mean," Bannon said.

"All we know is whoever this new entity is, they're a mystery. Highly secretive and completely off the grid as far as we can tell."

"Maybe our six would-be assassins can shed some light."

"We might have one other thing," Hornsby said. "Which is why Agent Quinn is up here from the New York field office. Because of her rather unique specialization."

Bannon turned his attention to the beautiful redhead. "Which is?"

"I investigate smuggled cultural properties, art, and antiquities."

Bannon asked the obvious question. "And what's that got to do with this?"

CHAPTER FIFTEEN

A SEAGULL CAWED AND danced around the table at the Barking Crab. McMurphy popped a littleneck clam in his mouth. A waitress came over. Bannon ordered another round of beers for the table.

"What's an Oklahoma country girl know about investigating smuggled cultural property, art, and antiquities?" McMurphy asked.

"I trained in partnership with the U.S. Department of State's Cultural Heritage Center and the Smithsonian Institute, among others. Learned how to identify, authenticate, and handle these objects and artifacts. Oh, and I went to college, too, y'all." She emphasized her southern drawl.

McMurphy held up his hands, surrendering. "Ouch. Just asking."

"Artifact smuggling is a multi-billion dollar a year problem," she said. "During the past fifteen years alone, HSI agents like myself have recovered over twelve thousand pieces and returned them to their rightful place or owners in over thirty countries."

"No one's questioning the value of your work," Bannon said. "But what's it got to do with this?"

Parker explained, "Six months ago, we were wrapping up a case in New York. A dealer of Southeast Asian art and antiquities who'd routinely sold looted pieces to museums and auction houses. We charged him with wire fraud, smuggling, conspiracy, and other theft-related offenses. In an attempt to lower or expunge the charges—which didn't happen— he offered information about the whereabouts of a number of specific items known to be stolen or missing that were available or at least bantered about on the black market. One item, in particular, caught our attention."

"Which was?" Bannon asked.

Parker drained her beer mug and reached for another. She then looked around as if concerned someone was eavesdropping. She leaned into the table and lowered her voice. "Have you ever heard of the Honjō Masamune sword?"

Bannon immediately stole her thunder.

"Sure. Japan's perfect sword. Forged seven hundred years ago by Gorō Nyūdō Masamune. Considered to be one of the greatest swordsmiths in all of Japan. A samurai sword. Masterfully crafted and exceptionally balanced. Believed to be nearly perfect in design. A great source of national pride for the Japanese people. I also know it's been lost to history for over seventy-five years."

"Do you know what happened to it?" Parker asked.

McMurphy threw his hands up in the air. "Oh, don't get him started."

As way of explanation, Bannon said, "I'm a bit of a nautical history buff—"

McMurphy rolled his eyes. "A bit?"

He raised his hand and signaled for more beer.

"Naturally," Bannon said, ignoring his old friend. "Much of nautical history coincides with military history. The two often overlap. As for the Honjō Masamune sword, it was passed down the line of shoguns during the Edo period and featured in many stories of battle—"

"Here he goes." McMurphy grabbed a fresh beer from the waitress and drank.

Bannon continued, "As a condition of surrender at the end of World War II, to comply with the disarmament agreement, Tokugawa Iemasa willingly turned over his family's sword collection. Fourteen swords, including the Honjō Masamune."

Clearly impressed, Parker said, "Very good, Commander. And as you've said, the sword's been lost ever since."

McMurphy sat forward. "Wait a dang minute. You can't stop there. How'd the damn thing get lost?"

"As the commander said, the sword was turned over to the American military. The Foreign Liquidations Commission of the Army Forces, West Pacific, specifically, according to records. To a sergeant Coldy Bimore."

"Let me guess," McMurphy said. "There's no such person."

"Exactly," Parker said.

"While this is all fascinating," Bannon said. "How is any of it relevant?"

"I'm getting to that," Parker said. "For you to understand, you'll need some context. A missing Masamune sword, not the Honjō but another one, was recovered two years ago. One of only two to ever be found. One of the few swords that didn't end up in Tokyo Bay after the war. That's where most people think the Honjō ended up, too. This recovered sword belonged to Toyotomi Hidetsugu, one of the swords Tokugawa Lemasa turned over during the occupation with the Honjō."

"I wasn't aware of this," Bannon said.

"It was kept very hush-hush. The owner didn't want the notoriety that comes from such a discovery. Quietly authenticated by the Japanese government, it was turned over anonymously to a museum in Kyoto."

"Where had it been?" Bannon asked.

"On a farm in Minnesota. In a barn. Brought back by a soldier and left in a black lacquer box in a hayloft. The man's adult grandson found it going through his effects after he passed away. An amateur enthusiast himself, he had an idea he had something special."

"He knew enough to get a good price for it," Bannon said.

Parker nodded. "He was quiet about it. Not stupid."

"How's that help us locate the Honjō Masamune?" Bannon asked.

"In and of itself, it doesn't," Parker admitted. "But the dark web's been abuzz about the Honjō ever since. The renewed interest. It's the sort of thing that gets collectors excited. But, often, as time goes by without any new reveals, interest begins to fade again."

She popped a shrimp into her mouth.

"But not this time. With our singing canary on the hook, we made progress in the search for the Honjō Masamune. We learned it had been acquired by a Saudi prince. How? We don't know. This was after rumors it was back here in the States. And in England. Some reports even placed it back in Japan."

"But it wasn't."

"No," Parker said. "We were confident in our intel. We secured all the proper paperwork, clearances, cut through all the red tape, but when we got to the Saudi's palace, the Honjō was gone."

"Or it wasn't there in the first place," McMurphy said. "Sounds like a wild goose chase to me."

"Is he always like this?" Parker asked.

McMurphy sat forward. "All I'm saying is we're wasting time talking about a sword that's probably on the bottom of Tokyo Bay, been melted down and sold for scrap, or in such poor condition it's worthless. While the people responsible for putting a bunch of women in a container and nearly sending them to the bottom of the ocean, and who just tried to kill us a few hours ago, and who killed your agent, is out there free as a bird."

"He makes a point," Bannon said.

"Here's where it might help," Parker said. "The intel we've gotten from a number of our operations, especially the chatter around the Honjō Masamune, a singular phrase kept coming up in different contexts. *Skaduwee*."

"What's that?" McMurphy asked.

"Wait a minute," Bannon said. "We've heard that phrase recently. Letty told us the locals get lost to *Skaduwee*. The shadow."

Hornsby piped in. "Angula used the term when referencing those responsible for the abductions, the trafficking. *Skaduwee*."

"Fine," McMurphy said. "The shadow. What's it mean?"

A smile formed on Bannon's lips. "A connection."

Parker smiled. "Exactly. It's thin, but we believe the shadow, whether it's a person or a code name, or an organization, we don't know, is key to both investigations."

"But do you know what or who *Skaduwee* is?" Bannon asked. "Or the location of the Honjō Masamune?"

"No," Parker admitted. "But if we did, we could use it to draw this *Skaduwee* out. Maybe it can lead us to him or her. Them."

"Sure," McMurphy said, "Not to be a Debbie Downer here. Again. *If* we had it."

"We could lie," Hornsby offered. "Put out false intel that it's been discovered. That we have it."

Bannon shook his head. "If our person is as secretive as you say he is, he'll be too cautious. He'll have feelers out. It must be the real thing, or it won't work."

"Absolutely," Parker agreed. "These people, art thieves and the like, if I've learned anything tracking them down, it's they're smart. Smarter than your average criminals."

"Putting us back to square one," McMurphy said. "Because here's another thought. Maybe *Skaduwee* already had the sword. Maybe that's why your Saudi prince didn't have it."

"Boy, you *are* the Debbie Downer," Parker said. "But I think it's the right lead to pursue. Suppose we could recover the Honjō Masamune sword and return it to the Japanese people. That would be a bucket load of goodwill for Uncle Sam."

"And get us our big bad," Bannon said. "I agree. It's worth following up on."

"Especially since we have nothing else to go on," Hornsby said.

"Hold on," McMurphy said. "This enigma? This super careful, cagey man—or woman—of mystery. Who we can't ID in the technology age of the twenty-first century, where we can read a postage stamp from space—"

"Who uses postage stamps?" Hornsby asked.

"And," McMurphy went on, "is thought to be running a, I don't know how big, criminal operation, encroaching on North America. Are they really going to risk all that, expose themselves for a sword?"

"That would have to be some sword," Hornsby had to admit.

"It's Japan's perfect sword," Bannon said. "A national treasure."

"And," Parker said. "We can't know its exact worth until it's found and appraised. The conservative estimate of its value is over one-hundred-five million dollars."

McMurphy whistled. "Some sword indeed."

CHAPTER SIXTEEN

Keel Haul Tavern
Hampton Beach, N.H.

CURTIS MARTIN PUSHED THROUGH the Keel Haul's front door. Inside was dark and cool. Just like his last visit, the place was packed. Once more, mostly young people gathered around tables and in booths and lining the bar. Talking. Laughing. And drinking. From the jukebox, Kenny Chesney sang about when the sun goes down.

Martin made his way to the bar. He dropped into a vacant seat at the corner.

Tara came down to his end of the bar. She looked great in black slacks, a sleeveless white shirt opened halfway to her navel. Her full black hair fanned out and framed her dark face. She dropped a napkin in front of him. Then, put a mug of beer on the napkin.

"Rough day?"

"Yeah. You could say," Martin said, drinking. He hadn't slept in over thirty hours. His eyes felt like beach sand was grinding into them. He hoisted the mug. "Thanks. I needed this."

Kayla Clarke emerged from a set of swinging doors, which Martin assumed led to a kitchen. She wore brown sandals, blue jean shorts, and an orange, open men's style dress shirt with rolled-up sleeves. A black t-shirt underneath. Her auburn hair fluffed and feathered out.

"Hey, look," Floyd called out from the same seat he'd been in the last time Martin was there. "Tootie's lover boy's back."

Tara threw a lemon slice at him. "Keep it up, and it's O'Doul's for you from now on."

Floyd seized his chest in mocking pain. "Oh, geez. You know that would kill me."

"One could only hope," Tara said.

"Hey," Kayla said with a welcoming smile. She put her open laptop on the bar and sat beside Martin. Smelling of suntan lotion and coconut, she sipped a greenish-blue drink with an umbrella and a pineapple slice. "What brings you out here?"

"News," Martin said. "And not the good kind."

Tara signaled to a second bartender to pick up her slack. She folded her arms and leaned over the teak wood bar. "Tell us."

"Yang Wang. He's dead. As far as I can tell, you and I were the last to see him alive."

"What happened?" Tara asked. "Exactly."

"After we left," Martin said, "the store remained closed. I don't know how much later or who. But someone noticed and got concerned. They called 911." He drank his beer. "Patrol went over to do a wellness check."

"And?" Tara prompted.

"Through the closed slates of the blinds, they saw the woman. Still handcuffed to the pole. They broke in. They found her and Wang's three mutts all dead. Slaughtered. I got called to the scene. It was a blood bath."

"How?" Tara asked.

"Knifed. All of them. Including Wang upstairs in his office. It looked like he took a hell of a beating first, too."

"The camera? Was there video?" Tara asked.

"They found the machine. The hard drive was gone."

"Why were you called to the scene?" Kayla asked. "I thought you were Family Justice?"

Not that they didn't deal with homicides, Martin thought. They did. Far too often. "Patrol did a canvas of the neighborhood. They found a security camera outside. The bank on the corner. It picked up Tara and me crossing the street together."

"What did you tell them?" Tara asked.

"I told 'em you were a tourist, asking me for directions. You're in the clear." He didn't add, for now.

"How did you explain your presence there?" Tara asked.

"I went there to see Wang," Martin said. "Because of Kwon's massage parlor and prostitution activities, the Yakuza are suspects in several of my open investigations. Nothing unusual about that. I'm often rattling their cages."

"You're not a suspect in his death?" Kayla asked.

"No. Of course not." He finished his beer. Tara got him another one. "I told them Wang was alive and well when I left him. It actually helped them establish a timeline."

"Which is?" Kayla asked.

Martin shrugged. "The call came into 911 about forty-five minutes after we left. It's a small window."

"Suspects?" Tara asked.

"We know someone's trying to muscle in on their territory. We talked about the turf battles, the shootouts, and drive-byes. Maybe the takeover campaign's escalating."

"The start of a gang war," Tara said.

Martin nodded. "It is getting to be like a war out there, for sure. Look, I know you people know more than you're saying."

Tara lowered her voice. "I told you everything I can say about that."

Kayla leaned closer. "We've learned there is someone new trying to take over. We think it's international in scope. South Africa. Namibia specifically."

"Who?" Martin asked.

"We don't know," Kayla said.

"Don't know or just won't tell me?"

"Stop it, Curtis," Tara said. "You sound like a child. There's more at stake here than the local Yakuza and your other little Boston gangs."

"Oh, really? What?" he asked. "Bodies are dropping like flies, Blades."

"Did the cameras or witnesses pick up anything else?" Kayla asked.

The camera that got us didn't directly cover the dry cleaner. Just a random street shot. There are others in the neighborhood. They're being reviewed. But that's a lot of footage to review. A lot of people to look at. If the killer's on them, there's no way to pick them out unless they're dumb enough to be carrying a bloody knife or something as incriminating."

"Doubt we can count on that," Kayla said.

"If we can ID a suspect, we'll maybe be able to match something up then."

"Or they slipped out another way," Tara offered. "Maybe through the back. Avoiding the cameras."

"Either way, can you get me the footage?" Kayla asked.

"All of it?"

"All of it. I've got people who can run it through our facial recognition software."

"We're doing that now," Martin said.

"But they don't have the international databases I have access to. NSA. FBI. DHS. DoD. Friendly foreign nations."

Martin held up his hand, surrendering.

"Got it. I'll get you the footage." Martin hoped they would be true to their word and share intel. "Tell me how you know this new player is…what'd you say international?"

Taking turns, Tara and Kayla filled him in on the information they'd learned from Letty Kamati and the discovery of Agent Simon Angula's body on the sunken *Marken*.

Martin began to piece it together. "You think a South African organization is responsible for all this? Here, trying to take over the criminal syndicate here directly? Without proxies? That would be… unprecedented."

"Eliminate the middlemen. Tighter control. Makes sense, business-wise," Kayla said.

Martin glanced around the bar. Luke Combs sang about when it rains, it pours.

Though the bar was crowded, no one paid much attention to the three of them, hunched over and talking in low tones. "What's Bannon's take on all this?" Martin asked. "Speaking of. Where is he anyway?"

"He and Skyjack are meeting with a couple of DHS agents to get more information about the South African angle," Kayla said.

"They ran into some trouble in Boston Harbor," Tara said.

"*Some* trouble? That was them? Four dead. One in a coma. Bullets flying everywhere," Martin said. "I thought you said you people keep a low profile?"

Tara shrugged. "Things happen."

"What's next?" Martin asked.

"We've got investigators talking with the rescued women," Kayla said. "They're cooperating thanks to Letty Kamati," Kayla said. "I'm meeting with her later today to see what else she can give us about her kidnapping and anything more she might know about the Namibia operation."

"Authorities are grilling the *Marken's* crew, too," Tara said. "Pressing them hard. Whatever we learn, we'll pass it along."

Will you? he wondered. Suddenly feeling sidelined.

"I guess I'll take another crack at what the streets have got to say. Ever since you people ripped the syndicate inside out, things have been a mess. Nothing makes sense."

"We were trying to help," Tara said.

"That wasn't a denial." Was he making headway? "Well, your helping has had a lot of unforeseen consequences."

"We couldn't have known," Tara said.

"That's the definition of unforeseen, isn't it?" Martin tossed back the last of his beer. "One more thing. A witness did tell the cops they saw a man and woman leave the dry cleaners around the time of the murder. The cops haven't figured out what to do with that yet."

"You think they meant us?" Tara asked.

"Don't know. But I'd suggest you keep a low profile for now."

Tara gave him a sour expression. "Just as well. My skill set doesn't really come into play until we know who needs to be taken down."

The ice in her voice sent a chill down Martin's spine. He declined another beer. "I'd better go. But watch your six. Whoever's behind this, they're dangerous." He thought about the Wang crime scene, up there with one of the worse he'd ever been to. "Deadly."

He pushed through the door and left the bar. Outside, the air was hot and muggy, filled with the salty scent of the sea. Squinting in the bright afternoon sun, he slipped on his dark sunglasses and walked along the boulevard to his car.

JADE VAN WYK SAT on a bench across from the Keel Haul. Ocean Boulevard was choked with people and cars. Families dragging wheeled coolers, juggling beach chairs, and holding on to children with towels draped over their shoulders. Loud groups of teens were yelling and laughing and roughhousing. A rollerblader wearing short shorts and a cropped top t-shirt zoomed past her, carrying a pizza box over his head. He zigzagged through the crowd. His skates clacked over the seams in the sidewalk.

A cloudless summer day. The sidewalks remained wet from the previous day's rain. The air was sticky and thick.

She wore oversized dark sunglasses. Her dark skin gleamed in the sunlight under a yellow bikini top, short white shorts, and matching, strappy sandals. Mzobe stood looming over her. He wore white linen slacks and a brightly colored Hawaiian shirt over a black muscle t-shirt.

They watched Curtis Martin leave the bar, slip on his sunglasses, and walk down the street.

"The cop," Mzobe guessed.

"It would seem."

"Do we follow him?" Mzobe asked.

"No," Jade said carefully, thinking. "I can keep tabs on him through our police contacts."

A line of cars drove by slowly. Rap music blared out of one. Jade winced at the horrible noise. She shook her head. "They call that music. Shameful."

Mzobe shook his head in stoic agreement.

Jade returned her attention to the bar. "No," she said again. "I am more interested in the women."

"Sardana?" Mzobe asked. "The bartender?"

"Yes. And the Coast Guard woman." She'd learned her name was Kayla Clarke. A lieutenant assigned to the Judge

Advocate Office in Boston. She'd been part of something called a Deployable Operations Group. A command formed in the wake of 9/11 to be the Coast Guard's answer to a Navy SEAL team. She saw action in the Persian Gulf before returning Stateside when the DOG command was decommissioned. At that time, she took her current position in Boston.

She'd also learned Clarke had worked for Bannon in the desert campaign.

"They are a very interesting little group, don't you think, Arno?"

He grunted.

"We wait," Jade said. "I think it'll be much more productive to see where the ladies lead us than the men."

Mzobe grunted again.

She smiled. "I'd like to try that powdery fired dough stuff. That looks interesting, don't you think?"

CHAPTER SEVENTEEN

Maritime Museum & Gift Shop
Kittery, M.E.

WHILE JADE VAN WYK AND Arno Mzobe pretended to enjoy the weather and seacoast activities of Hampton Beach outside the Keel Haul Tavern, Bannon and McMurphy rode with Parker Quinn in her government sedan up the coast to Kittery, Maine.

Parker had spent the better part of the past year tracking the Honjō Masamune sword and other artifacts believed to be of interest to *Skaduwee*, only to have lost the trail. Now, rumored to be back in the United States, she'd confessed that her leads had run cold.

But Bannon believed he knew a guy who could point them in the right direction.

Thaddeus Michael Perry ran the maritime museum and gift shop at the end of New Armory Place in Kittery. His shop overlooked the Piscataqua River.

A plain, nautical gray building with white trim. It looked more like a converted and renovated barn than much of a museum. Draped from the awning were red, white, and blue bunting. A flagpole stood in a patch of grass rimmed with white-painted rocks. An American flag and a POW flag hung limp in the still air. With the flagpole were several granite monuments and a granite bench. Flowers were planted in front of the monuments.

Parker pulled into the crushed seashell-covered parking lot. The shells crunched under the tires. The tired motor pool car clicked as she shut it down and extracted the keys. There was only one other car in the lot.

Getting out, Parker slipped on her sunglasses. "Tell me about this ole boy of yours."

"Thad's about a hundred years old. Or so it seems," Bannon said. "He's run this place for the last ten years. It's a great place. You'll love it."

"Get the two of them started. We ain't never getting out of here," McMurphy warned as they strolled toward the museum. He held the door open for them, pocketing his cell phone after checking an incoming text message. Parker and Bannon passed him and entered the shop.

"At least the *ole boy* keeps ice-cold beer on hand," McMurphy said. "So, there's that."

The bell over the door jingled.

A man with a leather-tanned face and thick white hair glanced up from behind a glass counter. He had a round face, a white goatee, and alert eyes. His craggy face broke into a wide grin of big, white teeth when he saw Bannon.

"Hey, there he is." Perry got to his feet and came around from behind the counter. Of average height and stocky build, he wore a work shirt over a black t-shirt with the museum's logo and blue jeans.

Spry for an old guy, Parker thought.

The old man clasped Bannon's hand and gave him a back-slapping hug. The two men slapped each other's backs. Perry shook McMurphy's hand. "Good to see ya, Skyjack. Steal any helicopters lately?"

"Not this week, TM. But it's only Tuesday." McMurphy pointed at a wine barrel and arched a thick eyebrow.

Perry smiled widely. "Have at it, son."

McMurphy opened the wine barrel. The old man always had something different on hand. He extracted a can of Grey Sail Captain's Daughter Double IPA. He grinned appreciatively. "You've outdone yourself this time, TM. Anyone else want one?"

Bannon and Parker shook their heads.

Perry's attention was on Parker Quinn. "Who is this magnificent young lady you've got with you?"

119

DAVID DELEE

Bannon made the introductions. "Parker's a DHS agent with their Cultural Property, Art and Antiquities program out of New York."

"How do," Parker said.

"Ah," Perry smiled broadly. He shook her hand, patting the back of it. "Pete Peterson still running the show down there?"

Parker smiled warmly. "You know Pete? He retired last year. Chad Mazzarelli's in charge now."

"Mazz," Perry said. "Good choice. Good man."

"How do you—"

"Know 'em? Worked with them on a couple of things. Back in the day."

"You were DHS?"

Perry laughed. "Honey, I've worked for just about every alphabet soup government agency you can name. And some you haven't and won't ever hear about. You get back to the Big Apple, ask Mazz to tell you about the time we tangled with a pair of unscrupulous treasure hunters over the booty from the *Royal Dutch*."

He led her to a display case. "This was long before Homeland Security was a twinkle in old George Bush's eye."

"And, here we go," McMurphy said, settling into an oversized, plush chair with his beer, scrolling through his cell phone.

Bannon had heard the tale dozens of times but tagged along anyway.

In a display case, under glass, was a cigar-box-size chest. Inside it were dozens of gold and silver coins. "The *Dutchie*, as I call her, went down in seventeen-seventy-seven. Returning to Cape Cod from Jamaica after plundering dozens of ships along the way. They got caught up in a powerful nor'easter. It's said the crew was too drunk to properly navigate in the storm."

"A crew of one-hundred-forty-three perished," Bannon said, "Only two survived, right?"

"Correct. One-hundred-eight bags of gold and silver went down with her. The wreck was discovered in the late 1990s and immediately preyed upon by treasure hunters."

"How is it you have this?" Parker pointed at the small chest.

Perry smiled. "On loan from the Smithsonian. A small sampling of what Mazz and our boys recovered from the treasure hunters, bent and determined to steal it."

"Worth one-hundred-fifty million dollars," Parker said, reading the placard under the display case.

From his chair, McMurphy said, "Can we get on with it, boys and girls, or someone's gonna need to fetch me another Captain's Daughter."

Returning to the sales counter, Bannon said, "The reason we're here, Thad. It might be a little outside your wheelhouse, but we're looking for information about the Honjō Masamune."

"Ah, Japan's perfect sword. What about it?"

"We're looking for it," Bannon said. "Part of a thing we're working on."

"Ah," Perry said. "Funny."

"What's funny?" Bannon asked.

"Your timing."

"How so?" Parker asked.

"There's been chatter on the black market about that thing for years, of course. Possible sightings. Claims of ownership. Rumored to have been found here in the States, but then there were sightings overseas, too. England. Saudi Arabia. Even back in Japan at one point."

"That's just what you told us," Bannon said.

Parker nodded. "Yes, we firmly believe it was once in the hands of a Saudi prince. It disappeared before we could get the proper documents together and filed in time to seize it. When we did, it was gone again."

"That's too bad. But you might be in luck." Perry sat heavily in his chair behind his counter.

McMurphy grabbed two more beers from the barrel and handed one to Perry. "I'm guessing we're gonna be here awhile."

He settled back down in his chair. The leather creaked. He popped the top of his beer can.

At the counter, Perry sipped his beer.

"I scour the Internet, haunting sites and groups looking for worthwhile items to add to the collection here. I also spend a lot of time on the dark web." He looked around the museum. "As you can see, people aren't much interested in history anymore. Leaves me with a lot of time on my hands. Anyway, six months, maybe a year ago. I noticed the chatter about that damn sword started to pick up. Seems somebody new was interested in acquiring it in a uber-serious way."

"That's why we're here," Bannon said. "That's who we're after."

"Because of the sword?" Perry asked.

"No, they're responsible for other…things."

"What sorts of things?"

"Human trafficking, for one," Bannon said. "Murder. And the list is growing."

"A real bad apple, huh? Okay, then. What do you know about the sword's whereabouts?" Perry asked Parker. "After 1945?"

"Like you said. Rumors. Unsubstantiated claims, nothing that ever panned out," Parker admitted. "Except for our near miss in Saudi Arabia. Which, I have to admit, might also have been a false lead, too." She looked over at McMurphy. "I'm starting to wonder. Maybe he never had it either."

"You weren't wrong," Perry assured her. "He had it. Your prince spirited it out of the country. Snuck out by his security detail."

"How do you know this?"

Perry finished his beer. "Because I know the scoundrel the prince sold it to."

"No way," Parker exclaimed.

Even McMurphy perked up from his chair, hearing that.

Perry held up his hands, stop sign fashion. "At least, I think I do. You know how these things go. But there's one interested party in particular who's been leading the charge to find this thing for years. And they're relentless as hell. One thread I've been watching pretty closely reported he knew of someone who'd bought the Honjō a year ago."

"Who is it?" Parker said.

"It's the Internet. So, started with screen names only," Perry told them. "You know the drill. But the handle mentioned is one I'm familiar with. One I've been following for quite some time for my own reasons. As I said before, a rather unscrupulous collector. His forte is lost, as in stolen swords and other bladed weapons. The more historical value they have, the better."

"Why such an interest in a sword collector?" Parker asked. "Seems a bit far afield from," she waved a hand around the museum, "your interest."

"Swords and other bladed weapons do play a big part in nautical history, but my interest in this particular individual," Perry said, "is also personal."

Bannon asked, "Do you have more than his screen name?"

"I do," Perry said. "And I'm convinced he's the buyer of the Honjō Masamune sword. Whether he's still got it… "

McMurphy climbed out of his chair. "Could this be *Skaduwee*? Our shadow?"

"From the stuff you've said he's done, I wouldn't think so. This individual is more your garden variety former Wall Street dirtbag. But you can ask him. I know exactly who he is and where he lives. And best of all," Perry smiled. "He's local."

"Local where?" Bannon asked.

"Not all that far from here, actually. Lives up the coast in York. He's an ex-hedge fund guy named Peter Jorgen."

BANNON, PARKER, AND McMURPHY took all the information Perry had to give, bid their goodbyes and thanks to Thaddeus Michael Perry, and left the museum.

Outside, Bannon put his sunglasses on and frowned. McMurphy was on his cellphone again, thumbing the screen.

"What's it with you and your phone today?" Bannon asked. "You're like an addicted Gen Z kid with ADHD."

A trait most unusual for his old friend.

McMurphy looked up. "Huh?"

"Speaking of phones," Parker said. "I think I left mine on the counter back there."

She went back into the museum.

"What? This?" McMurphy held up his phone. "It's nothing. A bad penny that keeps turning up."

"You want to share with the class?"

"No," McMurphy said. "But once Parker drops us off, there's a place I gotta go. This thing I've gotta deal with."

"Do what you've gotta do," Bannon said, asking again, "Anything you want to talk about? Or need help with?"

"Nope. I'm good. But thanks."

Before Bannon could probe further, the museum's overhead doorbell jangled loudly. Parker came out, holding her phone in the air. "Got it."

"Great," Bannon said. "We ready to go then?"

McMurphy pocketed his phone and put on his sunglasses. "Lead on, Kemosabe."

CHAPTER EIGHTEEN

Massachusetts Correction Institution
Cedar Junction, South Walpole, M.A.

LATER THAT AFTERNOON, McMURPHY sat at a table in the visitor's center of the MCI-Cedar Junction Correctional facility. They called 'em institutions now like they're a university. A place for higher learning.

McMurphy glanced at the iron grilles welded over the frosted windows. The smudged, scarred cinderblock walls were painted two-tone blue. The twelve square tables with connected chairs. Everything bolted to the floor. The dirty floor tiles, permanently scuffed black. The hollow, distant buzz of gates being opened and the metal clang of them shutting again. The convex mirrors and the tinted domes covering a dozen or so cameras.

Call it what it is, he thought. A prison. A maximum-security prison for the state's most hard-core criminals.

The door to the room buzzed. A guard pushed it open.

James "Paddy" Flanagan shuffled in. They had him in white tennis shoes, an orange jumpsuit, and restraints. His hands and ankles were cuffed. Connected by chains threaded through a thick leather belt around his waist.

McMurphy's old man had lost a lot of weight in prison and had grown a beard. His bright red hair streaked with gray. His eyes were hooded and had lost some of their intimidating intensity. Especially the one swollen shut. The skin around it a dark eggplant color.

"What happened to you?" McMurphy asked as Flanagan sat.

"A disagreement. You should see the other guy, boy-o."

The guard nodded. "Fractured nose. Two broken teeth. Four busted ribs. And, last I heard, the guy's still pissing blood. This one?" He jutted his chin at Flannagan. "Three days in solitary."

"Got to catch up on my beauty sleep."

To McMurphy, the guard said, "You need anything. I'm right over there." The guard returned to the door and stood, looking straight ahead but watching their every move.

"What do you want, old man?"

"Can't a father want to see his son?"

"Cut the crap. You're after something. What is it?"

Anger colored Flanagan's ruddy face. "I should want something, boy-o. You betrayed me. You made a deal and you went back on your word."

"Is that what this is?" McMurphy asked. "Why you got the warden all wound up, got him blowing up my phone when I wouldn't take your calls. All 'cause you wanna cry about me betraying you?"

"Ain't no thinking about it, boy-o. We're a narc, and that's that."

"You couldn't hold on to what you wanted. Poor you. We took LaScala and Kwon off the board for you."

"Because of me," Paddy hissed. His voice low. "With my help."

"You got what you wanted," McMurphy said. "To run the Boston criminal underworld. It was all yours."

Flanagan slammed his fists into the table. The chains rattled. "For a day!"

"Settle down," the guard warned.

"And now you've got what you deserved," McMurphy insisted. "You got swept up in the largest drug seizure the state's ever seen. How's that my fault?"

"You tipped them off, boy-o. You're a rat. I know you did."

"Poor you. Treated so badly. All the lives you've ruined over the years. Destroyed. People you killed or had killed. If I told what I knew, all of it, you'd be on death row. They wouldn't be able to jab the needle into your arm fast enough."

McMurphy got up. "I don't have time for you, Paddy."

"Wait."

"You're right where you belong," McMurphy said. "And if there's any justice in the world, you'll rot here until the day you die."

"Wait! Sit down." Flannagan glared at him. "Don't you disrespect your father by walking out on me."

McMurphy gave it a minute, then sat back down.

Flannagan leaned in and lowered his voice. "Look. You think I'm not still in charge just cause I'm in here?"

McMurphy recalled their meeting with Martin at the Keel Haul and wondered, was he? "One can hope."

"You're naive, boy-o. But I'll admit. There's limitations."

"What? The Black Rose," the old man's favorite Irish pub, "won't deliver?"

"Funny."

"Get on with it."

Finally, Flannagan continued. "You heard about Kwon? They got to him."

"You mean Wang. The son-in-law."

"What? Wang's dead, too." Flanagan wasn't used to not being in the know. The news rocked him. "They whacked Kwon in his cell. His cellie, too. Last week. Hacked them up good. That's cause of that thing you and Bannon are working on. Them girls."

"What do you know about that?"

"They get cable in here. You know that, right?" Flannagan shook his head, like a parent disappointed with his dimwitted child. "Saw you flying into Boston in the middle of the night. Then, that harbor thing the other day. I saw the footage. What were there? Three? Five dead? You wanna talk about *my* body count?"

"Get on with it, Paddy."

"Someone's making a play."

"That's the word. A new player—or players—in town," McMurphy said. "What do you know about it?"

"Not a lot. Like I said, being in here… there's limitations."

For the first time, McMurphy got the sense his old man was being straight with him. He also thought the old man sounded... afraid.

"That was what your beef was?" McMurphy asked, indicating his shiner. "They tried to get you?"

"Naw. That was typical prison yard territory stuff. But it's probably only a matter of time."

Unless they think you're irrelevant, old man, McMurphy thought. "The cops say even New York's clueless, or afraid, of these new players."

"Yeah," Flanagan said. "That's the word in here, too. Ain't the Russians or the Czechs. Not the Mexicans, either."

"What do you know?"

"Honestly, not much," Flanagan said. "Just that they're very secretive. And well-funded with a lot of muscle they're not afraid to use. Very dangerous."

"Lots of violent encounters on the streets."

Flannagan nodded. "But here's the thing, son. They've put a hit out."

"A hit? On you?"

"On me? Maybe," Flannagan said. "But the day ole Paddy can't take care of himself, then I deserve to be taken out of her wearing a toe tag. No. It's why I've been trying to get word to you, dummy. They're looking for you and your goodie-two-shoes buddy there, Bannon. Grabbing those girls. It pissed them off. They're gunning for you. Make sure you two can't do something like that again."

"But you don't know who?"

"Just that it's real. And whoever they are. They're dangerous. Deadly dangerous."

"This is because you and Kwon got locked up?" McMurphy didn't admit his part in their downfalls. Now Kwon was dead.

Flanagan sat back in his chair, contemplative for the first time. "Maybe. I don't know. Things ain't the way they've been. Not for a long time. What I do know, this is going to be like a storm. And it's gonna sweep through Boston, Providence, and maybe even New York. The streets are gonna run red with blood the likes ain't been seen since the Capone days."

"That's a little dramatic, isn't it?"

"Tell that to Kwon's family. Wang's wife."

McMurphy frowned. Martin had warned them. Gangsters were already getting cut down in the streets. What they originally thought of as turf wars between rival factions was turning out to be genocide of the existing criminal underworld. It wouldn't be long before innocent civilians got caught in the crosshairs.

"I ain't gonna lie to ya, boy-o," Flanagan said. "You might've done me a favor locking me up in here."

"You think you're safe?" McMurphy asked.

"If they really wanna get to me?" He shrugged, noncommittal over his own lack of status. "Naw. But I've got guys here to protect me. And I've got the bulls on my side. Better odds than if I were out wandering the streets. Besides. In here. Who cares about me? I'm no threat to what's going on out in the streets."

"That didn't help Kwon?"

"He got whacked because he wouldn't let go. Kept pushing that idiot Wang to step up, to be the next big cheese. Ain't nobody in my crew has what it takes to step up. I'm content to sit back and keep a low profile. Let the storm blow itself out. See what's left when the dust settles."

His old man wasn't one to sit out a fight. But now he sat, shoulders stooped, looking very old.

"But you two gotta watch your backs. The word is they're big guns out there after you. Whoever these people are, they're not messing around. They want you two seriously dead."

McMurphy thought back to the assault on them in Boston Harbor. "That's it then. That's why you wanted to see me?"

"Is that so hard to believe? A Da wanting to make sure his boy-o's okay?"

"You?" McMurphy admitted, "A little. Look. I've gotta go. I've got to get out in front of this." McMurphy stood up. He patted his father's hands, noticing the dark age spots.

"Be careful out there, son. I mean that."

"Will do. You too, old man."

When McMurphy passed the guard at the door, he said, "Keep an eye on him, would ya?"

The guard nodded and McMurphy left.

CHAPTER NINETEEN

Jake's Seafood Restaurant
North Hampton, N.H.

WHILE McMURPHY VISITED HIS Da in prison, Kayla Clarke leaned against the rear of her car. A 1975 bright yellow Volkswagen Type 181, marketed in the U.S. as the VW Thing. In truth, the vehicle looked like the offspring of a VW beetle and an Army Jeep ever mated. Originally designed for the German Army, the Thing had a square, boxy frame, a removable convertible top, a windshield that folded flat, and four detachable doors. She had the top and doors off. Its 1.6-liter flat-four engine was rear-mounted, of course, with a 4-speed manual transmission.

The car was all she had left after a long-ago, lousy breakup with an ex.

Painstakingly restored and lovingly maintained by McMurphy. She smiled, thinking about him tinkering with the car for hours, refusing any form of payment beyond the copious amounts of beers she provided.

She removed her hair tie and tossed her head, fluffing out her thick, tangled auburn hair. She wore sunglasses, a white linen blazer over a peach-colored blouse, distressed blue jeans, and white sneakers. The blazer concealed her Gen3 Glock 19, the newly issued gun replacing her Coast Guard-issued .40 caliber Sig Sauer P229. She wore the weapon snuggly in a tactical pancake holster, which tilted the gun forward for a swift, natural draw.

Behind her was one of her favorite seafood eateries.

Jake's Seafood Restaurant and Market. A side-of-the-road kind of place. Two connected barn-style buildings. Vertical pinewood siding painted blue with white trim. Window boxes overflowed with brightly colored, fragrant flowers. One side was a market specializing in fresh-caught seafood, a specialty the seacoast offered. The other had an order and pickup window, with a large blackboard colorfully listing the daily offerings. Picnic tables with blue and white striped umbrellas filled the side yard.

The afternoon sun blazed warm in the sky. The air was sticky and heavy. Thick with the promise of an imminent early summer storm. More Florida weather than New England, but the gentle, cool ocean breeze made the humid weather not totally miserable.

Kayla removed her sunglasses and squinted, checking her watch. They were five minutes late. She was a stickler for punctuality, but that wasn't what bothered her about their tardiness. The line at the service window had already reached the end of the building and was snaking around the parked cars into the parking lot. She'd only had a light breakfast that morning and had skipped lunch altogether. Her mouth watered for a plate of fantail shrimp and scallops sauteed with olive oil, basil, garlic, salt and pepper.

She put her sunglasses back on, trying to ignore her complaining stomach, just as Agent Hornsby pulled an old green sedan into the space Kayla had saved for them.

Letty sat in the passenger seat. Hornsby got out. He adjusted his dark-framed glasses and put a cowboy hat on. He wore snake-skinned boots and a blue suit. He rushed to the other side of the car and opened the door for Letty. They came around the back end of the car together.

He tipped his hat. "I'm assuming you're Lieutenant Clarke."

"I am." They shook hands. "A pleasure to meet you, Agent Hornsby."

"Oh, go with Darren, ma'am. Please."

She smiled. "It's Kayla, then. Letty. How are you?"

"Very nice. Thank you."

Following Grayson's visit to the detention center, Homeland Security had put the rescued girls up at a hotel in

Boston. ICE Agent Abioye had been assigned to oversee their protection, handling, and debriefings. During that time, they'd been given the opportunity to shower, eat, and sleep. Clothes had been bought for them.

Letty wore a white sundress and sunglasses. Her dark skin was radiant in the warm summer sun. She appeared almost giddy. "The hotel is very pleasant. It even has a pool." She clasped Kayla's hand in hers. "Thank you for all you've done for us."

"You're welcome, but it's not really me," Kayla said. "Are you two hungry? We should get in line." They moved along the row of parked cars toward the end of the line. "Everything is wonderful. But the baked haddock, it is to die for."

"I'm looking forward to experiencing it all," Letty said.

"And you, Agent Hornsby. Any favorites?"

"Being from Texas, I'm partial to barbeque, but I'm sure I'll find something."

"They do great grilled marinated steak tips," Kayla said, continuing to sing the praises of Jake's. "But they also grill Atlantic salmon, and swordfish, and—"

A loud screech of tires and the blast of a car horn cut her off, causing Kayla to turn.

Down the street, a black Jeep Wrangler had changed lanes quickly, cutting off an SUV. Its top and doors were removed. It had a heavy black roll bar and grille guard. The reckless driving had put the Jeep in the lane closest to the sidewalk and to Jake's.

Kayla expected the vehicle to hook into the parking lot.

It didn't.

Odd, she thought, getting a sense of danger at the base of her neck. Hornsby had much the same reaction. He put himself between the two women and the street. His hand was under his suit jacket.

Kayla's attention was on the Jeep. In the closest lane and driving past the restaurant.

A tall, thin black woman was behind the wheel. She wore a white sundress, oversized dark sunglasses, and a large-brim, floppy hat. A large bald man, also black, occupied the passenger seat. He had on a bright-colored Hawaiian shirt and a black t-shirt under a white line jacket and sunglasses.

A little too *Miami Vice*, Kayla thought, putting a cautionary hand on her Glock.

Time slowed down for her, bringing with it a clarity of detail.

She watched as the man pulled a weapon from the footwell. A Heckler & Koch MP7 compact submachine gun. A short, close-quarter personal defense weapon with a folding front grip and a rate of fire of nine-hundred-fifty rounds a minute. She knew 4.6x30mm hardened steel ammunition was unique to the MP7. Rounds created with the specific purpose of piercing soft body armor in mind.

She shouted, "Gun!"

Hornsby had already drawn his weapon.

She was seconds behind him when the guy in the Jeep opened fire. Gunfire chattered with the sound and intensity of a fireworks display. Bullets dug into the fenders of cars and pinged off bumpers. A line of bullet holes stitched across the face of Jake's. Glass windows shattered. Car alarms blared, their lights flashing. People on the street and in line screamed and scattered, ducking for cover.

Hornsby shoved Kayla to the side. She crashed into Letty and dragged the frightened woman to the pavement, pushing her between two cars. Letty covered her head with her arms and curled into a fetal position.

Kayla scrambled to her knees and fired at the Jeep from over the car's trunk.

Hornsby was on one knee, firing. Out in the open. Exposed. Saving the women had left him nowhere to go.

The shooter dropped the MP7's magazine and slammed a second one home. He opened fire again. A second spray of bullets tracked across the front of the restaurant. More car horns blew amid the sounds of tires screeching in the street and cars smashing into one another.

Kayla shouted, "Hornsby, get down!"

He popped off two more rounds before a line of bullets cut across his chest. He cried out. His body jerked as bullets slammed into him. He keeled over to the side and slumped to the pavement.

Kayla cried out, "No!"

She broke cover and bolted for the escaping Jeep. With her Glock extended, she fired several times. The shooter grabbed his upper arm. A red stain of blood blossomed on the sleeve of his linen jacket.

The driver tried to make a right turn at the corner. She cut it too close. The Jeep jumped the curb. She cut the wheel back sharply to avoid a metal table and four chairs set up to sell t-shirts. Chairs and shirts went flying. The table collapsed. The right front wheel rode up the table like a ramp, lifting and tipping the speeding Jeep. The engine revved. A high-pitched whine. The Jeep slammed to the street and skidded on its side.

Kayla ran toward the crash. She dropped her weapon's magazine for a fresh one. She thumbed the slide lock off, racking a round in the chamber. Cautiously, she approached the flipped-over Jeep. She noted the strong whiff of leaking gasoline. She stepped around to the front seats. Her Glock pointed in a two-handed grip.

The vehicle was empty. Only the discarded MP7, the woman's floppy hat, and the bloody linen jacket were left behind.

Kayla spun, searching the melee, but she didn't see them. Their assailants had escaped.

Kayla called 911 as she ran back to Hornsby. Already, the air filled with the sound of approaching sirens. Her gun holstered. She ignored the chaos around her as emergency units arrived. She dropped to her knees beside Hornsby.

Letty had scooted under him, cradled his head in her lap. Tears stained her dark cheeks. Hornsby's eyes were closed, but he was breathing, taking in raspy, shallow breaths.

"Hang in there, agent." Kayla squeezed his hand as she counted seven bullet wounds across his chest. Two still bubbling blood. "Helps almost here."

He shook his head. "Protect, Letty."

He coughed. His voice raspy. "Finish…what they started. Get the bastards. For Simon." Blood gurgled from the corner of his mouth. He coughed again and was gone.

CHAPTER TWENTY

Keel Haul Tavern
Hampton Beach, N.H.

THAT NIGHT, A SIGN hung on the locked door of the Keel Haul. *Closed. Death in the family.* It wasn't the first time the sign had been used. It wouldn't be the last. Inside, the jukebox was off. The bar was quiet. Dimly lit. Not even Captain Floyd had been allowed in. The somber air of a funeral parlor had settled over the bar.

Bannon wiped down the bar with a soggy rag. McMurphy sat in the corner. In his usual seat. A mug of beer in his meaty hands. With them, Tara and Kayla sat at the bar. Their drinks remained untouched. Parker Quinn had been introduced to the others. She sat, stirring a swizzle stick around her Alabama Slammer.

McMurphy broke the silence. "You know Hornsby long?"

Parker looked up from her drink. "No. Only met him at the airport when I came in this morning. Just an hour before we met up with y'all at the harbor. I was told he was a good agent."

"Did he have family?" Tara asked.

"Single. No kids," Bannon said. "Grayson says his mother and two brothers live in Texas. The brothers. They've got families. So, nephews and nieces. Married to the job, Grayson said."

"What about the girl?" Tara asked. "Letty?"

"Greyson's moved her, all the girls, to a safe house out of state. They're under Secret Service protection until we can figure this out."

Kayla wiped away a tear that tracked down her cheek. Bannon noticed.

He came out from around the bar and touched her shoulder. When she looked up, he nodded toward the back booth. His reserved booth. They slid into the seats, drinks in hand.

"How are you holding up?" he asked.

"I'm fine." Her voice had an edge to it. "Why?"

"You've had a rough couple of days of it. Just want to know you're okay."

"You think I'm not?"

"Didn't say that." He sighed. "What happened today. And the other day on the *Lightfoot*. It's a lot."

"It's not like I haven't—" She snapped her mouth shut. "I… I didn't even know the guy, and he…he pushed me, us, out of the way. He saved our lives."

"A good agent doing his job. You would have done the same. If circumstances were reversed."

"Of course, but—"

"Survivor's guilt. It sucks." He forced a smile. "Funny. I had this very same conversation with Hornsby this afternoon. What happened to Angula. He took hold of it. And it ate at him."

"I've had people die on my watch before," Kayla said. "This isn't any different."

"Not saying it is. And you'll get through it. Like we all have. But…."

"What?"

"It's fresh. The wounds will heal. Scar over. You'll get past it. But that's down the road."

"What are you saying, Brice?"

He took a sip of beer. "If you wanted to. If you decide to take some time off. That'd be okay. There'd be no shame in that."

"You're sitting me down? You're benching me?"

"No. Giving you the option to give yourself time."

She glanced over at McMurphy and Tara, talking quietly with Parker Quinn.

"Would you ask them to sit out?"

"Comparing yourself to others is never a good idea, Kayla. You need to do you."

"Would you ask them to stand down?"

He looked at his two best friends in the world, his brother and sister-in-arms, as was Kayla. He looked back at her. "No. And I'm not asking you to." He held up a hand, cutting off her protest. "But yes. I'd make the same offer to them. And I have. Many times."

"And my answer's the same as I know theirs were."

He smiled sympathetically. "To prove something to me? Or yourself?"

"Neither," she said definitively. "To get the people who did this to Hornsby. To get justice for him, for Angula and Petrus Luiperth."

The woman who'd died in the container.

"To find the people who would sell human beings like cattle and shove women in boxes and drown them. To stop them from doing that again. Stop them from killing anyone more. To make sure they pay for what they've done."

Bannon gave her a full-on smile this time. "Now you're talking." He patted her hand and stood up. "Let's go do that."

Back at the bar, Bannon refilled his mug from the beer tap and passed around fresh drinks to his friends. To his team. "What do we know?"

McMurphy recapped his visit with Paddy Flanagan, ending with his warning that he and Bannon had been targeted. "Maybe we ain't the only two in their crosshairs." He glanced at Kayla. "Sorry, kid. It never dawned on me that you might...."

Be targeted, too. She shook his apology again. "You couldn't have known. It's not your fault."

"Forgetting for a moment you're a crime lord's kid," Parker said. "I'm still wrapping my little ole brain around that. They might still have been after Letty."

"Taking her out does tie up a loose end," Tara suggested. "Maybe she knew more than she thought. Killing Hornsby or making another attempt on her life might frighten her enough to shut her up. And while killing an agent doesn't stop an investigation—"

"And tends to piss said agency off," McMurphy added.

"It could stall the investigation," Tara finished. "Give this *Skaduwee* time to cover his tracks."

"Either way," Bannon said. "It does bring up a thorny question. How'd they know where Kayla, Letty, and Hornsby would be? That would require inside information."

McMurphy put down his beer. He glared at Parker. "Goes back to the conversation we had at the harbor—"

She got to her feet, shoving her stool back noisily. "That's twice you've gone and accused me of being a spy. Or something. We ain't getting on that merry-go-round again, mister."

"Ever since those goons came at us at the harbor," McMurphy said. "Somebody knew we were gonna be there. Someone knew about the meeting today. There's a rat."

"Well, it ain't me, buckaroo. I didn't even know where we were going to meet. Not 'til Hornsby drove me to the harbor," Parker said. "I was on a plane for two hours coming out of New York. No way I could've organized them wave runner boys."

"Sit down." Bannon didn't have to use his command voice often. He did now. "It couldn't be Parker, Skyjack. She's right about this morning. As for the attack at Jake's? She was with us all day."

"She could've slipped word to someone," McMurphy said rather unconvincingly.

"I didn't even know there was going to be a meeting," Parker said, slipping back onto her stool. "I never even met this lass before right now."

Bannon asked Kayla, "Who knew about your meeting with Hornsby and Letty?"

"No one," she said. "Wait. I mentioned it to Detective Martin, but not the time or location. We hadn't even settled on a location where to meet. I was on my way into Boston. I got hungry and thought I hadn't been to Jake's in a while. I called Hornsby on the road. He thought it was a great idea. Thought it would be good for Letty. She was feeling cooped up at the hotel."

"Hornsby or Letty could be the leak," Parker said. "Could've told someone else about the change in location. Maybe inadvertently."

"Still smells like a rat to me," McMurphy said.

"Agreed," Bannon said. "But it's not any of us."

"You seriously think I was the target?" Kayla asked.

"I don't know what to think," Bannon admitted.

"Maybe the incident at Wang's was meant for me," Tara said. "Maybe we just left too early, or the ones who took out Wang showed up late."

"If that's the case, we've all got targets on our backs," Bannon said.

"Still doesn't tell us who the mole is or how these hit squads are getting their information," McMurphy said. "Hell, *we* hardly know where we're going before we get there."

Bannon looked at Kayla. "What have we got from the crime scene?"

"By some miracle, Hornsby was the only casualty. Civilians were hurt, but nothing serious. Bumps and bruises. Cuts from flying glass. Letty's scared, but she's more committed to helping now than ever."

"Forensics?"

"Blood was recovered from the Jeep. I winged the shooter. The FBI's running DNA. No hits so far. No matches in the system. Street cameras picked up the Jeep in the area, but facial recognition hasn't produced anything. Big floppy hat. Big dark glasses will do that. The H&K recovered is obviously illegal. All identifying marks were filed down."

"The Jeep?" Bannon asked.

"Stolen. Elimination prints have traced back to the owner. A high school kid from Merrimack. White. Seventeen. Lived his whole life here in New Hampshire. Same goes for his parents. No trouble outside of parking tickets and open container complaints with his friends at the local lakes. Nothing noteworthy on his computer, phone, or social media. All typical teenage stuff."

"Where was the Jeep taken?" Bannon asked.

"Here," Kayla said. "Parked up the road at North Hampton beach." She sat back in her stool. "Damn it. I *was* followed."

"Not your fault," Bannon said. "They must've been surveilling the Keel Haul. None of us caught it."

"No reason we should've," McMurphy said, but his tone belayed that statement. Guilt gnawed at him for not being ahead of the assassins.

Bannon felt a muscle twitch in his set jaw. "Well, we know now. From this point forward, we're on our own," he said. "Everything we say. Everything we do. Stays here. With us. No outside contact, especially with our respective agencies."

"Including me?" Parker directed her question at Bannon, but she looked at McMurphy.

"Yes." Bannon glanced at McMurphy.

The big, ruddy pilot drank his beer. "Sure."

"And we partner up. Two-by-two, minimum, until this is over." Bannon stared at Parker. "We're officially off the grid. All channels, official or otherwise. Off-limits. Dark."

"Radio silent," McMurphy said.

"Blacked out," Tara said.

"Ghosting," Kayla added.

"Got it. I got it. Y'all made your point."

"You good with that?" Bannon asked.

Without hesitation, Parker said, "What's next?"

"We follow the only lead we have," Bannon said. "Get the bait we need to finish this once and for all. We get the Honjō Masamune sword."

CHAPTER TWENTY-ONE

Skyjack's Folly
One mile offshore of York, M.E.

THE 32-FOOT, ALUMINUM, FLAT-BOTTOM, monohull dive boat was a beast. Outfitted with a landing craft-style hydraulic drop-down bow door, it had an enclosed, walk-around wheelhouse. Powered by twin, three hundred horsepower Yamaha outboard engines, *Skyjack's Folly* had a top speed of thirty-eight knots. The boat had removable passenger benches, a dive bottle rack that held up to fifteen tanks, port and starboard side dive doors with fold-out ladders and handrails, and a deck crane McMurphy used for salvage jobs when they came along. When he felt like doing them.

Dive equipment littered the deck of the flat-bottom boat. They'd dropped anchor a mile east of York Cliffs. He'd raised the dive flag, though they had no intention of diving. All done for appearances.

The sun hung low in the sky over the mainland, coloring the ribbon of dark clouds in a variety of maroons, scarlets and purples. Another hour and the sun would be gone. With the humidity still high, the cool ocean breeze made the early evening more tolerable weather-wise than the day had been.

McMurphy wore a black Afghanistan veteran t-shirt under an open denim work shirt and blue jeans. His black baseball cap read Captain with a pirate skull and crossed swords emblem. A lit cigar jammed into the corner of his mouth puffed ember red as he dug through a cooler full of ice.

"You want to fill me in on what you've got planned?"

Bannon lowered a pair of binoculars. "I would. If I actually had a plan."

McMurphy handed Bannon a beer. He popped a can for himself. He leaned against the gunwale.

Bannon joined him.

From the information Thaddeus Michael Perry gave them, utilizing every resource at her disposal, Kayla did a thorough, deep-dive background check on ex-hedge fund guy Peter Jorgen. Fifty-five years old. Retired young after making more money on Wall Street than any one person could ever spend. He was married to Jennifer 'Jenny' Rhodes. His high school sweetheart. They had two grown kids. One away at college, completing his last year at Harvard. Their oldest, a daughter, was a junior executive in an advertising agency. She lived in Manhattan.

Jorgen and his wife lived in an eight-thousand-square-foot mansion north of York Cliffs. Nestled on a rocky cove, on a two-acre lot. The ten-million-dollar, two-story residence had a separate three-car garage, a guest house, and a poolside cabana. They wintered in Florida. Palm Beach, of course.

Kayla came out of the wheelhouse carrying her laptop computer. She set it down on the fish cleaning table and slipped her sunglasses down from her forehead. "You boys the only ones who get to drink on this trip?"

"No, ma'am," McMurphy said with a laugh. He handed her a cold can of Coors Light.

"We should be all set," Kayla said, popping the top of her beer.

"Should be?" Bannon glanced over at the house.

"Figure of speech. We'll capture the call when it's made."

McMurphy furrowed his wide brow. "For not having a plan. There's a lot going on here. Want to catch me up?"

"Making it up as we go along," Bannon said. "The first step is to verify the information Thad gave us."

"Meaning does this Jorgen guy even have your magic sword—"

"Perfect sword."

"Whatever. How we doing that?"

"A simple intelligence-gathering op. We search the house."

"In broad daylight?"

Kayla shushed them. Her fingers danced across her computer keyboard. "Calls coming in." She pressed her earpiece to her ear. "NATCO Security Services. This is Kayla. How may I help you?"

She smiled. "Your security code, Mr. Jorgen?" A pause. "Thank you. We did dispatch two technicians to your location, sir. They are Sarah Tucker and Patricia Zane. Did they show you their IDs, sir?"

Another moment passed.

"They did. That's great. You're in good hands." Another pause. Kayla sipped her beer. "We've been getting intermittent power interruptions in the neighborhood. Have you been experiencing any electrical blackouts or brownouts over the past few hours?"

Off to one side, Bannon explained. "Tara and Parker have been driving around the neighborhood hitting houses with random EMP bursts all morning," They'd used an EMP ray cannon obtained from DARPA, the Defense Advanced Research Projects Agency, based on the Air Force Research Laboratory's ground-breaking Tactical High power microwave Operational Responder technology called THOR. A weapon capable of emitting an EM burst that could take down a swarm of incoming attack drones.

Kayla paused, listened, then told the caller, "That's what we thought. No. We don't believe it's damaged your alarm system. But to be on the safe side, our technicians will run a diagnostic on your control panel and conduct a complete inspection to make sure everything is operating properly and connecting to the central station. No. There's no extra charge to you at all, Mr. Jorgen. Just part of the excellent service we provide here at NATCO Security Services."

Another pause. "Thank you. You have a nice day as well, sir." Kayla disconnected the call with a grin.

"What the hell just happened?" McMurphy asked.

"You mean what *is* happening," Bannon said, passing out fresh beers.

TARA AND PARKER WERE dressed in dark blue coveralls with the NATCO Security patch on their right sleeves and an American flag on their left. They both carried a tool kit pouch over their shoulders and wore NATCO baseball caps. Parker had had a time of it trying to wrangle her mane of red hair into a ponytail that she could tuck up under her hat. Each cap concealed a camera in the brim, wirelessly transmitting video back to Kayla's laptop on *Skyjack's Folly.*

They were with Peter Jorgen in the mudroom off the pool and patio area.

He hung up his call to what he thought was the NATCO central alarm center. Kayla had used an eavesdropping device called an IMSI catcher that acted like a fake cell phone tower. It hijacked and rerouted his call to her cell phone and computer.

"Okay," Jorgen said, pocketing the phone. "What do you need to do?"

"I'll get started here," Tara said, opening the alarm control panel. She took an OMI-meter from her tool pouch and unwound the leads.

Parker said, "I'll need to physically inspect each point of protection individually. Run a test on each of them to make sure the panel's getting a signal."

"Each one? That'll take forever."

Parker smiled. "Less than an hour. We'll let you know when we're done."

"You're not wandering around my house unsupervised," Jorgen said.

"We're fully licensed and bonded, sir." Parker pretended to be offended without showing it. "There's no risk we would ever—"

Jorgen tried to walk his protest back. "No. I didn't mean to suggest—there's areas in the house that are locked. I'll need to open them up for you."

"Of course." Parker gave him her winningest smile. "Lead the way."

"We can start in the basement," Jorgen said.

Leaving Tara at the control panel, Parker winked.

Earlier, they'd downloaded the floor plans of the house from a website run by the real estate company who'd sold the house to Jorgen seven years earlier. There had been no mention of a basement.

Jorgen led Parker to the kitchen. He opened a door beside the refrigerator. Activated by motion sensor, the lights in the stairwell leading down snapped on. The walls were painted a soft cream color. At the base of the carpeted stairs was a second door. This one was black steel and set in a chrome frame. As much a vault door as Parker had ever seen.

It operated on a keypad. Parker pretended to look away but memorized the four-digit code Jorgen punched in. The door opened with a click and a puff of air.

"Hermetically sealed," Parker said.

"And environmentally controlled. Temperature. Humidity. All precisely regulated. I'm something of a collector," Jorgen said, feigning modesty poorly. "Some of the pieces I own are quite valuable."

Inside the basement room, the lights went on automatically.

Jorgen shut the heavy door behind them. Parker didn't like that but noted the door didn't lock. The basement consisted of two rooms. One larger than the other. The second room, off to the left, had an archway opening and a glass panel in the partition separating the two rooms. The rooms were carpeted. Recessed ceiling lighting softly lit the beige walls. The basement was a comfortable seventy-two degrees.

There was no secondary exit. A code violation, Parker was sure, confirming the basement had been built illegally after he'd bought the house. "This is some setup."

Jorgen beamed. "Thanks."

Parker approached a red felt board on one wall. Displayed on it were nine swords, each blade pointed downward to a single point, so the weapons formed a fan. A ceiling spotlight highlighted it.

"You like knives," Parker said.

Jorgen bristled. "Those are important swords from British history. From the Middle Ages through the Renaissance to the period of Enlightenment, dating back to the mid-8th century. AD."

"They're nice." She pointed to a device in the ceiling. "Smoke and heat sensors."

Jorgen nodded. "In both rooms. Carbon monoxide detectors, as well. Motion detectors and glass break protection on all the display cases. Pressure alarms on the openly displayed items. Magnetic contacts on the door, of course, and as you can see, there are no windows or any other egress. We are completely underground. One way in. One way out."

Parker whistled. "Fort Knox ain't got nothing on you."

"Ready to start testing?" Jorgen asked impatiently.

Parker called Tara, cradling her cell phone between her cheek and shoulder.

With the system in test mode, no alarms would transmit to the central alarm system. But to be safe, Kayla told them, she'd keep her IMSI catcher active, capturing any wireless transmissions from the house. Going in, they knew the alarm had dual-path connectivity, meaning any signal would transmit wirelessly via a Wi-Fi network and over a hard-wired landline. Tara had instructions to unplug the phone line before they began.

"We're a go," Parker said, informing Jorgen.

She put her phone on speaker, trying to keep any undue attention from the centerpiece of Jorgen's immense collection. The Honjō Masamune sword was displayed on a central pedestal. It was cradled in a lacquer sword stand. An overhead spotlight on it.

The weapon was sheathed in a scabbard. A black *sageo* wrapped around its end. The hilt was wrapped in black *samegawa,* and the sword had a small round *tsuba,* or guard. All consistent with what Parker knew of the sword's appearance and craftsmanship.

"This one you don't cover?" Parker asked. "It looks expensive."

"Even I don't know how expensive it is," Jorgen said. "Several million at least."

Parker whistled.

"As for how it is protected." Jorgen pointed at devices on opposite walls, aimed at the sword. "Proximity alarms. Pressure alarms under the carpeting. Anyone steps within five feet of it, light and audio alarms go off all over the house. The door locks." He indicated the closed vault door. "Try to lift the sword, additional pressure-sensitive switches in the stand activate." He stood, staring at the Honjō sword. "A lot of people want to own this," he said. "It's known as the perfect sword."

"Ready when you are," Tara said over the open line.

Parker instructed Jorgen to re-open the vault door. Tara reported getting the signal. Parker donned a pair of latex gloves Jorgen gave her. Over the next half hour, she activated each alarm point in the two rooms. Those that couldn't be actively tripped, glass break protection, for example, Parker affixed the leads of her OMI-meter and registered the electrical signals. While she worked, her baseball cap cam captured on video every item on display. The footage transmitted to Kayla's computer on *Skyjack's Folly*.

As promised, an hour after their arrival, they wrapped up with one final task.

Back at the control panel in the mudroom, Tara asked Jorgen to activate the system. He did so with a six-digit code. Unbeknownst to him, that code was captured by Tara and Parker's cap cameras.

Once he deactivated the alarms again, Tara and Parker declared the system one hundred percent operational.

"We shouldn't need to disturb you again," Parker said.

"The system's fully functional?" Jorgen asked. "I'm protected? You're sure?"

"Yes. We've tested every aspect of your system. It's top-notch. I even replaced the backup battery," Tara said, lying, "to make sure it's fully juiced. Our people are working with the power company to resolve the rolling energy disruptions.

We've been assured they've identified the problem and are working to correct it. You shouldn't have any more issues."

"And if there is?"

"The backup battery will give you at least twenty-four hours of protection should an outage occur."

"You've nothing to worry about, Mr. Jorgen," Parker said. "Your knives and swords are perfectly safe."

They packed up and said their goodbyes, apologizing for disturbing the man's afternoon and again assuring him his collection was in good hands.

CHAPTER TWENTY-TWO

Keel Haul Tavern
Hampton Beach, N.H.

THE CLOSED SIGN HUNG on the door of the Keel Haul once again.

In what was becoming their regular spots, Kayla and Parker sat at the bar. McMurphy was on his stool in the corner. Bannon and Tara were behind the bar. Tara kept everyone's drinks fresh. Unlike the last time they were together there, the drinks were being consumed in copious amounts. There was a buzz in the air. An electric energy Bannon enjoyed.

None of them had forgotten why they were there. The importance of the mission. The losses they'd already sustained. The lives they had to avenge. That was why they did what they did.

But there was also the undeniable thrill, the heart-pounding excitement of planning and conducting a dangerous mission. To put a plan into action. And to *be in* the action. That adrenaline-fueled rush only soldiers and first responders like cops and firemen felt. A runner's high, but on steroids.

During the season, Wednesdays began the build of business that led up to the typical wild weekends on the seacoast. While the financial loss of business meant nothing to Bannon—the bar was simply a cover for him—he had always dreamed of owning and operating such a place. He'd found he enjoyed running it even more fun than he had imagined. Something to do with the youthful energy. The buzz of the young people, the crowds, there, letting off steam.

Bannon contacted Lieutenant Ng earlier in the day, asking if she and her team were up for a little off-the-books operation.

It must be strictly volunteer, he said. With no repercussions if they said no. Ellis and Connell were immediately on board.

Ng posted the two ensigns outside the bar, in civilian clothes, to surveil the Keel Haul. They were to identify anyone with an undue interest in the bar or those coming and going. She would provide a roving, vehicle surveillance, expand their physical search, and provide immediate backup if required.

The boulevard was choked with traffic and kids drinking and hollering. And cops. But, from their perspective, Ng reported everything outside the bar as quiet.

Inside, Parker declared, fuming, "It's there! Missing for all these years. And it's just sitting there in plain sight." The stand the Honjō Masamune sword was displayed on had a pressure-sensitive switch. She'd picked the sword up to activate the alarm point for their test of the system. "I held it in my hands."

She tossed down a beer and pushed her empty mug forward. Behind the bar, Tara filled it from the tap while McMurphy and Bannon crowded around Kayla's laptop on the teak bar. They were watching Parker's transmitted video again.

"And that's not all," Parker went on. "In that second room. The three swords mounted on the wall. The two daggers under glass in that display case. Those are the Truman swords."

Bannon, Kayla, and McMurphy glanced over at her.

"Gifts at various times to President Truman from the Shah of Iran, Mohammad Reza Pahlavi, the Crown Prince Amir Saud of Saudi Arabia, and the Saudi Arabian king himself. Nineteen-seventy-eight. Thieves broke in and stole the collection from the Truman Library in Independence, Missouri. A simple smash-and-grab. At the time, the weaponry was worth over a million dollars. Obviously, it's all worth much more today. But their historical value? Priceless."

Parker paused to sip her beer, then continued her tirade, voicing her outrage. "He's in possession of pilfered national—international—treasures."

When they finished viewing the tape, Bannon said, "Jorgen will get what's coming to him. For now, can you tell us for sure? Is that the Honjō sword? Is it real?"

"No," Parker said.

"No, it's not," McMurphy said. "Or no, you don't know?"

"I'm not qualified to authentic such an item," she said. "We'll need to bring in an expert—experts—to examine it. And the other items there. Even then, there'll be debates. Differences of opinions."

"Not the concern right now," Bannon said. "Do we have what we need to draw out *Sakduwee* or not?"

"Yes," she said. "As a betting gal, I'd say it's the real deal. And we can sell that."

McMurphy went back to his stool. He sipped his beer. "Swell, we've found our bait. Now what?"

"We go ahead with the plan," Bannon said.

"The one you said you didn't have?" McMurphy asked.

Bannon smiled. "A work in progress. But without question, the next step is to get the sword."

"By that, you mean breaking and entering," Kayla said.

"Burglaring a private residence," McMurphy said. "Stealing someone's private property—"

"It's not his!" Parker insisted. "He stole it first."

McMurphy continued, "Worth millions of dollars. Sounds a lot like grand larceny to me."

"Only have to worry about that if we get caught," Bannon said.

McMurphy raised his mug and grinned. "I'm in."

"Kayla," Bannon said.

She looked up from her computer. "What? Oh. Sure. We've got the codes to disarm the alarms and get into the trophy room. Thanks to Tara and Parker. If the central station calls to check on why the alarm's been deactivated—they shouldn't, but—we'll catch that incoming call with the IMSI catcher. Same as we did outgoing calls this afternoon. Same thing if something goes wrong and the alarm's tripped accidentally."

"And I'll disconnect the landline," Tara said. "Again."

Bannon walked through it from there. "Kayla, you and Skyjack will be on the *Folly,* just like this afternoon. Blades, Parker, and I will get inside and deactivate the alarm. Blades will stand watch. Parker and I'll go downstairs, grab the sword, and skedaddle out of there."

"No one the wiser." Tara poured shots all around.

Bannon raised his glass. "What could go wrong?"

Tara frowned. "You didn't just say that?"

"He did," Kayla said.

"We're doomed." McMurphy threw his shot back and chased it with his beer.

"Well, aren't y'all the superstitious bunch," Parker said. "There is one more thing. We don't want to keep this quiet."

"What do you mean?" Tara asked.

"The theft. It needs to go viral," Parker said. "If word doesn't get out, no one will believe we have the sword."

"I don't see Jorgen listing stolen magic Japanese sword—"

"Perfect sword," Bannon corrected.

"On the police report and insurance claims," McMurphy finished.

"No," Parker said, agreeing. "But a police response, even if for a false alarm. Will lend credibility to any claim we make of possession."

Bannon smiled, following her train of thought. "Publicize through whatever dark web backchannels the black marketers and back-alley dealers use to know we have the sword."

"Letting our big fish know we have what he's looking for," McMurphy said.

"Exactly," Bannon said. "That the Honjō sword's in play."

"Sound like a big ocean to fish in," McMurphy asked. "How do we make sure the right circles hear the chatter?"

"I have channels I can exploit. And your friend Perry. He's dialed in," Parker said. "Maybe he can—"

"I've got a better way." Kayla waved for everyone to gather around her and her computer again.

Displayed on her screen was an announcement for the Devon-Arbuckle Masterpiece Auction. A fundraiser and charity event being held at the recently completed Rye Harbor Spa & Inn off Route 1A.

"They mentioned this at the last town hall meeting before the season started," Bannon said. "Part of the hotel's grand opening hoopla. Big corporate involvement, government lobbyists, celebrities, and politicians. It'll be a big media circus."

"What's it do for us?" McMurphy said. "We get the sword, and what? You wanna put it up for auction?"

Parker said, smiling. "Exactly. Kayla's right. These events. They're held all around the world. Where buyers and sellers of art and antiquities from all over the world get together. Places like Christie's, Sotheby's, and Bonhams. But the real action takes place—"

"In the back rooms," Bannon guessed. "The out of the public eye, side deals. Off-the-books."

"Yes," Parker said. "It's the perfect front for selling stolen items on the black market. What better way to do it than under the nose of a legitimately run auction house?"

"Hiding in plain sight," Tara said.

"Great," Bannon said. "How do we get the word out that we're open for business?"

"We need to actually *get* the sword first, don't we?" McMurphy asked.

"We're planning ahead," Bannon said. "Thought you'd like that."

Kayla said, "I can do a deep-dive into the dark web, put feelers out."

"I can help with the wording and descriptions," Parker said. "There's keywords and phrases these bottom feeders. Code."

"Good. Thad can probably help with that, too," Bannon said. "When is this event?"

"This weekend," Kayla said. "Friday, Saturday, Sunday."

"That's a tight window," Bannon said. "But we've got a plan." He nodded to McMurphy. "Happy?"

"Can barely contain myself." He downed his beer.

Bannon laughed. "Good. Then let's go steal a sword."

CHAPTER TWENTY-THREE

Jorgen's Residence
York, M.E.

THE NEXT NIGHT, BANNON, Parker, and Tara were crowded in the cab of his F-350. They were pulled off on the side of the road, a half mile south of Jorgen's home.

Two in the morning, Bannon checked his Omega Seamaster dive watch. It was the only thing that had traveled with him since childhood. His parents were killed in a car accident when he was an infant. With no other family, Bannon grew up in the system. Shuttled from one foster home to another. Never making any meaningful connections. Not with the parents or the other kids.

One of his better foster moms told him the watch had been his father's. Recovered from the car wreck. Bannon had no idea if that was true or not. But he'd held onto the idea. And had kept the watch. He didn't even have a first memory of owning it. It was just always with him, always his. The only constant in an unstable, ever-changing childhood.

Until he joined the Coast Guard.

The watch now told him it was oh-two-ten. The plan was for them to deactivate the alarm at two-thirty. "We move out in five."

From his earpiece, McMurphy reported in. He and Kayla were in position on *Skyjack's Folly,* drifting five hundred feet out in the cove. They were ready.

"Go time," Bannon said.

They exited the truck. They were all dressed in black tactical shirts and pants. He and Tara had Glocks strapped to their waists. Parker preferred the .40 caliber Sig Sauer P320.

She'd proven her proficiency with the weapon at the harbor. She and Tara had their hair in tight ponytails under black wool caps. Parker wore a black backpack strapped to her shoulders and carried a seven-foot-long Pelican hard plastic case. Tara also carried a urumi. A sword with a flexible, whip-like blade she wore around her waist like a belt.

While the plan didn't call for any face-to-face encounters, Bannon had seen her use the weapon with deadly precision.

They made their way along the side of the road until they came to a line of trees providing a privacy barrier between properties. Staying low, they followed that until they were directly across from Jorgen's mudroom. From Parker and Tara's earlier visit, they knew there were no security cameras, but they had to deal with the motion sensor lights.

The thing about motion-activated alarms and security lights is they are easily defeated. Especially outdoor ones, which are usually adjusted very low to reduce the number of annoying false activations triggered by animals and the like.

All they had to do was move so slowly the devices didn't register their movement. Simple.

After a torturous twelve minutes, they'd moved the four feet from the trees to the house. Now, crouched around the mudroom door, Tara made quick use of a set of lockpicks and unlocked the door. Once opened, they had thirty seconds to deactivate the alarm.

Tara stepped over a pile of shoes and wet towels on the floor and punched in the alarm code.

Bannon unconsciously held his breath until the little red light glowed green.

Tara remained at the panel. Parker knew her way around the house from her previous visit. She led Bannon through the kitchen to the basement door.

"The master bedroom's upstairs. End of the hall," she said.

Bannon found the staircase in the large foyer. He took the carpeted stairs two at a time, swiftly and silently. The hallway was dark except for a pale nightlight plugged into the wall socket close to the open bedroom door.

Bannon crept closer. At the open door, he peeked into the bedroom. Two forms were asleep in a king-size bed. One of them snoring loudly.

He gingerly swung the door shut and latched it with the quietest of clicks. Then he pulled a hallway chair over and jammed the back under the doorknob, locking the sleeping couple inside the room.

A precaution. If all went well, they'd remain undisturbed until the heist was over.

As silently as he approached, Bannon retreated down the hallway and back downstairs. He found the door to the basement open.

The lights were still on.

In the trophy room, he joined Parker.

She stared with reverence at the Honjō Masamune sword still on its acrylic display stand. He looked around the room and whistled. "You think these are all authentic?"

"Can't say with certainty," she said. "But if they are, you're looking at stolen items valued in the multi-millions."

Bannon glanced through the glass partition to the room at their left. There were two empty wall displays and a smaller katana display rack on a table. "What was there?"

"The Truman Collection." Parker knelt beside the hard plastic case she had on the floor. She opened it up. Two diamond, ruby, and sapphire-encrusted swords and a dagger. All in scabbards and fitted firmly in the form-rubber padding.

"I can't leave them here," she said. "I just can't."

He frowned. "That's not part of the plan."

"You want convincing, don't you?" she asked. "No art thief in the world who's gone through all this trouble would pass them up."

There wasn't any time to argue.

Parker covered the swords and dagger with a gray foam liner. Back on her feet, she carefully lifted the Honjō sword from its display stand. Bannon half expected to hear alarm sirens even though he knew they'd taken steps to prevent that.

Parker must have had the same anxiety because she let out a held breath.

She placed their prize in the case, covered it with another piece of foam padding, and snapped the hard plastic cover closed. With case in hand, she stood up. "Mission accomplished."

"Skyjack's always warning me to not count my chickens," Bannon said.

"That pilot of yours does seem to worry a lot," Parker said with a smile.

"I'm alive because of his concerns, many times over."

"Oh, I don't doubt that," Parker said, heading back to the heavy vault door.

Bannon raised a finger. "Hold up a sec."

He looked away, listening to Charlotte Ng's voice in his earpiece. "All's clear, Commander. No sign of a tail."

"Copy."

Believing Kayla had been tailed from the Keel Haul to her meeting with Letty and Hornsby, he'd assigned Ng and her team to follow them, keep a loose surveillance, to make sure no one was on their tails.

"Okay," he said to Parker.

They crept upstairs and through the dark house to the mudroom.

Tara moved out from the shadows where she'd been practically invisible. "All set?"

"Like clockwork." Bannon tapped his earpiece. "Skyjack. Kayla. We're good to go."

A minute passed while Kayla turned off her IMSI catcher. Once done, Bannon nodded to Tara. "Arm it."

She keyed in the code. The panel light went from green to red. Bannon pulled the exterior door open. They exited. Once outside, they stood with the door open. Waiting. Intentionally wanting to set off the alarm which would trigger a police and security response. Reports of the alarm, even if Jorgen insisted it was a false alarm, would be made. It was all the public response they needed to lend weight to the claim the

Honjō Masamune sword had been stolen. The story would circulate throughout the Internet and dark web.

Parker theorized Jorgen would put up a bounty, further legitimizing their claim.

Bannon counted down thirty seconds.

The alarm didn't sound.

He looked at Tara with an arched eyebrow for an explanation.

She shrugged her shoulders. "It should have—"

Tara's next words were drowned out by the sudden, ear-piercing screech of the alarm sirens. A split second later, bright white lights snapped on around the property with the intensity of a night game at Fenway Park.

"Happy?" Tara shouted, smiling.

"Let's get out of here."

Staying in the shadows, they darted across the lawn and retraced their approach down the privacy tree line and out to the street. There, they ran for his F-350. Even if the police kept to their impressive three-minute response time—Kayla had looked it up—they would be two minutes too late.

Approaching his truck, Bannon alerted to Charlotte Ng's voice in his ear. "Commander. You've got company. A black SVU traveling southbound down Bayberry. Two more traveling north."

Three vehicles on a remote loop in a quiet, well-to-do residential neighborhood in the dead of night. Bannon's hackles rose.

"Where'd they come from? Belay that. Doesn't matter. Positions?" Bannon asked.

"They were parked. Lying in wait," Ng said. "I'm tailing the southbound vehicle. Three minutes out from your location. Ellis and Connell are on the two northbound boogies."

"Copy." Picking up his pace, Bannon aimed his key fob at his truck and heard the door locks pop with a tiny beep. A pair of headlights appeared behind them. "We've gotta move."

He stepped into the street, heading for the driver's side while Tara and Parker moved faster along the curb, going toward the passenger door. Parker had her backpack on. She carried the hard plastic case.

Where the road looped toward Shore Road, south of them, high-beam headlights from two vehicles appeared. Blinded, Bannon threw his arm up to cover his eyes. The vehicles were almost on top of them already. Tires screeched to a stop. He heard car doors opening.

They were trapped between the vehicles, Bannon cursed. Lying in wait. How'd they know where they'd be?

His expletive was drowned out by gunfire.

Bannon ducked, spinning away for his truck. Bullets pinged and ricocheted off the F-350's fenders, bumpers, and grille.

Next, he heard the thump of an M72 LAW rocket launcher firing. The hollow whoosh of the shoulder-fired light anti-tank weapon was familiar to his ears. He dove away from the F-350. The truck exploded into a fireball of boiling orange and yellow. Glass shards flew in every direction. Black smoke roiled into the night sky.

"Beach!" he shouted. His ears rang from the explosion.

He picked himself up off the pavement and fired at the two SUVs.

On the opposite side of the road, crouched among the trees, Parker and Tara shot at the third black vehicle, giving him cover.

Bannon darted across the road, blindly popping off rounds. His efforts were rewarded with a grunt and the sound of a body hitting the ground.

"Skyjack, we need an extraction!" he yelled into his commlink.

"We caught your smoke signal," McMurphy responded. "Already on the move."

Bannon zigzagged across the open road past his burning truck. Rounds chewed up the pavement around his feet. More shots snapped branches off the trees around where Tara and Parker were pinned down. He heard the thump of a second launched missile.

This one exploded into a tree trunk to his left. It set the dry leaves ablaze like the biblical burning bush. As he ran, he tried to determine how many shooters there were. He counted seven silhouettes, but he guessed there were more from the barrage of gunfire they were under.

Tara and Parker knelt low in a copse of trees that wasn't burning and provided additional cover fire for Bannon until he cleared the street and dove in beside them.

Bannon shouted to Ng on comms. "Lieutenant. Back off. Repeat. Break off pursuit. Do not engage."

"Retreat, sir?" Ng asked. "What about you?"

"We've got our ride out of here. There's too many for you to take on. Go."

"Copy that, sir."

"How the hell'd they find us?" Parker shouted.

"Later," Bannon said, again returning fire. "Get to the beach. Now!"

They ran past Jorgen's house. The yard and pool were awash with bright, white light. Even the lights inside the house were on now. Jorgen and his wife must have busted their way out of their bedroom.

Bannon pushed Parker and Tara past the fenced-in pool. Each took turns returning fire behind them, slowing down the group chasing them. They leaped from a retaining wall onto the rocky beach as *Skyjack's Folly* scraped across the shallow shoreline. McMurphy was at the hydraulic controls, lowering the bow gate.

Kayla was in the wheelhouse, at the boat's helm.

With the gate only three-quarters of the way down, McMurphy stood to one side, wearing his Captain's baseball cap, with a lit cigar jammed in the corner of his mouth. The tip glowed bright red. He picked up an M16 rifle and pocketed the stock to his shoulder.

"Stay low," he shouted.

He opened up with the weapon on full automatic. Two thirty-round banana clips taped together extended from the weapon's magazine port. Rounds chattered out of the firearm's barrel at eight-hundred rounds a minute.

Bannon and the others ducked low and splashed through knee-high water as McMurphy sprayed the shoreline with bullets. A few pops of return fire could be heard over the roar of his automatic gunfire.

Bannon grabbed Parker's arm—she clutched the hard plastic case—and pushed her up over the still-dropping bow gate. The hydraulics whining. She reached for Tara's hand and pulled her up while McMurphy flipped his magazine and started firing again.

Together, Parker and Tara hauled Bannon into the boat. He tumbled across the wet deck, shouting, "Get us out of here!"

The throaty, twin, three hundred horsepower engines rumbled, frothing up water as *Skyjack's Folly* backed away from the beach. Tara lunged for the gate's controls and began to raise it. The hydraulics were laboriously slow. It felt like an eternity before they could all crouch behind it and pepper the beach with gunfire while McMurphy emptied his next taped-together bundle of magazines.

Four people in dark clothes lined the beach, shooting. A fifth person ran to join them. Behind them, six or seven more figures emerged from the shadows. Bannon focused his attention on what the fifth man carried.

"Rocket launcher!"

"You've got to be kidding me," McMurphy said.

"It's what took out my truck," Bannon said.

"Hard starboard!" McMurphy shouted.

The engines roared as Kayla swung the boat in a tight turn and opened up the throttle. *Skyjack's Folly* swerved hard left.

"Firing!" Tara shouted.

Bannon, Parker, and Tara opened fire with their handguns.

The man on the beach jerked. Struck by a bullet. A bright yellow and red flame blew out of the back of the M72 tube. The tendril of white-gray smoke made the missile easy to track.

Kayla spun *Skyjack's Folly* hard to the right.

The unexpected evasive maneuver tossed everyone to the other side of the deck. McMurphy grabbed Parker's arm, keeping her from pitching over the gunwale.

The missile sailed about a foot left of the boat and splashed into the water.

Bannon slumped to the deck with an exhaustive sigh. "Kayla, get us out of here."

The sound of the house alarm horns, joined by approaching police sirens, faded as *Skyjack's Folly* powered east at full speed out to deeper waters. Flashing blue and white lights traced along Shore Road.

McMurphy put the emptied M16 down and leaned against the gunwale. He scissored his cigar with his meaty fingers and indicated the Pelican case. "That it?"

Parker smiled. "We got it."

"At least that part worked out."

"My truck," Bannon said. "I just made the last payment on it this month."

"Look on the bright side," McMurphy offered, tossing him a beer. "Whatever's left of it will probably fit on your souvenir wall back at the Keel Haul."

TWENTY-FOUR

JADE VAN WYK WATCHED the ugly, flat-bottom boat speed away. She raged into the night sky. Beside her, Hendrik Maharero, a disgraced former member of the Namibia Defense Force and number two man on her father's security detail, held the rocket launcher loosely by his side. The six-pound tube suddenly felt heavy in his hand. He clasped his bloody upper arm, winged by automatic gunfire, just before pulling the trigger on the weapon.

Jade slapped his wounded arm for missing.

He ground his teeth and winced.

Electric blue and white emergency lights splashed over the dark trees shrouding the prestigious homes along Shore Road. The blaring sirens of approaching patrol cars added to the annoying whoop of the house alarms. Neighbors' lights were starting to snap on.

"Take the men and go," Jade ordered. "And Hendrik? If any of your men are captured by the American police, it is you who will pay the price for their failure."

"Yes, ma'am."

"Now go!"

Jade stormed up the beach toward the house. The closer she got to the house, the louder the alarms sounded. Along with the bright halogen lights and the escape of the American agents, it all served to intensify her already painful and annoying headache.

Mzobe stood on the patio near the open sliders off the living room. With him was a man in his early fifties, wearing striped pajamas under a white bathrobe. His dyed hair was mussed from sleep. His eyes were wide. Mzobe had him pinned to the outside wall.

"The wife?" Jade asked.

"Locked up in the bedroom," Mzobe said.

"Who are you people?" Jorgen asked. "Are you the police?"

Dressed in skin-tight black tactical overalls, she wore a gun belt around her waist, a holstered Vektor 9mm pistol, and a Gerber Mark II fixed blade knife strapped to her thigh.

"Do you believe we are the police?"

"Well, um, like SWAT. Maybe." He swallowed hard. "But, if not, then who are you?"

The local authorities would be there in seconds. Time was fleeting.

"What was taken?" she asked.

"Nothing. It was just…just a false alarm. Happens a lot."

"You are lying," Jade said.

Mzobe seized him by the throat, pushing him hard against the wall behind him. Jade pulled her pistol and pressed it to his temple. "Tell me what was taken."

She saw the fear in his eyes, yet still, he asked, "Who are you?"

She pressed the barrel harder against his head. "Tell me."

"Speak," Mzobe said, his voice low and threatening. He pulled his combat knife and held it so Jorgen got a very good look at it. "Or I slit your wife's throat."

"Swords. They took a bunch of swords. I collect 'em."

"Which? Tell me."

Jade heard the first patrol cars screech to a halt on the street in front of the house. As doors opened, the static-filled crackle of voices over the police radios added to the cacophony of noises.

"We must go," Mzobe warned.

"Which swords?"

"A bunch. I…have, um, Truman swords. Others."

"The Honjō Masamune sword," Jade screamed. "Did they take the Honjō?"

"Yes. Damn it. Yes, they did."

"You are sure it was real?" Jade asked. "It was *the* Honjō Masamune?"

"Of course. I had it appraised. It's worth millions. Tens of millions. And the Truman swords. They cost me a bundle, too."

"Jade," Mzobe said. "Now."

"Tell no one what was taken here today."

"And admit I've had national treasures illegally in my possession. Stolen property. No way."

"If you do," Jade said, stepping away. "Missing swords will be the smallest of your concerns."

"Yes. Yes. Of course." Then, an idea struck Jorgen. Excited, he asked, "Can you get them back?"

Mzobe pushed Jade toward the stairs down to the beach.

Jorgen called out. "I'll pay you. A reward. I'll make it worth your while."

They reached the rocky beach as the first two officers rounded the side of the house. They pointed their guns at Jorgen. "Freeze!"

Jade and Mzobe crouched below the low rock barrier and darted toward the tree line between properties. They melted into the shadows and disappeared, making good their escape.

CHAPTER TWENTY-FIVE

Rye Harbor Spa & Inn
Rye, N.H.

TWO NIGHTS LATER. NINE P.M.
Dressed in a black tuxedo, with Parker on his arm, Bannon led her up the drive toward the line of beautiful people being directed toward the main entrance of the newly opened Rye Harbor Spa & Inn. A project begun two years earlier, the facility was built on a naturally occurring bay with terraced landscaping out back and a commanding view of the Atlantic Ocean.

Adjacent was a rundown fishing and whale-watching charter service and a boat repair company that refused to be bought out by the giant corporation that owned the spa. And a chain of others.

The harbor was full of sailboats, speed boats, and yachts of every conceivable size with lights on their masts and strung along their guide ropes. The sound of cleats knocking against metal poles rang in the air with rubbery squeaks of bumpers squeezed between the dock and boat hulls.

Considered small but exclusive, the sprawling, shingle-style, ninety-room hotel boosted full-service suites overlooking the harbor's marina. Three full-service restaurants, poolside and marina-side eateries and bars, two outdoor pools, and spa services that included salt therapy, hydra-facials, holistic treatments, and other European healing techniques.

Bannon had read about it on their website.

He and Parker joined the line of Hollywood celebrities, pro-athletes, top local, state, and national business leaders, along with several famous foreign dignitaries. The auction attendees also included some of the most important politicians from around the state, Washington, DC, and the country. A seen and be seen event. It was an election year, after all.

The DHS agent dazzled in a form-hugging, long, blue sequined dress with a slit up to her hip. She wore her mane of red hair free and wild, with a single blue flag iris pinned over her left ear. The line moved toward the front. Many of the well-known stepped out onto a red carpet to get their pictures taken by the media and the paparazzi. Blinding white flashbulbs popped constantly.

Reaching the steps to the main entrance, Bannon handed their invitations to a burly man in a dark suit. A wire ran from under his collar, up the side of his neck, to an earpiece. His jacket bulged from the sidearm he wore in a hip holster. He scrutinized Parker with a wry smile almost as hard as he studied the invites presented to him. Muggy, the air was heavy with moisture. A storm had been forecast to roll in overnight but hadn't arrived yet.

Parker smiled and patted at her hair. "This humidity's terrible. Just playing havoc with my hair."

"Not from what I'm seeing," Bannon said.

She fluttered her eyes and exaggerated her southern accent. "Why, thank you. That's mighty kind of you to say, sir."

He laughed.

And even the stoic guard smiled. He told them they could move on.

Concealed inside an arch festooned with colorful, fragrant flowers was a metal detector.

Having anticipated the security measures, they arrived without weapons. Parker handed her clutch purse to another guard. He examined the contents while Bannon emptied his pockets into a gray bin. They passed through the detector without incident.

Heading into the hotel, they joined a pop star singer with only one name, a famous former big league baseball player, two U.S. Senators—one who'd recently thrown her hat in as a presidential candidate, granting her Secret Service protection—a Saudi oil magnate, and the CEO of one of the largest online cryptocurrency companies in the world.

Once inside, Bannon guided Parker to the right, out of the large foyer crowded with people and circulating hostesses serving hors d'oeuvres and champagne. They moved down a carpeted corridor while the other guests were urged gently to proceed to the main lobby area.

"I feel naked without my gun," Parker whispered in his ear. Her arm still threaded through his.

"We've got that covered." Bannon cast an eye over his shoulder at the crowd behind them, looking to see if they'd elicited any undue attention.

They had no idea who their enemy was. Which, of course, was the point of all this, to draw them out. Bannon was sure the bait they dangled would be enticing, but with the mystery identity of *Skaduwee* unknown, not knowing where or from whom any threat might come concerned him.

After the heist of the Honjō Masamune, Bannon ordered everyone to ground. His team had established protocols for times when they'd been compromised. They separated. Kept moving. Stayed off the grid and away from all their normal haunts. No Keel Haul for him and Blades. No JAG office for Kayla. They went radio silent, including no contact with Secretary Grayson.

Moving down the corridor, Bannon ran through Thursday's encounter at Jorgen's home in his head for the millionth time. He'd anticipated the Keel Haul had been under surveillance. That they'd be followed, as Kayla must have been for her fateful meeting with Letty and Hornsby. Thus, the point of bringing in Ng and her team.

He'd been prepared to shake a tail on their way to steal the sword if necessary. But, when no tail was spotted, either by him and his team or by Ng's MSRTs, he'd felt confident they were in the clear. They could swipe the sword and be on their way.

He'd been wrong.

They *had* been followed. But neither of his teams had spotted them. That was near impossible. Which meant either their adversaries were very, very good, or he'd missed something. He racked his brain to figure out what, but so far, he'd come up empty.

Over the two days since the theft, Kayla worked her Internet and dark web magic. She'd orchestrated various chatter, misinformation, planted seeds, and whetted appetites with the potential that the Honjō Masamune might be back in play. Once she got the black market antiquities sites in a lather with buzz about the sword, she arranged for the bombshell mic-drop.

The Honjō Masamune sword would be auctioned off to the highest bidder at the Devon-Arbuckle Masterpiece Auction's unsanctioned, underground, black market event on Saturday night.

One problem they still needed to contend with was separating the wheat from the chaff. *Skaduwee* would not be the only unscrupulous art and antiquities aficionado interested in adding Japan's perfect sword to their collection.

Bannon had considered contacting Grayson for help but decided against it. While he trusted her with his life, if there were a mole, or moles, they'd be high up in the bureaucracy that was Washington, D.C. Any moves she made to support their op, regardless of how well covered up, would be like firing a flare into the night sky.

No. Until they knew more, they were on their own.

Bannon escorted Parker to a set of stairs roped off with a velveteen rope and brass stanchions. Still under construction, that wing was closed off. Checking that no one was watching, they slipped around the stanchions and down the carpeted steps to the floor below. He pulled her to a stop across from the women's room.

"Second stall," he said. "There's a loose tile behind the toilet. Inside, you'll find a silver, five-round .38 Smith & Wesson and a speed loader. It's not much, but—"

"How?" she asked. "The place had to have been swept."

"Skyjack looked smashing in an ACE outfit."

Parker arched an eyebrow, suggesting Bannon's words explained nothing.

"This affair is a major public event," he said. "The legitimate piece of it anyway. The organizers hired one of the premier security firms out of Boston. For most of the Northeast, actually. ACE Security. Run by an ex-LAPD police commissioner I happen to know. He put McMurphy on this detail the day before yesterday."

"This ex-commissioner knows what it is y'all do?"

Bannon gave her a wry smile. "Has an idea. What he does know is we're the good guys."

"Did Skyjack leave *you* any little goodies?" she asked.

"My old Sig, he said. 'And a surprise.'"

They went and retrieved their weapons. When they regrouped, Parker was zipping closed her clutch purse. "I've gotta know. What's the surprise?"

Bannon checked the corridor for cameras and to ensure they were alone. He opened his jacket label. Hung on his belt was....

"A grenade?" Parker said. "What in tarnation's you gonna need that for?"

Bannon shrugged. "That's Skyjack for you.'"

Parker shook her head but with a smile on her face. "Can't say that ole boy ain't wrong. I've found myself in a pickle or two where a hand grenade would've come in handy. What now?"

Bannon handed her an earpiece. "We find Tara and Skyjack. They should be at the loading dock.

"Let me guess," Parker said. "Skyjack's handled the inspections of incoming items."

"His talents know no bounds." Bannon offered her his arm and directed her toward the stairs. "Come on."

The stairwell opened up onto a service corridor. Here, the floor was concrete, the lighting was harsh, and the overhead service pipes, ductwork, and cables were exposed. Their footfalls rang in the hollow space as they passed room service carts and stacked chairs.

They found a set of double doors marked LOADING DOCK.

Reaching for the doors, Bannon froze when the doors burst open from the other side.

He and Parker step back. They reached for their recently acquired weapons.

Facing them, McMurphy came to an abrupt halt. He wore a yellow Polo shirt. Event Security embroidered where a breast pocket would go. He raised a hand. "Easy, cowboys."

McMurphy added, being inclusive, "And cowgirls."

Tara was with him. She carried a beautifully crafted cherry wood case. It was long and flat. The case contained the Honjō Masamune. It had been custom-made by a swordsmith friend of Tara's.

"Ah, Perfect timing," Bannon said.

Tara handed the case to Bannon. On the end, a red square had been painted. An identifying marker Kayla had posted in her dark web conversations to potential buyers so they could identify them.

"Now what?" Parker asked.

"We join the party," Bannon said. "Mingle and see whose attention we pique."

"Hopefully, that's where the bar is," McMurphy said.

"Hold on." Tara leaned a hand against the wall and unzipped her delivery service coveralls. She stripped out of it. Underneath, she wore a single-sleeve, off-white, stretchy bodycon dress. It hugged her figure with a mid-thigh hem and a jersey modal fabric belt. She tossed off her baseball cap and shook out her flowing black hair.

The off-white material complimented her dark, sun-kissed skin nicely.

Parker whistled. "That's a stunning outfit."

Tara surveyed Parker's sequined blue dress. "Same to you. The flower's a nice touch."

"A blue flag iris," Parker said. "The official flower of Tennessee."

"Love the tux, bro. What is it? Vera Wang or Ralph Lauren?" McMurphy asked, rolling his eyes. "Can we get going now? I wanna see what kind of beer this fancy-schmancy place is serving." He stalked off toward the stairs.

The others fell in step behind him.

CHAPTER TWENTY-SIX

THEY RETURNED TO THE main floor.

McMurphy and Tara split off before they reached the front lobby, where the attendees congregated, drinking and eating more hors d'oeuvres before the auction began. There had been talk of holding the event outside, in the courtyard, to take advantage of the spectacular view of the harbor and the Atlantic beyond. The threatening forecast of rain and high winds dampened those plans.

Bannon and Parker stepped into the lobby.

"A drink?" Bannon asked. The case containing their bait clutched in his left hand.

On his opposite side, with her arm slipped through his, Parker said, "Don't mind if I do."

McMurphy had beaten them to the open bar. At the far end, he ordered a beer.

Looking at his yellow security shirt, the bartender frowned.

"I'm off duty."

The bartender shrugged and drew him a draft beer from the tap. Scaled, an IPA from Boston brewery Trillium. A good choice, Bannon thought. He followed his friend's lead and ordered two Scaled IPAs as well.

Waiting, he turned to survey the room. A smile ticked at the corner of his lips when every man, and a good number of the women, turned to take in the exquisite sight that was Tara Sardana entering the room in her off-white dress.

"She makes quite the entrance," Parker said as they turned back to the bar to receive their drinks.

"Yes, she does." Bannon slipped a twenty into the bartender's tip jar and clinked his pilsner glass to Parker's. "Cheers."

Behind him, a man said, "Commander Bannon. A word, if I may?"

Well, that simplified things, Bannon thought.

There was no reason to believe anyone at the event would know him outside of the current mission objective. As for the off-book auction, his real name had not been used in the dark web queries Kayla had planted. Nothing identified him as the possessor of the sword except to inform potential buyers to look for the red decal placed on the case. Only one faction could connect him, as Bannon, to the sword.

This had to be *Skaduwee.*

Or, at least, his representative.

Bannon sipped his drink before putting it down on the bar and turning.

He faced a tall, thin black man. Mid-to-late fifties, the man wore a custom-tailored gray tuxedo with black lapels, a white shirt, and black bow tie. Black shoes polished to a mirror shine. He had a thin silver ring on his right pinky.

Tense, thought Bannon, like a coiled snake, ready to strike.

Beside him stood an attractive black woman. Much younger, she had a scrim of short black hair, dark skin, high cheekbones, and cold, green eyes. Her plunging low-cut, long yellow dress had a slit up the side to her hip and clung to her like a second skin.

No one needed a DNA test to tell these two were father and daughter.

"You have me at a disadvantage, friend."

"A word, Commander. In private," the man said. "I must insist." He glanced down where he held a small Vektor 9mm pistol pointed at Bannon's gut.

Bannon tightened his grip on the case and gestured toward the front foyer. "After you."

The woman took the lead.

Bannon and Parker followed.

The armed man fell in step behind them.

They were taken to a meeting room down the hall. Bannon caught sight of two dark-skinned, dark-suited men approaching as he and Parker were led inside the room. Guards. They would take up positions on either side of the doors as they closed. The bulges from their shoulder holsters did not go unnoticed.

Inside the meeting room, rows of chairs faced the front wall where a screen extended down from the ceiling. There was a podium to one side of a long conference table lined with more chairs. The room had been set up for a panel discussion of some kind. Another set of long tables lined the left wall. For a buffet, more than likely. The tables were empty except for beige cloths draped over them.

The woman in the yellow dress took up a position at the door. A Vektor pistol suddenly in her hand. The small, blunt-edged handgun was perfect for a garter belt holster. No other place she could've concealed it.

"We finally meet," the man said.

"Not really," Bannon said. "Not without a proper introduction. You are?"

"Who I am isn't of concern. What matters is I am a man with little tolerance for wasting time. You have the Honjō Masamune sword. I intend to have it."

"That is why we're here," Bannon said. "Friend."

"The sword. Show it to me."

Bannon crossed the room and laid the case on the buffet table but did not open it. "There's to be an auction. You can see it, but no deals will be made until then."

The man waved a hand dismissively. "Let's disperse with the charades, shall we, Commander Bannon? You are a government agent who believes I am a criminal."

"I don't even know who you are," Bannon said.

"Not my identity, no. But this is your clumsy attempt at drawing me out, of luring me into a trap. Now, show me your bait."

Bannon unsnapped the custom-made pinewood case's latches and opened the top of two lids. The secondary lid was made of glass, framed by the pine wood. The Honjō Masamune sword lay displayed on a bed of red velvet under the glass.

The man stood over the sword, marveling at it. He glanced at his daughter, unable to conceal the wolf-like grin on his face. He reached for the brass latches to open the inner case. "I must hold it."

Parker rushed forward. "Not without gloves."

She produced a pair of black latex gloves from her clutch purse. She handed them to the man, leaving her purse open.

He snapped the gloves on, opened the case, and picked the sword up from the hilt and the blade's tip. He held it out and then twisted it, examining every intricate detail of the hilt, its pommel, the wrap. He balanced the blade. Holding it by one finger a few centimeters from the guard. He gripped the handle and swung the blade in a quick figure eight.

The blade cut through the still air with a quiet whisper.

"It is… amazing."

His reverence for the weapon was apparent. Like a kid in Willie Wonka's chocolate factory, he grinned. "Do you see, daughter?" He held the sword up in the air.

From Bannon's perspective, he saw little interest in the woman's eyes.

"The perfect sword," the man said. "And, yes, Commander, the perfect bait. Except, the tables have turned."

"How so?" Bannon asked.

The man ignored the question as he returned to the table. With exaggerated reverence, he carefully laid the sword in its place on the red velvet and closed the inner cover, latching it. Then he closed the outer lid. Slowly.

"I am here to take the sword and be on my way," the man said. "Any attempt to stop me and you will die."

He glanced at his daughter. She raised the 9mm. Her gun arm as steady as steel.

"Since you know who I am," Bannon said, unfazed by having a weapon pointed at his head. "You know I can't let you take it. Or leave, for that matter."

The man pulled his pistol. He leveled it at Parker. "And how shall you stop me, Commander? The sword will be mine."

As if on cue, the sound of the two back doors opening caught everyone's attention.

McMurphy and Tara entered the room through opposite sides, guns drawn.

The distraction gave Bannon and Parker time to draw their own service weapons.

"Four against two," McMurphy snarled. "Don't sound like good odds for you, Mister…."

The man smiled. "What happens now, Commander?"

"We arrest you."

"On what charge? I've done nothing illegal. At least not that you can prove. Even a black ops operator like yourself—"

"We're not black ops," Bannon insisted.

"Working on behalf of the Secretary of Homeland Security are bound by your country's due process laws. Probable cause. Etc., etc., etc."

"Perhaps," Bannon said. "But you can be held until it all gets sorted out. During that time, we'll learn what we came here to learn. Who you are, and what illegal activities you're up to."

"We have diplomatic immunity."

Which told Bannon something. A lot, actually.

"Good. We kick you out of the country. Banished from ever coming back," Bannon said. "It's a start."

"You are a fool if you think I don't have more than two men posted outside with me. I've an army."

"I don't care how many goons you've got," Bannon said. "They come through those doors. They're all dead."

The man laughed at that.

"You misunderstand. My men won't come in here in some ill-fated rescue attempt. They're planted all around the building and the grounds. Gardeners. Caterers. Flower delivery people." He glanced at Tara. "Bartenders. If anything should happen to either of us." He indicated his daughter. "If we are to be harmed in any way or taken into custody, they have orders to gun down as many of your important politicians, your famous celebrities and captains of industry as they can—"

If what he said was true, sure, there were Secret Service agents and dozens of police and armed private security around, but that would only add to the carnage. It would be a bloodbath. The loss of life would be catastrophic.

"He's lying," Parker said.

The man holstered his gun. "Am I?" He smiled. "Stalemate."

Bannon lowered his gun. "For now."

The man glanced wistfully at the sword case. "But know this, Commander. That sword will be mine. I simply need greater leverage than I currently have. But rest assured. I will get it. And then, friend, you will beg to give me the Honjō Masamune sword."

"Fat chance," Bannon said.

To his daughter, the man said, "Come."

He pushed the conference room door open and guided her through it.

"That's it?" Parker asked. "We're just gonna let them walk out of here?"

"For now," Bannon said. "For now."

McMurphy frowned. "For this, I left a cold brewski on the bar. Sheesh."

CHAPTER TWENTY-SEVEN

OUTSIDE THE RYE HARBOR Spa & Inn, Kayla Clarke had parked near the main entrance. She's spent the last hour taking pictures of the guests as they arrived. She stopped when she received a text message.

She stared at her phone screen. *The white van at the end of the driveway. Meet me there.*

Kayla had been using her phone to take pictures, capturing the faces of the attendees as they presented their invitations to security and entered the auction. Most of the people in attendance were a who's who of the rich and famous. Those that she didn't recognize on her own, she'd run through facial recognition software after the night was over. It would be a tedious task. One which would've been far simpler, far more efficient, if she'd had access to the government equipment she was accustomed to using. That she'd be using right now if they hadn't been forced to go to ground. While it wasn't the first time she'd had to compromise, to go low-tech—more than half her time in the sandbox, that was all they had. But she still didn't like it.

Speaking of being irritated, the text message had interrupted her efforts. She would've ignored it, except for the signature. *Eagle.*

Secretary Grayson's call sign.

The promised rain had started to fall. Misty for the time being, but forecast to get heavier as the night wore on. The low dark clouds were a threatening harbinger of the coming storm.

Kayla found the van easily enough. A flower delivery van. A bouquet of red and white roses painted on the side. The windows were tinted. She brushed a damp lock of hair from her face.

She banged on the back door, heard a metallic click from inside, and stepped back.

One door opened.

A man she did not know wearing black utility fatigues motioned for her to come inside. She climbed in. After a quick survey of their outside surroundings, the man closed and relocked the door.

As Kayla expected, it was a surveillance van.

Two shelves lined the length of the van. The walls were equipped with the most up-to-date, state-of-the-art monitoring and electronics equipment the government and military had at its disposal. Screens mounted high on both walls displayed various images in and around the resort. At the consoles, two men and a woman dressed in black fatigues with no identifying emblems or patches scrolled through surveillance footage captured by the Rye Harbor Inn security cameras. Other screens were running the images through sophisticated, high-speed facial recognition software. This was the type of surveillance van and equipment and software Kayla was accustomed to using.

Near the cab of the van sat Elizabeth Grayson and her Secret Service detail's lead, Special Agent Franklin Gregg. They knew each other and exchanged nods.

To Grayson, Kayla said, "Ma'am. Why are you here? How'd you know we were here?"

Grayson gave her a sly smile. "I was invited to tonight's event. Along with the President's Chief of Staff and the Secretary of the Treasury."

Kayla knew both positions, like Grayson's, came with Secret Service protection details. The secretaries by law. The Chief of Staff by presidential order.

"While reviewing the advance team's preparations, I spied a familiar face among the private security personnel assigned and vetted for the event."

"Skyjack."

She nodded. "And since Brice—all of you—have gone radio silent on me, as well as DHS Agent Quinn, I thought while I was here, I'd better see for myself what you're all up to."

Kayla glanced at the three people operating the surveillance and facial recognition equipment. Before she could voice her concerns, Grayson said, "Brice suspects a mole. I think he's right. And going off the grid was the right call. For the right reasons. These operatives, I called in some old favors from some very dear friends. They're from Japan, England, and Israel security services. In the country as part of a joint international educational exchange program. They have no ties to anyone here. This is simply a field training exercise. That's the cover story, anyway. Now. Why are we here, Lieutenant?"

Kayla cleared her throat. "We believe we have a lead. A means by which to identify *Skaduwee*."

"The so-called shadow." Grayson smiled. "It's that damn sword, isn't it? Brice has it."

"How'd you know—"

Grayson smiled. "DHS reports to me. I'm kept abreast of what my Arts and Antiquities agents are investigating. And I'm well aware of the frequency in which these types of events masquerade black market activities. As for the Honjō Masamune sword? I know Quinn's been working that angle in conjunction with Hornsby. She believes the sword is *Skaduwee's* great white whale."

"You disagree?"

"No," Grayson admitted. "But it's thin. And does nothing to tie him into the human trafficking issue."

"It's all we've got at the moment, ma'am."

"A Hail Mary, but fine," Grayson said. "How did you get the sword?"

"Are you sure you want to know?"

"No," she said. "I'm sure I don't. Do we know for sure it's real?"

"Agent Quinn believes so," Kayla said. "Pending scrutiny and verification. But I think she's right."

"That's… " Grayson started to say impossible. "Incredible. Is it intact? What condition is it in?"

"Intact and in impeccable condition," Kayla said.

"Have you any idea what it's worth?" Grayson asked rhetorically. "Or what its recovery will mean to the Japanese people." What she left unsaid was the goodwill they would gain, further cementing the friendly relationship they enjoy with the Japanese government and people.

Kayla said, "I don't have Blade's appreciation for edged weaponry, but it's…it's a thing of beauty."

She'd been eyeing the monitors while she spoke with Grayson.

On one screen, she watched as Bannon and Parker were led from the lobby to a meeting room, well away from the main event. Bannon carried a long, wooden case.

"See for yourself." Kayla leaned toward the monitors and pointed at the hallway screen as the meeting room door closed. Two dark-skinned men took up guard positions on either side. "Can we see inside that room?"

The operative, a young Asian woman, said, "I think so. Give me a minute. Yes."

Grayson and Gregg crowded around the screen behind Kayla. The image flickered and changed, now showing an empty conference room. Kayla caught a shadowy movement in the corner of the screen. She pointed.

"There. They're under the camera."

"They're avoiding the camera," Grayson said.

"Okay." The operative tapped keys on her keyboard. The image switched. "There's a second camera in there." The image changed again. This time, it showed Bannon and Parker talking with a man. His back was to the camera.

The woman with them stood by the door, away from the others.

Gregg pointed. "She's got a gun on them."

Kayla sucked in a breath. "That's…she's the one who was driving the Jeep. With the bald man who killed Hornsby at Jake's. That's her."

"You're sure?"

Kayla nodded. "She was wearing a floppy hat and large sunglasses at the time, but I'm sure of it. It was her."

On the screen, Bannon laid the long pinewood case on a table. The man approached. As he did, Bannon stepped to the side, allowing him to open it. The camera caught the man's face. Full-frame.

"Nicely done, Brice," Grayson said. He couldn't know anyone was watching, but he'd know it was reasonable to assume the cameras were being recorded, providing them with a facial recognition-capable image, even if post-mortem.

They silently watched as the man lifted the sword from the case, examined it, and swung it around before returning it to the case and closing it.

The operative pointed at the male on screen. "He's got one, too."

Meaning a gun.

Kayla said, "No worries." McMurphy and Tara came in through two doors at the front of the room. Weapons drawn. Bannon and Parker drew weapons as well. "Four against two."

"So, we can have a shootout like at the OK Corral at one of the biggest social events of the summer?" Grayson shook her head. "Clearly, it's time I reminded you all what low profile means."

Kayla asked the operative. "Are you able to run facial recognition? We need-to-know who those people are."

"We won't need facial recognition for that," Grayson said. "I know who they are. The man is Bernardor van Wyk. And with him is his daughter Jade."

Kayla sat back. "Who are they?"

Grayson returned to her chair at the van's cab. "South African nation—"

An explosion cut Grayson off. The blast blew a hole through the van's double doors below the locking mechanism. Shards of metal and smoke blew through the van. The hole where the lock had been was charred and burning.

Kayla fell back. Her face stung where shrapnel cut her. She covered her ears. They rang deafeningly.

The back doors were pulled open. Two armed gunmen dressed in black, including face masks and night vision goggles, filled the open space. They opened fire with automatic weapons.

The three seated operatives took the brunt of the barrage. Their bodies jerked and spasmed. Catching most of the rounds of fire.

Gregg shielded Grayson with his body.

Kayla rolled onto her back and opened fire with her Glock. One of the shooters cried out and dropped to the ground. The other disappeared out of her line of fire.

With his gun out, Gregg slapped at the side panel door. He got it open. Covering Grayson, he pushed through the opening. They fell to the ground.

Rolling onto her back, Kayla aimed her weapon out of the open side panel door. A gunman appeared and aimed his rifle at Gregg's back. Kayla shot him twice. Double tap. One to the chest. The other in the man's head.

Kayla scrambled out of the van and yanked at Gregg's arm. "Get up! Go! Go! Go!"

CHAPTER TWENTY-EIGHT

THE BLAST OF WET, outside air was the only welcoming thing to come from opening the side door. As predicted, a steady rain had started to fall.

The van had filled with bitter, acrid smoke from the explosion. Kayla's eyes stung. A muffled ringing filled her ears. It was like having her ears stuffed with cotton balls. She crouched over Gregg as he got Grayson to her feet. He held her under her arm, steadying her while he pushed toward the front of the van.

Kayla moved with them, covering their rear.

One of the gunmen who'd blasted open the back door tried to get a shot off from around the back of the van. Kayla fired, brushing him back.

She twisted around as more gunfire stitched the side of the van.

Gregg pushed Grayson down to the ground. He fired over her at two more black-clad gunmen. One took a bullet in the shoulder, spun around, and fired a round wildly into the air.

Kayla shot the second one in the throat, her arm extended past Gregg's shoulder. He shouted in pain and covered his ear.

Another shooter, farther back, fired.

Gregg took the round in his arm. His hand went from his ear to his bicep, where blood leaked through his fingers. Kayla shot Gregg's shooter in the face, but not before Gregg took another round in the gut. His body armor prevented it from being a kill shot, but he clutched his stomach and went down.

Kayla pushed past him and crouched over Grayson. She fired at two approaching gunmen, brushing them back. Two more men charged her from behind. They tried to toss Kayla aside, making a grab for Grayson.

They're not out to kill her. Kayla realized. This is a kidnapping attempt.

"No!" she shouted.

She twisted and slammed her arm across the man's forearm, breaking his grip on Grayson. She kicked out and brought the man to his knees.

Kayla fought a second assailant off. He backhanded her across the face with the butt of his gun. The metal cut through her skin. Adding to the scraps she'd already received. She cried out. Blood tracked down her cheek.

Gregg got halfway to his feet and pulled Grayson back, away from the hands grabbing for her.

From somewhere in the darkness, a deep voice shouted, "Get her. We have to go."

The attackers made a second grab for Grayson. Kayla charged. She hurled herself into the closest one. She brought her gun up under his chin and fired. The bullet slammed his jaw shut and sprayed blood in Kayla's face. She twisted away and spit blood and gore from her mouth.

The deep voice shouted again, "Get her. Let's go."

The man Kayla shot slipped away from her, but a second attacker replaced him. This one slapped her gun away, then seized her throat with a gloved hand. He squeezed.

Kayla gurgled, trying to breathe.

Pulled away from Grayson and Gregg, her vision faded, dimming to black, closing in around her.

Gregg remained crouched over Grayson's body. He swung his gun back and forth, frantic, desperate to protect his boss. His black sweater was shiny. The blood from his arm wound soaked the material. He fired indiscriminately, but it kept Grayson's kidnappers at bay.

"Take the other one. Let's go!"

Kayla's vision collapsed in on itself. She got woozy, barely registering that she'd been thrown into the back of yet another van. The man with the deep voice jumped in behind her and slammed the doors shut.

But the vise-like grasp on her throat was gone. She coughed, able to breathe again.

He banged on the roof. "Go! Go! Go!"

Large, bald, and black.

Kayla passed out, recognizing him. He was the one with the woman who'd attacked them at Jake's. The man who'd killed Darren Hornsby.

THEY HEARD THE EXPLOSION inside the hotel.

Thoughts of a terrorist attack, never far from one's mind these days, caused the attendees inside to scatter. Many ran. Some screamed hysterically. Others fell and were stepped on and kicked. Panicked, they ran for exits. The on-site police officers and contract security personnel tried to evacuate the masses without causing a stampede. At the same time, close personal protection details of the rich and famous and the Secret Service worked at spiriting their protectees away from danger.

Among those running for the doors were Bannon, Tara, and McMurphy. But they were running toward the danger, not away from it. Bannon clung tightly to the sword case. Following the explosion, they heard the cacophony of gunfire.

Even through the heavy sheets of rain that had started to fall, McMurphy saw a thin column of gray smoke rising over the trees near where the driveway wound down to the street.

At the top of the outdoor steps, he pointed. "There."

Not waiting for the others, he charged down the rain-slick granite steps, slipping once, then charging toward the smoke. Bannon and Tara were hot on his heels.

McMurphy rounded a bend in the driveway, getting past a copse of trees in time to see Kayla fighting off two men clad in black. Secret Service agent Franklin Gregg was on the ground, defending Grayson.

It was clear the assailants were trying to grab Secretary Grayson.

McMurphy sprinted faster, too far away to do anything but watch helplessly.

Kayla shot and killed one man but was swarmed over by two more. One, a large black man with a bald head. They dragged her from the florist's van toward a waiting black one with the engine running.

McMurphy chugged after them as fast as he could go. He'd closed the gap but wasn't nearly close enough to get there before the doors slammed shut and the van peeled away with Kayla inside. The back wheels spun, slick on the wet pavement. The driver floored the gas. The wheels caught traction, and the van shot out of the driveway.

McMurphy reached the area and quickly took stock of the scene. Several black-clad gunmen were on the ground. Some dead. The others moaned, too wounded to put up any more fight. Gregg crouched over Grayson, shielding her with his body. The secret service agent was wounded but alive. As was Lizzy.

At the foot of the driveway, McMurphy spotted an unattended police motorcycle.

He ran for it.

As he approached, a cop shouted. He moved to intercept McMurphy.

McMurphy swept him aside with ease, knocking him to the ground. McMurphy jumped on the motorcycle, righted it from its kickstand, revved it, and squeezed the throttle.

With a roar of the engine, he sped out in pursuit of the escaping van. Traveling south through the sleeting rain on Ocean Boulevard, a winding road that hugged the dramatic coastline from Maine to Massachusetts. McMurphy knew the road well, like the back of his hand.

The pavement was wet and slick. A steady rain falling.

Helmetless, rain lashed at his face and soaked his hair. McMurphy blinked the water from his eyes, focusing on the road ahead. Because he knew the road so well, he could make the turns at breakneck speeds. It didn't take him long to spot the taillights of the dark van ahead.

McMurphy squeezed the throttle, closing the gap between them. The motorcycle's engine roared in his ears.

He got to about three car lengths behind when the van's back doors opened. A gunman sat on one leg and steadied a long rifle on his opposite knee, sighting in.

McMurphy narrowed his eyes and sped up. He waited a hair's breadth, then swerved, anticipating the gunman's timing. The bullet whizzed past his ear. McMurphy pulled his Glock and fired. Shooting while driving a motorcycle one-handed isn't as easy as Hollywood makes it seem. His bullet pinged off the open door, sending the gunman scrambling.

McMurphy fired a second time before the gunman could reappear in the back door. He aimed lower this time. His bullet dinged off the rear bumper. The van swerved. Precisely what McMurphy was hoping for. With the van's flank exposed, McMurphy's next shot hit the back tire. With a loud bang, the tire blew.

The van veered.

McMurphy grimaced with satisfaction.

A gust of wind blasted at him from the left.

They were closing in on the traffic circle junction of Ocean Boulevard and Sea Road at the historic, private Rye Beach Club. The van's brake lights flared. A momentary indecision on the part of the driver.

The shooter in the back leaned against the van's door frame, lining up another shot.

But the van hooked left at the circle to continue south on Ocean. Fishtailed. The shooter got thrown off his perch again.

McMurphy heard the burb of a siren behind him. He caught sight of a patrol car in his rearview. Between the rain and the flashing lights, He couldn't make out the driver, but he did see there was someone riding shotgun.

At the junction, the van fishtailed to the left and slowed considerably. The shot-out tire shredded away. The van rode noisily on the rim. Sparks flew from the metal rim across the pavement.

The shooter reappeared at the back door. This time, the rifle was gone. He'd replaced it with an M-16.

Murphy swore, sure the weapon would be locked on full automatic. "Oh, come on. That's my move."

McMurphy prepared to swerve, but he had nowhere to go. If the shooter opened up on him, McMurphy was a sitting duck.

He hated being right. Before he completed the thought, the shooter opened fire. He swept a wide swath of gunfire across the road. The automatic fire rattled with a quick *tat-a-tat-tat*. Empty brass clanged, littering the roadway. Rounds chewed up the pavement. A round pinged off the motorcycle's fender. Another one pierced the windshield, spiderwebbing the glass.

McMurphy swerved. Too far. The machine slipped on the wet pavement, going out from under him. A blast of cold, rainy wind swept across him.

Another round blew out the motorcycle's front tire. McMurphy went down in a slide. He held tight to the handlebars and yanked his right leg free before it got trapped between the machine and the pavement. More bullets sprayed across the front grille and fender of the pursuing police car.

In what was like a slow-motion dream, as McMurphy clung to the topside of the motorcycle skidding across the pavement, he saw Tara sitting on the sill of the passenger side window of the police car. Her long black hair billowed out behind her. Her white dress soaked to her skin. A raven hair angel of vengeance.

She pulled the pin of the hand grenade and threw it.

With the accuracy of an outfielder pegging a running at home plate, the grenade hit the pavement and bounced under the van. It exploded, lifting the back end of the van in the air.

McMurphy shouted, "Yes! Knew that would come in handy."

The motorcycle slammed into the curb. It bounced, tilted, and sent McMurphy careening through the air. He hit the wet ground and tumbled across the rocky gravel that served as the front yard of the house on the corner. He rolled, got up, and ran—limping—across the street as the battered van swerved into the Beach Club's parking lot.

The police car skidded to a stop in front of the club.

Bannon and Tara jumped out. Their Glocks aimed at the van. Bannon nodded at McMurphy as he reached them. Together, they moved through the sleeting rain and the shadows cast by the clubhouse toward the van. It had stopped at an angle near boulders separating the lot from the beach below.

The passenger side flank faced them. The back doors hung open.

Tara moved toward the cab, staying low. Her gun held in a two-handed grip.

Bannon and McMurphy moved cautiously toward the rear.

Bannon reached the door, hanging half open.

McMurphy said, "Go."

Bannon yanked the door open further.

Gun forward, McMurphy charged. But the cargo space was empty.

From the cab, Tara shouted, "Clear."

McMurphy spun around, angry. "Where? How?"

He wiped rain from his face.

From the row of boulders, Bannon called out. "There."

He leaned over. A trail of rocky steps led down to the beach below.

Two men, shadowy figures, had dragged a third figure across the narrow strip of beach. They'd already reached the frothy white-capped surf, splashing through the waves. A sleek speedboat without running lights angled in toward the shore. Slowed to pick them up.

McMurphy raised his gun, aimed.

Bannon tapped his arm. "They're too far."

McMurphy lowered his gun. "Damn it!"

CHAPTER TWENTY-NINE

Versteek Island
Isles of Shoals

BERNARDOR VAN WYK STOOD on the portico overlooking the inlet. Protected from the rain by the overhang, the downpour had begun to lighten. The outdoor furniture had been removed and stored. The lighted pool glowed ethereally. Raindrops hit the water, rippling the surface with concentric circles. The tiki torches were gone, but the plantings around the pool and patio area were lit with bright white accent lights. The leaves of the trees shimmered wetly in the rain and the still-heavy breeze.

Members of his security detail had returned him to the island after the disastrous mainland meeting with Bannon. He'd underestimated the man. A move he'd been warned against. It was a mistake he would not make again.

Still in his tuxedo, he'd discarded the bow tie and had the throat of his collar open. He held a glass of bourbon in his hand. His thoughts raced. Amped up, like an engine stuck on full throttle. He took a long, deep breath, trying to calm his mind. Through the sheets of rain, he watched his daughter's sleek twenty-five-foot Talon riding the rough white-capped waves into the dock.

Jade was at the wheel. A skilled pilot. The speedboat powered down. It jostled dangerously on the storm-swollen seas.

Their dockmaster, a man named Nangolo, caught the ropes tossed to him by Mzobe. He cinched the tie-down ropes to the dock cleats and stepped to one side. Mzobe climbed from the rocking boat, holding a woman by the arm. A black hood over her head.

Mzobe held her while Jade climbed from the boat.

The third man from the detail remained in the back of the boat, cradling his arm. Apparently, the fool had gotten himself injured.

Van Wyk twirled the glass in his hand. The ice cubes rattled against the sides.

He continued to watch as Jade, Mzobe, and their forced guest traversed the sawtooth series of weathered steps and landings up the hillside to the main house. When they reached the walkway below the pool, van Wyk crossed to the bar and freshened his drink.

Jade came onto the portico first.

Drenched from the pounding rain, her yellow dress clung to her body like a second skin. Rain beaded on her shoulders and dripped down her arms and off the slope of her nose. She wiped a hand down her face.

"I see you have succeeded, Daughter."

Jade took the glass from him and swallowed the remaining bourbon in one swig, ice and all. "There were complications."

"What complications?"

Mzobe dragged the struggling woman through the gathering room to the patio. Her arms were zip-tied behind her back. Yet she fought fiercely. The two of them were as soaked and disheveled as Jade. Mzobe jerked the woman's arm. "Stand still!"

When she settled down, Mzobe tore the hood off her head.

The woman blew her tangled auburn hair from her blood-streaked face. She had a deep cut across her cheek. Other superficial wounds leaked little droplets of blood.

Van Wyk narrowed his eyes and frowned. "This is not Elizabeth Grayson."

"No, it's—"

Van Wyk exploded. "I don't care who it is! It's not Grayson."

He snatched the empty glass from Jade's hand and threw it across the portico. It shattered against the stucco wall. At the bar, below the overhang, he dropped two ice cubes into a new glass and filled it with three fingers of bourbon. His hands shook with rage.

"I told you, Father. We had complications."

Van Wyk pointed at the woman. "This is *not* a complication, Daughter! This is a mistake. Van Wyk's don't make mistakes." He swallowed half his drink. "You *said* you had this handled. You *assured* me it was handled. *This* is not handled."

"Careful, Father."

Van Wyk threw this glass at the side of the house, too. It shattered and rained bourbon down the stucco. Glass shards littered the tile floor like diamonds. He growled in frustration.

"I had it. I had it in my hands." He fisted his hand. "The sword. And I let it slip through my fingers. All you had to do was pick up one little old lady. One job to do. We needed Grayson to get Bannon to give up the Honjō sword. And you bring me...."

He waved his hand angrily. "A nobody. You failed me, Daughter."

Jade remained calm in the face of his outrage. She let the sting of his criticism fade before she found her voice and spoke again. "Grayson proved too difficult to grab. Too well protected. But this woman. She will do as well."

"Is she as important as a Secretary of Homeland Security?" van Wyk asked.

"To Bannon, she is."

That caused van Wyk to pause. He stood face-to-face with the disheveled woman. He chucked her chin with his finger. She shook her head away.

"Don't touch me!"

He seized her jaw and snapped her face forward. She struggled against him, but his grip was like iron. Defiant. A fighter. A bruise had started to form around her left eye.

"Who is she?"

"Kayla Clarke," Jade said.

Van Wyk shrugged, remaining unimpressed.

"Lieutenant Kayla Clarke, United States Coast Guard."

Van Wyk smiled. "She works for Bannon?"

"Yes, Father. One of his team. Part of his most inner circle."

"He'll come for her?"

"He'll come for me all right," Kayla said. "And he'll reign fire down on you and on this place like you've never seen before. This was the last mistake of your suddenly cut-short life."

Van Wyk stepped back and laughed. "Spirited, isn't she? I'll give the Americans that. They are very, very spirited." He grabbed her face again. "It'll be fun to see that great American spirit broken. Defeated. Stomped out and destroyed as every last hope you and Bannon ever had is ripped away."

He pushed her away.

"Mzobe, Take her." To Jade, van Wyk said, "If what you say about Bannon is true, Daughter. We have much planning to do."

Mzobe grabbed Kayla's arm. He yanked her toward the gathering room, then took her deeper into the house.

When they were gone, Jade said, "This will work, Father. I've watched these people. Studied them. I know how they think. How they operate."

Van Wyk stared out over the dark, storm-swollen ocean. Black with violent whitecaps. The moon and stars unseen behind a low ceiling of slow-moving black clouds. The predictions were for a damaging nor'easter to arrive over the next twenty-four hours.

"They all must die, Daughter. All of them."

Jade came up behind him. She put a hand on his arm and on his shoulder. She rested her cheek against his back. "And they will, Father. You have my word."

"But first," he said. "We get the Honjō Masamune sword."

She kissed his ear. Through a sinister smile, she said, "Yes. Then I kill them all."

CHAPTER THIRTY

Keel Haul Tavern
Hampton Beach, N.H.

SUNDAY MORNING, McMURPHY SAT at his seat at the bar.

After Kayla's kidnapping, no one had slept. The storm hadn't let up. The boulevard and the beach were as empty as a post-apocalyptic Hollywood movie, everyone driven indoors. The rain lashed at the windows. Bannon hadn't even bothered with a closed sign for the door.

A plate of scrambled eggs, bacon, and toast sat on the bar, untouched in front of McMurphy. Instead, he drank. Switching from coffee to a mug of Guinness since they returned to the bar in the middle of the night.

There was nowhere else for them to go. Nothing they could do.

Bannon stood behind the bar. His cell phone pressed to his ear. His cup of coffee had grown cold for the umpteenth time.

Seated at the bar, Tara picked at her eggs and toast as well. Parker sipped her coffee.

No one spoke.

Bannon concluded his call without telling anyone who he'd been talking with. His side of the conversation too cryptic to give anyone a clue.

They all glanced around as the Keel Haul door opened up.

A shaft of overcast gray knifed through the gloomy bar. Rain lashed across the heavy door and puddled on the floor. Elizabeth Grayson came in, wearing a casual outfit under a black raincoat, shiny and wet. Behind her, Franklin Gregg closed the door. He had on a dark suit and his arm in a black sling.

Seeing the Secret Service agent, McMurphy's eyes narrowed.

Without warning, McMurphy launched off his stool and charged across the room. He plowed into Gregg with a forearm across the man's chest and a hand to his throat, slamming the agent into the doorframe with a thud.

"You could have stopped them. You could have saved her."

Grayson tugged at McMurphy's arm. She'd have had a better chance of tipping over a hundred-year-old oak tree by herself than pulling McMurphy back.

"John. Stand down. Stand down! That's an order."

Bannon rushed from behind the bar and patted McMurphy's shoulder and arm. He knew better than to try and pull them apart. As such, he had no better success than Grayson had. Careful to not get on the receiving end of McMurphy's aggression, he patted the man's shoulder.

"Come on, Skyjack," he said, keeping his eyes on the big man's hands. "There's no time for this. Come on."

"He was protecting me, John," Grayson said. "He was doing his job. The same as Kayla. Now stand down and stop this nonsense. This minute."

Gregg gurgled. His eyes had gone wide.

Bannon continued to pat McMurphy's shoulder. Only calm reason would cut through the man's rage, not brute force. "Come on, man. Come on."

McMurphy relented. He stepped back with a grunt.

Gregg pushed himself off the door frame.

McMurphy shoved him back again. A final brush-off before walking away. He returned to his place at the bar and downed half a mug of Guinness.

Gregg leaned heavily against the wall. He caressed his throat, then cradled his injured arm.

McMurphy stared at Gregg again. His face was flush with anger. He picked up his plate of food and hurled it across the room.

Tara and Parker ducked.

The plate smashed against the closed kitchen door. Shards of broken plate and eggs fell to the floor.

Grayson patted Gregg's good shoulder. "You should go wait in the car, Franklin."

He frowned, staring daggers at McMurphy.

"It's okay," Grayson said. "I'll be fine."

Still, the big black man hesitated.

"That's an order, Agent."

Gregg relented. "Yes. Ma'am." His voice raspy. He pushed the door open and plunged into the heavy storm and sleeting rain.

Grayson exchanged glances with Bannon. She kept her voice low. But, not so soft the others didn't hear her. "You need to pull your team together, Commander. Now."

Bannon returned to the bar, looking no happier than McMurphy. "Why are you here?" he asked, adding, "General."

"A drink, Brice. Then, important information you need to hear."

Behind the bar, Tara poured three fingers of bourbon into a tumbler and plopped one ice cube in. She dropped a napkin on the bar and set the drink in front of Grayson.

"We're listening," Bannon said.

"Your adversary," she said after sipping her drink. "The man you encountered last night. He is a South African national named Bernardor van Wyk. With him was his daughter Jade. There is no Mrs. van Wyk. There are no reports of who Jade's mother is. Forbes and Fortune Magazine list van Wyk as number nine of the top one hundred richest men in Africa. He made his fortune mining diamonds and other rare gems. An orphan conscripted to the mines at an early age, and if reports are true, later kidnapped to be a child soldier. His rise to power in the private sector, by all accounts, was as meteoric as it was brutal. Ambitious and impatient, he didn't rely on hard work, integrity, or a remarkable expertise in business to rise up the ranks. He did it by savagely eliminating those he worked for and his competitors. And I'm not talking in the metaphorical sense. African authorities and Interpol link many of those eliminations to his daughter, Jade. A rather nasty piece of work she is. Several ruthless murders are attributed to her, though with no proof."

"I look forward to meeting her," Tara said.

"Don't get ahead of yourself," Grayson warned. "As is often the case, with that level of business success and the acquisition of more financial wealth than most third world countries, van Wyk has managed to secure tremendous capital. It is said he rules the entire political infrastructure of Namibia and a good portion of South Africa with an iron grip. He has tremendous sway over the military and more than likely has the whole of law enforcement in his pocket."

"Does the intelligence community believe he is *Skaduwee*?"

"In light of recent events, it stands to reason. According to sources, van Wyk works hard to maintain his persona as an upstanding, legitimate contributing member of the business community and society. While we know his business dealings are ruthless, and may even be morally questionable, officially, he's not run afoul of authorities over so much as a parking ticket."

"Van Wyk's a name I'm familiar with," Parker said, speaking up for the first time. "A very private person, as the Secretary has mentioned, it is believed he's an avid collector of art. Much of it rumored to be stolen or possessed illegally. This rascals' cagey. No one's built a case against him, but I bet a search of his properties would be eye-opening."

Grayson sipped her drink. "For years, he's been the focal point of investigations. On the shady side of everything from corruption and securities fraud to human trafficking, the illegal drug trade, and multiple murders. But nothing's moved past the suspicion stage."

"He's never attempted to expand into the U.S. before?" Bannon asked.

"Not so far as anyone knows."

"Tell me about the woman. Jade," Tara said.

"Again, nothing verifiable. Rumors, innuendos, and theory. But if true, she's a piece of work. Van Wyk's enforcer, his chief muscle. She handles all the dirty work. And she's reportedly very good at it. Violent, ruthless, unmerciful. Romantically, she's tied to a man named Arno Mzobe. A man as deadly and as cruel as she is."

"Guess it's true then," McMurphy said. "There is someone for everyone."

"He led the attack on us last night," Grayson said. "Kayla also confirmed it was Mzobe and Jade who killed Hornsby. Willing to kill dozens more in the process."

"That sounds like more than a parking ticket," Bannon said.

"But without proof," Grayson said, "there's nothing we can do about it."

"That's going to change," Bannon said.

Grayson frowned. "Leading me to my second reason for being here."

Expecting a second shoe to drop, they waited.

She said, "We've been ordered to stand down."

"Stand down?" McMurphy shouted, coming to his feet. "By who?"

"You know damn well who, John. The President. The only person in the world authorized to give me such an order."

"Why?" Bannon ground his teeth. Felt the vein along his jaw pulse.

"The men you and John," Grayson turned toward Parker, "and you killed in the harbor the other day. They worked for a private security contractor."

"That makes them mercenaries," Bannon said.

"A South African company. The Namibian government has issued a formal protest. They're demanding an investigation. Demanding those responsible for their deaths be turned over. To stand trial in Namibia."

"You've got to be kidding?" McMurphy said.

"I wish I were. Now, the President has no intention of complying, but…"

"But what, Lizzie?" McMurphy demanded.

"He's ordering us to stand down."

"What about Kayla?" Tara asked. "We just let them kill her."

Grayson frowned. "The President wants to work that through diplomatic channels."

"Diplomatic channels!" McMurphy slammed his fist on the bar. "Screw this! I'm out of here."

Grayson called out, "John. Don't go. We can figure something out."

McMurphy waved his hand dismissively in the air. "A bunch of spineless diplomatic hacks talking at each other. I don't think so."

He pushed through the heavy door and was swallowed up by the storm.

In the silence that followed, Bannon said, "Kayla doesn't have that kind of time. If van Wyk doesn't get what he wants, he'll kill her."

"And we can't go off half-cocked," Grayson said. "We don't even know where she is? Our best option is—"

"What?" Bannon demanded. "Talk to van Wyk and ask him nicely to not hurt Kayla. To turn her over to us? In exchange for what? The man won't even admit to your diplomats he has her. And when you accuse him, that's her death sentence."

"I can't say you're wrong," Grayson admitted glumly. "But we need to stand down. Those are your orders. From me and from the President. This operation is shut down effective immediately."

Parker tried to reason one more time. "In the hands of people like that—"

"Kayla's dead," Tara concluded. "And you and the President are the ones who killed her."

Grayson sighed. "We need to do this right. Nations. Governments are involved now. Or, it becomes an international incident."

She stood up and tossed back the last of her drink. "Those are your orders." She headed for the door.

"Where are you going?" Bannon asked.

At the door, Grayson stopped. "Back to Washington. I've got my job to do. For now."

She pushed through the door. It closed behind her.

Bannon picked up a tumbler and threw it across the room. It hit the door to the kitchen and dropped to the floor where the broken plate and eggs had fallen.

"Really?" Tara asked.

Sitting in the quiet, Parker asked the question on everyone's mind. "What do we do now?"

Bannon frowned. "What we were told to do. We stand down."

CHAPTER THIRTY-ONE

THE KEEL HAUL REMAINED CLOSED for the rest of the day.

After Grayson left, Bannon sent Tara and Parker away. Sitting around sulking wouldn't do any of them any good. He contacted Lieutenant Ng and informed her of Grayson's—and the President's—decision to close down the operation. Pulling their detail, he told her and her people to go home, too.

He said he'd be in touch if anything changed.

Under the watchful eye of Agent Gregg and her Secret Service protection detail, Grayson started the forty-five-minute drive back to Manchester Airport. There, she'd take a private jet back to Washington.

Bannon rehung the Death in Family sign on the door.

The streets were deserted. A stream of debris-filled water rushed along the curb. Rain slashed across the road at nearly a forty-five-degree angle, with wind gusts whipping into small squalls. Jagged lightning bolts flashed over the ocean, streaking toward the turbulent, black sea.

Bannon returned to the bar. He poured a beer and busied himself with cleaning up the dishes left behind from the day. He'd just dunked a glass in the sudsy water when the bar door opened.

Jade van Wyk stepped inside. She wore a long red raincoat, wet and shiny. A garment good for concealing all manner of weapons.

Bannon had left the lights turned low. He hadn't even turned on the jukebox.

The door closed behind the woman. She was alone. "You should lock your doors when you're working all alone. Never know who might show up."

Bannon pulled the glass from the water, wrapped a towel around it, and smiled. "Hard for you to accept my invitation with the door locked."

Jade strolled cautiously across the room. "Is that what this is? An invitation."

"You're here, aren't you? Drink?"

"No."

"Pity. I hate drinking alone." Bannon refilled his glass mug with more Sam Adams seasonal. "Doesn't mean I won't."

"I have a message from my father."

Bannon leaned against the back wall. He sipped his beer. "I didn't peg you as an errand boy—sorry—person."

Jade ignored his banter. "We have your woman. We'll trade her for the sword."

"And no harm will come to either her or me if I turn it over. Blah, blah, blah," Bannon said. "I've heard that one before. Been there. Done that. I've got the t-shirt around here somewhere."

"Joke if you want. My father will have the sword."

"Or I could take you hostage," he said. "Then, I'll have two bargaining chips to your one."

Jade smiled. There was something sad about it. "If you believe my father would sacrifice…anything for me, you are either mistaken or misinformed."

The Keel Haul door opened. Mzobe stepped inside. He held a Vektor 9mm pistol alongside his leg.

"That doesn't mean I'm willing to be sacrificed," Jade said. "Not without a fight."

"Oh, we're playing this game again," Bannon said.

"Except," Jade said, "you have no one else here. Your friends are gone. Your leader is halfway to the airport. You dismissed your protection team."

"True," Bannon said. "But I'm not interested in playing these games. You're right. I'm all alone. I sent them all away."

He pushed off the back wall and reached for something behind the bar.

Mzobe stepped forward, his pistol raised. His arm steady as granite.

"Relax," Bannon said. "We actually do want the same thing." He placed the pine sword case on the bar. "Kayla for the Honjō Masamune. I accept your offer."

Jade eyed him suspiciously.

"All I care about is getting Kayla back. Unharmed. Here's the sword. Right here."

Jade's expression registered puzzlement, but she nodded to Mzobe. Her unspoken order was clear: *Take it.*

Bannon held up a hand. "But not so fast...." He walked out from behind the bar. Mzobe kept the pistol trained on him. Bannon remained unfazed. "You see, I don't trust you to keep your word. You know, it's easy to say the words. We won't harm you. You'll be free to go. But actions? They tell a different story. So, there are a few conditions—"

"You are in no position to make demands," Jade said. "You can't even stop us from taking it."

She nodded her head to Mzobe, ordering him to do just that.

"Actually, I can," Bannon said. "If you'd done a proper job of researching my team, you'd know what we are capable of. What our collective skill sets are."

When Jade didn't respond, Bannon said. "Let me enlighten you."

He popped the case's two latches. "Come on over. Take a look."

Cautiously, the two moved in closer.

Like the last time, the outer lid opened to reveal the glass and pine inner lid. The sword lay on display in its bed of red velvet. But there was something else. Something new inside. A square, black box with a blinking yellow light. Attached to it were wires to a block of what looked like gray modeling clay. Looped around the black box was an old fashion analog pocket watch. The second hand swept across the face.

"That's a block of C4. Plastic explosive. It's wired to a detonator that is also wired to several pressure switches along the edge of the inner lid. Inside the case. Since all the components are contained within…."

"The case can't be opened without activating the bomb," Jade concluded. "The bomb can't be deactivated without opening the case. Cleaver."

"Blades and Skyjack are really good at this stuff. Devious, in fact. Circuitry is embedded in the wood. If the circuits are broken, say by smashing through the wood. Boom. Also, there are glass break sensors. So, a no-go there, too. And the entire case is sealed. Airtight. No flooding it with foaming agents, corrosives, etc. The case is absolutely impenetrable. Impossible to—"

"To disarm," Jade said.

"Exactly. There's enough C4 in there to obliterate this entire room."

Mzobe took a step back.

"Only I can deactivate the bomb. Using a password-protected code," Bannon said, driving home his point. "Triple biometric protection, including body temperature readers. So, there'll be no killing me and cutting off my thumbs or carving out my eyeballs. The third biometric is a voiceprint analyzer. Meaning, I have to be alive to say the magic code. All DARPA-engineered, cutting-edge stuff."

Jade frowned. "What do you propose?"

"You bring Kayla here. I give you the case. I unlock it with the code. That triggers a thirty-minute countdown delay before the case can be safely opened. Enough time for us to part ways. We all walk away. If not happy, at least alive."

"That's not going to work for us. Lieutenant Clarke isn't here."

"Then take me to her. Same deal applies. We exchange. We walk away. Everyone lives."

He grabbed the case and pulled it roughly off the bar.

Jade and Mzobe both stepped back. Abruptly.

"Oh," Bannon added. "Also incorporated into the timer device is a twelve-hour countdown. If the case isn't deactivated or the alarms reset within that time—you get the picture."

With a humorless smile, he said, "We should get going, don't you think? Tick tock."

Bannon went to the door first. He shut off the lights and opened the door, holding it for them. "After you."

Jade and Mzobe passed him. He followed them out into the raging storm.

CHAPTER THIRTY-TWO

Bernie's Beach Bar
Hampton Beach, N. H.

McMURPHY SAT UNDER THE covered section of the outdoor bar. He'd been there most of the afternoon. Watching as the storm worsened with each passing hour. He wore an anorak rain jacket and a black baseball cap. Stitched across the front: I FIX STUFF.

When he arrived hours earlier, a full bar had greeted him. But since then, the crowd had dwindled to a handful of hearty young people huddled around the back end of the bar, braving the steady downpour of rain and listening to rock music. Trying to make the most of their washed-out vacation time. The uncovered dance floor was empty. The owners had brought in the umbrellas, tables, and chairs that normally filled the exposed deck overlooking Ocean Boulevard below and the beach beyond.

The bartender, a kid named Jeff, put another Corona on a napkin and slid it to McMurphy. He wore a bright yellow Hawaiian shirt, a deep tan, and sundrenched bleach-blond hair. He glanced out at the ocean. Dark, foreboding. The wind stirred the black water into rippling whitecaps. Breakers rolled into the beach and crashed across the sand. The rain had fallen steady for the last few hours, but now the wind had begun to pick up. The occasional gust blew through the bar, tearing at the thatch-roof covering.

"It's getting nasty out there," Jeff said. "We'll probably have to close up soon."

"No worries, buddy." McMurphy glanced at his phone. "Looks like I won't be here much longer."

"No rush." Jeff took McMurphy's empty. "Just putting it out there."

McMurphy's attention was on the app on his phone. On the screen, a map with a single blue flashing dot on it. The dot had started to move north, up Ocean Boulevard. Grayson had provided them with state-of-the-art tracking tech developed by DARPA. Grayson's answer to James Bond's Q. It was concealed in the one thing van Wyk's people couldn't check and wouldn't go anywhere without. The sword case.

Wearing an earpiece, McMurphy said, "Operation Jailbird is a go. Falcon is on the move. I repeat. We are a go."

McMurphy stood up and threw back the last of his Corona. He placed a hundred-dollar bill in the tip jar on the bar. He put a cigar in his mouth, tilted his head away from the wind and the rain, and lit up.

"Stay dry," Jeff said.

"Naw. It's time to get wet." McMurphy flipped the hood of his rain jacket over his head and crossed the empty, rain-lashed deck to the railing overlooking Ocean Boulevard. Standing in the brunt of the storm, he puffed his cigar. Rain dripped from the bill of his I FIX STUFF baseball cap.

Below, a dark sedan sat parked at the curb across the street. Its lights were off, but the engine was running. The windshield wipers cleared the glass of rain and thumped to a stop. The fogged windows were a dead giveaway. Someone was inside. And made it difficult for those inside to see out. The whole point of a surveillance.

"Amateurs," McMurphy said.

Unseen by the car's driver, a dark figure moved along the sidewalk behind the car, staying low. McMurphy enjoyed watching Charlotte Ng work. Dressed in black fatigues and a black baseball cap of her own. Hers had no logo. She'd tied her long black hair in a ponytail and threaded it through the back of her cap. She paused under the driver's side window and gave McMurphy a wave.

McMurphy smiled. "Quit showboating."

Ng blew him a kiss.

She used a bus mallet and quickly shattered the driver-side window. The driver ducked away from the door and the flying glass. Ng reached inside, unlocked the door, pulled it open, and dragged the driver out of the car. She pressed her Glock to his temple and forced him to the wet pavement. She pulled the driver's hands behind his back and zip-tied his wrist.

"Target one neutralized."

McMurphy threw her a salute. "Well done."

AJ's Axes & Archery
Portsmouth, N.H.

WHILE McMURPHY DRANK CORONAS at Bernie's, Tara had driven up the coast to Portsmouth. There, she'd spent the afternoon tossing various size axes at targets. AJ, a retired Boston cop and former SEAL Team commander, watched in stunned amazement at her accuracy. They had the place to themselves because of the weather.

She'd worked up a sweat. Her muscles were pleasantly fatigued.

Now, showered and changed, she stood at the window in AJ's office. Rain pelted the glass and rolled down the pane, turning the neon lights of the strip mall stores into a kaleidoscope of diffused colors.

AJ sat at his desk. He keyed information into his computer while keeping an eye on Tara. "Any chance you want to tell me what you're up against this time?"

"Can't." She spotted her tail in the vestibule of the Market Basket across the street.

A dark-skinned black man, he'd had to move around quite often to avoid raising suspicions inside the grocery store, but he never ventured out into the weather to conduct his surveillance. Tara shared McMurphy's same low opinion of the mercenaries tasked with keeping an eye on them.

AJ flipped through papers on his desk. Invoices from what Tara could see.

"Anything I can do to help?" he asked.

McMurphy's voice filled her ear. Tara pressed her earpiece. *"Operation Jailbird is a go. Falcon is on the move. I repeat. We are a go."*

"Thanks, AJ, but no. Everything's going according to plan. Surprisingly." Tara turned and smiled. "I've got to go."

"See you next week for practice?" he asked. "Not that you need it, but the competition's only a couple of weeks out."

"I'll be here."

She stepped out of the office and through the closed lobby. She had on a black rain slicker with a green hoodie underneath. Stepping into the rain, she didn't bother with the hood. She walked by the front windows of the Market Basket. Made it easy for her tail to spot her. Without glancing at the man surveilling her, she saw him match her pace inside the brightly lit grocery store, heading for the exit.

He frowned at the prospect of getting wet.

That'll be the least of your worries in a minute, Tara thought.

At the curb, she glanced around, feigning a cautionary look for traffic dangers. She spotted Ensign Connell approaching her location. She stepped off the curb, hearing the store's automatic store door fold open behind her.

She strolled through the parking lot. The dark-skinned mercenary, now between her and Connell, was so focused on Tara he never noticed he had a tail of his own. Not until Connell slipped an arm around the man's neck. He placed the other around the man's head, tilting it forward in a chokehold until the man passed out.

Tara reversed directions and quickly scooped the unconscious man's feet off the ground. Connell popped the hatch of their nearby black SUV with a key fob. They tossed the man inside seconds after he'd emerged from the store. Connell secured their adversary's arms behind his back and slammed the hatch closed.

"Target two neutralized," Connell said into comms.

Tuck Museum
Hampton, N.H.

MEANWHILE, PARKER QUINN HAD spent her day exploring the main building of the Tuck Museum on Park Ave. She'd last seen her surveillance detail rather conspicuously hiding in the shadows under the overhang of the Historical Society's barn across from the main entrance. A black man in dark clothes more concerned with staying out of the weather than staying out of sight.

Parker had returned to the door periodically. Pretending to check on the deluge of rain pouring down outside but really to make sure her tail remained in position.

The museum's curator, a sweet young woman named Amy, approached her. They'd had a pleasant and informative conversation earlier in the day. She was pursuing a BLS in Art History at Boston University. She worked at the museum part-time and for life credits.

"I'm sorry," Amy said, approaching Parker. "But we'll be closing soon." She forced a smile. "The weather is atrocious, isn't it?"

"A bad storm, yes." Parker checked her watch. "That's fine, darling. I'll just be a minute. Just waiting for someone who'll be along in two shakes of a lamb's tail, I'm sure."

"Of course. No hurry."

"You're so kind, Amy. Bless your heart."

In her ear, McMurphy said. *"Operation Jailbird is a go. Falcon is on the move. I repeat. We are a go."*

"There they are now." Parker pointed at the earpiece she wore and smiled. She remained visible in the doorway, knowing what would happen next.

Earlier in the day, even before Grayson announced the operation was over, Tara had surreptitiously handed out secure burner phones to each of them, along with the commlink earpieces. Bannon texted them all with instructions. Go out. Do things in public. Nothing that would look conspicuous or be out of character. He was sure they'd remain under surveillance by van Wyk people until a move was made.

He'd also instructed Lieutenant Ng's team to identify each tail, to follow, but not engage until instructed to do so. McMurphy had given the order. *Falcon was on the move.*

A second later, Parker heard what she was waiting to hear. Ensign Ellis' voice in her ear. "Target three neutralized."

The handsome young guardsman opened the door to the museum. He smiled at Parker. His hair plastered wet to his skull. His dark clothes were soaked to his skin. He grinned, "We're good to go, ma'am."

"We won't be you keep calling me ma'am. I'm only but a few years older than you."

Ellis blushed. "Yes, ma—Agent Quinn."

"Parker will do just fine."

She followed him out into the storm. "Bluebird's on the move. Back to the nest in twenty."

CHAPTER THIRTY-THREE

Keel Haul Tavern
Hampton Beach, N.H.

FREE OF WATCHFUL EYES, and with Charlotte Ng at his side, McMurphy unlocked the door to the Keel Haul and shouldered his way inside the bar. In his ear, Tara said, "Hawk's returning to the nest."

"Copy that."

"Next time, I want to pick the codenames," she complained. "I don't identify as a hawk."

"At least you're not called loon," McMurphy said.

"See, now that fits."

He could hear the glee in her voice. McMurphy terminated the call. He flipped the switches by the door. The lights came on, but on a dimmer switch, they remained low. Lieutenant Ng closed and locked the door behind them.

Elizabeth Grayson stood by the jukebox, her back to the door. She held a small snow globe in her hands. Her focus was on the replica of Tiamat Bluff inside, the so-called city under the sea. Its glass had a crack in it, reminiscent of the real-life damage caused to the prototype project by terrorists. The same terrorists who'd tried to assassinate her and the President a few months earlier.

Franklin Gregg stood by the door leading into the kitchen. His arm still in a black sling.

"The exterminator been here yet?" McMurphy asked.

"Yes," Grayson said.

McMurphy crossed the room and extended his hand out to Gregg. They shook hands. Gregg pulled him into an embrace. McMurphy pounded the man's back. "Apologies, brother."

"And the Oscar goes to," Gregg said with a grin, stepping back. "We're good. Always."

McMurphy went behind the bar. Four small audio listening devices and two small surveillance cameras were lined up on the spit-shined glossy bar. "These all of them? We're sure?"

Grayson put the snow globe down and picked up her glass of bourbon. "Swept twice. We're sure."

They were disconnected, deactivated.

McMurphy picked up a heavy glass mug and, one at a time, brought it down, smashing them into little bits of plastic and dust. He swept the pieces into his hand and dropped them into the trash. He clapped his hands, cleaning them.

After the attack at Jake's Restaurant that killed Hornsby, it was clear she'd been followed to the popular eatery. No inside person could've leaked the location. No one but Kayla knew it until the final minutes before the meeting. That meant someone had been tailed, probably her. Meaning the bar was under surveillance.

Bannon had figured that would still be the case when they went to steal the Honjō Masamune sword from Jorgen. He'd recruited Ng and her team to be spotters, but no tails were found. Instead, the assault team they encountered was already on-site.

The only possible conclusion could be the Keel Haul had been bugged.

Bannon used that to lay his trap. Feigning dissension in the ranks. Fracture the group. Make it appear as if the team had been pulled off, the operation shut down. Van Wyk would drop his guard and make his move on the sword, still known to be in Bannon's possession.

Re-baiting the hook.

And like clockwork, Jade appeared at his door.

McMurphy drew a beer for himself. Ng declined a drink. "If only all of Brice's plan worked this well."

"With the bugs kaput and their surveillance teams dealt with," Gregg said, "They'll know something's up."

Grayson had dispatched DHS agents to pick up the three mercenaries taken out of commission by Ng and her team. Tara and Parker were on their way back to the Keel Haul.

"It's too late to matter," McMurphy said, addressing Gregg's concern. "They'll already have taken Bannon to Kayla. Nothing to stop us now."

McMurphy held up his phone. The tracker app screen was a flat sea blue. The blinking blue dot was Falcon, aka Bannon, moving east. offshore. Based on speed and trajectory, that meant a boat.

"You have his location?"

"As we suspected. Out in the briny blue sea."

Based on intelligence reports Grayson had been given regarding the van Wyks, authorities had learned two years earlier a shell company belonging to another shell company belonging to a string of even more shell companies that eventually led to Bernardor van Wyk had purchased Versteek, one of the bigger islands of the Isles of Shoals.

Pleased, Grayson said, "The *Lightfoot* is on standby."

A lightning flash drew McMurphy's attention to the window. "Now, if not for this damn storm."

"On my abbreviated trip to the airport," Grayson said. "Inspiration struck. I called in a favor that should be able to help us with that."

"What?" McMurphy asked.

"I've upgraded your travel accommodations." Grayson glanced at her watch and finished her drink. She slipped off her barstool. "Shall we?"

Bemused and with a bit of trepidation, McMurphy joined his boss heading outside. Ng and Gregg followed behind them.

They crossed the rain-lashed street. Grayson wore a black trench coat. Very spy vs. spy, McMurphy thought.

She led them to the beach.

With heads down, they pushed through the near-zero visibility of the storm. Grayson held a rain hat to her head. Her coat's hem whipped around her legs as they trudged through the heavy, wet sand.

McMurphy held his cap to his head and squinted against the lashing rain.

When she stopped, McMurphy nearly bumped into her. He looked up.

"You've got to be kidding me?"

Sitting on its skids in the sand was an H225m Airbus helicopter. A twin-engine, long-range tactical transport platform. It could carry up to twenty-eight troops and crewed with one or two, depending on the mission.

Designed with a five-blade composite main rotor to reduce vibration. It had armor plating and was powered by two turboshaft engines mounted over the cabin with a cruising speed of 163 mph but capable of reaching 200 mph in a pinch. It also had a rate of climb of 1,460 feet per minute. It had an all-glass cockpit and was equipped with an integrated display system with a digital map and liquid-crystal display screen. This one was outfitted with a pair of 7.62mm machine guns, two 68mm side-mounted rocket launchers with nineteen rockets, and Hellfire air-to-surface missiles.

It was painted matte-black.

As McMurphy gawked, two cars pulled to the sidewalk on Ocean Boulevard.

Tara and Ellis climbed out of one. Parker and Connell emerged from the second one. They joined the others on the beach, staring at the impressively overpowered, weaponized helicopter. Its two large headlights blazing brightly.

To McMurphy specifically, Grayson said, "I'd ask you to bring it back in the same condition I'm giving it to you in, but we both know that would be a waste of breath."

"Lizzie, you are freakin' amazing."

"This I will ask of all of you." She affixed each of the six of them with a firm, stern gaze. "Go. Get our people. And bring them home safe."

CHAPTER THIRTY-FOUR

Versteek Island
Isles of Shoals

BERNARDOR VAN WYK ONCE more stood on his veranda, a drink in hand. This time, he wore a pair of black silk pajama bottoms and a paisley and black lapeled smoking jacket, cinched tightly around his waist. A cigar scissored between his fingers.

Again, he looked down, watching his daughter and Arno Mzobe navigate the Talon speedboat into the inlet. The swells were cresting to over three feet. Rain lashed in waves, pushed by the gale-force winds. It took Mzobe three attempts to get the boat close enough to the dock for Nangolo to catch the ropes Jade threw at him. He lashed the bow line around a cleat, then quickly caught the stern line. He pulled mightily to drag the boat close to the dock.

Jade leaped out as the heaving boat rode a violent wave.

Mzobe and Bannon jumped out as well. Bannon slipped on the wet, slick, bucking dock, clutching a wooden case to his chest. Van Wyk recognized the cherry wood case from their encounter at the Rye Harbor spa. The Honjō Masamune was almost his.

The lighthouse beacon swept the island. Its bright white light bathed the craggy rock and illuminated the pelting falling rain. Following Jade, Mzobe grabbed Bannon's arm and propelled him along the dock. The three of them pushed against the rain and the wind. Their heads down and their shoulders hunched. They reached the first flight of stairs that traversed the rugged slope uphill to the main house.

Jade and Mzobe hadn't bothered with a hood for Bannon. Knowing where he was wouldn't matter. There was no need for pretense any longer. Neither Bannon nor his girl would be leaving the island alive.

BANNON LEAPED OVER THE gunwale of the boat. He slipped before planting his feet firmly on the bucking dock. He wiped rain from his face. To his right was a lighthouse. Its beam swept across the island. Bannon's attention was on the large house set above them on the hill.

A split-level raised ranch-style house. The one-story main section was awash with yellow interior lights and white outdoor lighting. To the left, nestled between two rocky peaks, sat a couple of garage-size buildings. From the hum, loud enough to hear over the howling winds, Bannon assumed they housed the island's generators. Farther left, another two-story structure had been built into the hillside. It, too, glowed with yellow interior lights but had none of the big picture windows the main house boosted.

Mzobe grabbed Bannon's arm. "Move." He pushed Bannon forward.

Bannon didn't resist. He fell in step behind Jade van Wyk and concentrated on maintaining his grip on the sword case.

"Keep up," Jade shouted, spitting rain that dripped into her face. "Both of you."

The dock led to a set of twelve weathered steps. The first flight before another horizontal walkway that led across the face of the hillside, then to a second set of stairs. These were shorter before reaching another walkway that switch-backed across the layered granite inclines.

They zigzagged their way to a final walkway directly under the pool and patio before a last set of stairs brought them up to the same level as the house. From there, a white stone pathway led past a side door, which Jade ignored. She took them around to the front of the house.

Two large, heavy, ornate wooden doors were already open. "Inside," Jade said.

Bannon stepped into a large foyer. A maroon and navy-blue Oriental carpet laid over large square white tiles. A heavy wooden side table with drawers and thin decorative brass pull handles filled one wall. The piece would've looked at home in Victorian England. Two straight-back chairs with intricately etched wooden frames and crimson velvet padded seats played sentry to the table. Above them were two wall sconces. In them, thick white candles burned. The flames flicked with the sudden gust of outside wind and rain. Above the side table hung a large display case. Mounted behind glass were Medieval weapons. A polearm, a battle-ax, and a mace.

Across from the side table stood a suit of armor, tarnished. The hollow suit clutched a sword as if it were standing guard over the entrance. A painting of a foreboding, dark 15th-century castle on a craggy cliffside hung in a heavy, thick, gilded frame beside the armor.

"Keep moving," Mzobe said.

He pushed Bannon through the foyer and past a dark, burgundy-curtained archway.

Beyond that lay a vast room with a dark timber vaulted ceiling and dark leather furniture. A baby grand piano to one side. A large stone fireplace filled the opposing wall. Ahead, the far wall wasn't a wall. It opened directly onto a well-lit patio with a lighted infinity pool, an outdoor kitchen and bar, and a whirlpool tub.

Bernardor van Wyk stood in the opening. Water rained from the overhang behind him like they were on the inside of a waterfall looking out. With a drink in one hand and a cigar in the other, van Wyk wore black pajama pants, slippers, and a paisley smoking jacket.

Bannon thought, give me a break.

CHAPTER THIRTY-FIVE

VAN WYK TURNED AWAY from the storm.

Bannon strolled through the gathering room with more confidence than his situation warranted. Smug American arrogance. He wore khakis, boat shoes, and a black Polo shirt, all soaked to the skin. His unruly brown hair was plastered across his forehead. His shoes squeaked wetly across the marble tile floor.

"So, Commander. We meet again."

Bannon clutched the case tightly in his left hand. His right was balled into a fist. "Where's Kayla? I want to see her."

"The sword first." He reached for the case.

Bannon jerked his hand back.

Jade cried out, "Careful, Father. It's a bomb."

Van Wyk backpedaled. "What?"

"He's rigged the case with explosives," she said. "C4."

"Hope you're not offended to learn I don't trust you," Bannon said. "Kayla. Now."

Van Wyk frowned. "This is a most disturbing development."

Bannon pulled the triggering device from his pocket. It looked like a vehicle key fob. He held it in the air. "You think you're disturbed now. This will blow your mind. And everything else. Kayla. I'm waiting."

Van Wyk waved his hand at Mzobe. "Get the girl."

Mzobe left the room. He appeared grateful to be putting distance between himself and Bannon and the bomb.

Jade stood in the archway, keeping her distance as well.

"While we wait," van Wyk said. "Join me outside?"

He went to the outdoor bar. He needed to figure out this new angle. This development wasn't anything insurmountable. A bomb can be deactivated. Find someone, a disposal expert.

Pay him enough. It would take time, but he'd waited this long for the sword. What would a few more days mean?

Van Wyk heard Bannon's squeaky shoes behind him. "Drink?"

"I'm particular with whom I drink. So, no." As if reading van Wyk's mind, Bannon went on. "All the components are inside the case. Pressure switches all around. Shock sensors and glass break protection. Impossible to get to without, you know, opening the case. The only way to deactivate it is this." He again held up the fob. "All programmed to my distinct and living biometric signals. Oh, and if you're thinking, 'I'll just get some expert to deactivate it....'" Bannon turned to Jade. "Tell 'em."

"It's on a timer," she said.

"How did you allow this, Daughter? I'm very disappointed."

"Let's save the family drama for another time." Bannon checked his watch. "Less than nine hours and counting. Or counting down, should I say."

Van Wyk kept his back to Bannon while he ground his back teeth. He squeezed the bottle of bourbon in his hand until it shook. He'd been told Bannon was no fool. And yet, van Wyk had allowed his daughter to underestimate him.

When he was sure his hand wouldn't shake, van Wyk poured his drink.

"Mzobe's back," Jade announced.

Van Wyk turned.

Bannon pocketed the fob and moved quickly to greet the girl. He put the case down and held her by the arms. "Kayla. My God. What'd they do to you?"

She wore a nondescript gray sweatshirt, sweatpants, and slippers. She'd been allowed to clean and treat her wounds. While the scratches across her cheek were red and prominent, they no longer wept blood. Her blackened left eye had gotten worse. The area around it had become swollen and puffy. Tender to the touch. The bruised skin was a dark eggplant color.

"You should see the other guys," she said.

"I have." Bannon forced a smile. "So has the coroner."

"Grayson and Gregg?"

"Alive. Because of you." Still holding the girl's arm, as if afraid to let go, Bannon faced van Wyk. "What's your play here?"

Van Wyk held his glass of bourbon.

He took notice of how Bannon fisted his hands. The knuckles blanched white. A vein along his jawline throbbed. This was a man walking the dangerous tightrope of anger. Van Wyk's partners had filled him in on Bannon's exploits. Both while in service of the Coast Guard and since. Van Wyk hated to admit it, but the man seemed to live up to his reputation. He'd proven more dangerous and more cunning than van Wyk thought possible.

"Ah. Is this where I lay out my evil master plan to you, Commander? Like some poorly fleshed-out James Bond villain."

Bannon shrugged. "You might as well. Because before this night is over, you will be as dead as every one of those misguided megalomaniacs."

Van Wyk laughed, sipping his drink. "Is that what you think I am? A madman bent on world domination?"

"A madman, for sure. One that needs to be stopped."

"And there it is. That famous American arrogance. It must be exhausting, convincing yourself constantly you, your people, are on the right side of every issue, every conflict."

"We're not kidnapping and trafficking women into forced labor and the sex trade," Clarke said.

"Or trying to murder them by sending them to the bottom of the ocean."

"Or gunning down federal agents," Clarke added.

Van Wyk waved his hand dismissively. "As if they meant anything, these women, these people, you pretend to care so much about."

"They're human beings," Clarke shouted. "Of course, we care."

"They're pawns," van Wyk shouted back. "Little people. Of no consequence."

"Can you truly be that low?" Bannon asked. "That despicable."

"Please," van Wyk scoffed. "Destitute, drug-addled peasants who'd ruined their own lives long before our paths crossed. Not to be missed, and for some…a better life. Isn't that what America's all about? The American Dream."

"That's twisted," Bannon said. "All you offer is misery and death."

"Widgets. To be bought and sold. Exploited until they've outlived their usefulness. Depreciating assets. As my labor was used and exploited by others when I was young. You are aware I was kidnapped as a child. Forced to be a soldier in someone else's war. Then conscripted to work in the mines before I was sixteen. Simply a tool."

"That justifies it?" Clarke asked. "It happened to you, so it's okay to do it to others?"

"Don't be so melodramatic, girl." Van Wyk said. "There isn't some deep-seated psychological diagnosis to be found here. Important people use those…who are inferior. Powerful men do it. Powerful countries do it. Even your precious USA. They're a means to an end. Nothing more."

"And what end is that?" Bannon asked. "Trafficking your women here rather than through Eastern Europe and Asia? Why here all of a sudden?"

Van Wyk downed the last of his drink.

"It isn't all that complex or nefarious, Commander. I'm a businessman expanding my already thriving and lucrative global enterprise. Exploiting a new opportunity."

"Why are *you* here? Not at home, sitting safe and cozy in Namibia," Bannon asked. "You mean to take over the organized crime here in Boston. You're here because it needs the personal touch?"

"To start," van Wyk said. "Oh, and I would be remiss if I did not express my gratitude to you, Commander. From those I partner with, I've learned this particular business venture is thanks in large part to you and your team's efforts. Getting the ball rolling."

"And how is that?"

"If you hadn't so cleverly swept away the competition by taken Kwon, LaScala, and Flannagan off the board for me... You accelerated my take-over plans by years."

"For what purpose? Simply greed? To be wealthier than you already are? How much money do you need, van Wyk?"

"I'm disappointed. That is such limited thinking, Commander. I'd have expected better from you. Not all people, all entrepreneurs, are motivated by greed. Certainly, I enjoy the finer things money buys me, but no. Like the pathetic peasants you concern yourselves over, money is a tool. Capital. It is an asset, the lubricant, used to get to the ultimate goal, not the endgame."

"Then what is your endgame?"

"Ah, if I were to tell you that, then I truly would become your cartoon villain, wouldn't I?" Van Wyk contemplated another drink but decided against it. "Besides, you've already demonstrated a glaring inability to grasp the truly global picture. The long game. And...."

He eyed the case at Bannon's feet.

"And, this is all starting to really bore me. Let's get this done. How do you propose we proceed?"

"Kayla and I leave on that fancy speedboat of yours. Unharmed." He glanced at Kayla. "Any more than she already is. I deactivate the case. You wait twelve hours, then open 'er up."

"What stops me from killing you after you deactivate the case?"

Bannon held up the fob. "It's got a three-mile range. I can reactivate the bomb with the press of a button. Think you can kill me before I can press this? Go ahead. Try."

"Unacceptable," van Wyk countered. "I suggest I put a gun to Ms. Clarke's head and threaten to blow her brains all over this room if you don't deactivate the bomb now."

As he said it, Mzobe drew a handgun from behind his back. He stepped toward them. Jade made a move for a sideboard, where another weapon was stashed. She pressed a finger to her ear, listening. Her expression tightened. Whatever she'd been told, it hadn't been good news.

She whispered in Mzobe's ear. Barely above a whisper, she said, *Go. Prepare.*

The large bald man handed her his gun and left the room.

Jade aimed the gun at Clarke.

"What is it, Daughter?"

"The men we have watching Bannon's team. They missed their last check-in. It could mean trouble."

Bannon looked at his watch. He took Kayla by the hand and smiled. "Yeah," Bannon said. "It's certainly gonna be trouble."

The house shook as a massive explosion rocked the foundation. The artwork on the walls rattled. The ground vibrated under their feet. The lights flickered once and went dark.

CHAPTER THIRTY-SIX

Gulf of Maine
42°58'37.2" N - 70°39'15.4" W

THE H225m AIRBUS FLEW low over the churning black water of the Gulf. The main rotor cut through the rain and the wind, emitting a low, constant chuffing. The wipers swished across the windshield, unable to keep up with the deluge of pelting rain. Jagged lightning bolts streaked across the sky near the horizon.

They'd followed Bannon's signal six miles east of the mainland, approaching the archipelago Isles of Shoals out of the southwest. McMurphy banked slightly, aiming for the white beacon of the Versteek lighthouse. Its bright beam swept around at regular intervals, cutting through the darkness and rain, lighting the dark, foreboding landmass.

"Not exactly an island paradise, you ask me," McMurphy said. "Just a big rock in the middle of the water."

Waves crashed menacingly against the craggy rocks that rose from the sea. A walkway ran along a rock precipice from the lighthouse to a dark stone main structure. A split-level structure. The northern portion consisted of two levels judging by the illuminated row of windows. A single-story section ran along the ridgeline. Stopped where the island's topography dropped down to a valley between peaks. Nestled there in a fold were two smaller buildings. Each the size of an average two-car garage. Beyond that, another structure had been built into the sloping side of the southern peak. A two-story building, four thousand square feet from the looks of it.

Parker sat in the co-pilot's seat, clutching McMurphy's phone. Bannon's beacon flashed on the sea of black. "Reminds me of the gothic novels I read as a kid. But, as secret lairs go, it does take the rag off the bush."

"Say what now?"

"Never mind," Parker said with her infectious laugh.

McMurphy spoke into his mic. "Five minutes to DZ. Swimmers, get ready to get wet."

They had no idea how large a private security force van Wyk had on his little island getaway. But based on the skirmishes they'd already had in Boston Harbor and at the Rye Harbor Inn, McMurphy anticipated their insertion efforts would face fierce resistance.

Ng's DSF team was as skilled and capable as any SEAL team or Special Forces group out there. They were experienced and extensively trained to infiltrate the island and deal with just such a force.

McMurphy only wished they'd had more time to reconnoiter. He hated going in blind. But the inclement weather—getting worse by the minute—and with Bannon and Kayla in the devil's den, he wasn't about to waste time gathering intel.

Thus, operating on the fly, their half-baked plan was a simple one. The MSRT team would hit the water a mile off the island's windward side. Swim to shore. Climb the craggy shoal and approach the compound from that side.

McMurphy would fly around the island, find a suitable landing spot on the leeward side, and approach the house from that direction. The two-prong approach should trap van Wyk's detail between them. Simple. What could go wrong?

"What if we can't find a place to land?"

"Well, look who's being the Debbie Downer now?" McMurphy said, but Parker's question echoed his own thoughts.

"Point taken."

"One minute to drop zone," McMurphy announced over the comms. "Lieutenant, once you're onshore, proceed to the crest of the southern ridge. There, wait for my signal."

Over comms, Ng asked, "What will that signal be?"

In truth, McMurphy had no idea. To Parker's dreary point, he didn't even know if he could get this bird on the ground. If he couldn't, Parker and Tara would have to repel down alone while he remained in the chopper. He hated that prospect.

"You'll know it when you see it," McMurphy said, sounding much more confident than he felt.

"Copy that, Chief."

They reached the drop zone.

In the storm, they were far enough away from the island to not be seen. He hoped to maintain that element of surprise. It was one of the few advantages they had. McMurphy lowered the Airbus to ten feet over the choppy water. He struggled to hold the chopper steady against the buffering winds, kicking up to sixty miles an hour. Holding the stick, his forearm bulged from the herculean effort. A strong gust of wind rocked the chopper.

Over the comm, Tara shouted, "Keep her steady, Skyjack."

McMurphy grit his teeth. "Get a move on, kids. I know I make this look easy. It ain't."

"Swimmers away," Tara shouted. "I repeat. Swimmers are away."

McMurphy glanced out his side window, watching as the dark figures dropped one after the other into the black sea. Creating a concentric circle of white froth before they disappeared. Swallowed up by the turbulent waters.

It's what they do, McMurphy reminded himself. They'll be fine.

He lifted the Airbus higher, keeping an eye on the choppy black water.

"Can you see them?" Parker asked.

He grinned as three black hooded heads popped up in the water like corks. One of them, probably Ng as the team leader, gave him a wave.

"All accounted for." McMurphy lifted the Airbus up and away from the drop zone. Pros, he thought, proud to serve with them. "Godspeed."

To Parker, off mic, he said, "Let's go see what the other side of this vacation paradise has to offer."

He banked the chopper left, swinging in a wide arc around the island's southern tip. A craggy knoll rose from the sea, like a resting whale-back, forming a smaller, symmetrical counterbalance to the ridge section where the main house was built and protecting the ancillary buildings nestled between the two peaks. The lighthouse occupied the northwest curve of the boomerang-shaped island, towering over a naturally formed inlet.

Parker pointed. "There's a dock. They must use the inlet as a harbor."

McMurphy followed her line of sight. Noting the boats tied to the wharf. One was a sleek eighteen-foot speedboat. The other, a larger cabin cruiser, cradled in a harness above the thrashing water.

He grinned. "Momma McMurphy's smiling down on her boy today."

At the deepest part of the inlet, the ground was level and covered with sand. That had to have been imported, McMurphy thought. The island was just a big, old rock. Didn't matter. What did matter was that the manmade beach was flat enough and large enough to easily accommodate the Airbus.

"It's not exactly Cozumel," he said, "But it'll do."

Over the comms, he said, "Blades, we've found our parking space."

"Once we land, what then?" Parker asked.

"Rescue Brice and Kayla."

"What 'cha gonna do, sweetie? Just walk on in there and ask for them back?"

McMurphy grinned. "Naw. We knock first. And this bird's got the platform to do just that."

He brought the chopper down and level with the main house. They hoovered as if in a standoff. McMurphy targeted the small garage-like buildings tucked in the valley between the natural summits. "I doubt they're hooked up to the local power company."

"Those two small buildings? They house the island's generators?" Parker asked.

"That would be my guess."

Equipped with HMSD, monocular helmet-mounted sight and display technology, the helmet McMurphy wore enabled him to simply turn his head toward his target. His eye aimed a Hellfire air-to-surface missile at the selected structure. He pressed the red weapon release button on the flight control stick. The Hellfire missile launched.

It streaked toward the house, then banked, following his line of sight. McMurphy grinned. "Just like a damn video game."

The small buildings exploded in a fireball of red and yellow flame and black roiling clouds. The yellow lights in the main house and the ancillary buildings flickered and went out. A series of secondary internal explosions followed. Gas and propane tanks exploded, blowing out what remained of the building's stone walls after the initial strike.

"Yee-haw!"

"That's Texas, not Tennessee."

"Sorry," McMurphy said. "Got carried away."

"Now what?" Parker asked.

"That rings the doorbell. Now, let's see if our host is ready to party."

McMurphy pushed the flight control forward, down, and away, swinging the Airbus to the left while he armed the rocket launcher platform. He lined up the red targeting bullseye in his goggles with the boats at the dock. The one slung in a cradle, out of the water, was the first to go. McMurphy fired twice more. This time, taking out the speedboat and then the wharf itself.

Three up. Three down.

He spun the chopper away, swept them around in a tight circle.

When he approached the island this time, he aligned their left flank with the island, with the main house.

A dozen or more dark figures swarmed down the craggy face from the hillside house like ants scurrying from their holes. Van Wyk's army traversed down the rugged, striated slope toward the beach and what was left of the collapsed dock, floating, still on fire.

The bad guys were getting entrenched in the rocky folds of the terrain.

McMurphy pinched his mic. "Blades. You're up."

Before he was done speaking, Tara opened up with the 7.62mm machine gun mounted on the chopper's left side. The rat-a-tat-tat of rounds filled the cockpit while Tara sprayed the dark hillside with rapid-fired gunfire.

As she kept shooting, McMurphy settled the chopper onto the sandy beach and shut her down. He and Parker climbed into the crew cabin, hearing enemy fire pinging off the metal and starring the glass.

McMurphy winced with each bullet strike. "Lizzie's gonna kill me."

He pulled a CQBR carbine from the weapons rack and handed it to Parker along with two Glock pistols while arming himself similarly.

Tara kept firing the machine gun. The muzzle fire strobed through the compartment like flash lightning. The noise echoed in the cabin, deafening.

McMurphy threw open the opposite side crew door and shouted, "Time to exit. Stage right."

Parker leaped out first. She circled to the cowl of the chopper. She dropped to one knee and provided cover fire with the carbine. McMurphy jumped down. His boots hit the wet sand. Rain lashed at him, pelting his skin like driving needles.

He slapped the floor of the crew cabin and shouted over the storm and machine gun fire. "Blades! We've gotta go!"

She let loose a final barrage of firepower, rolled across the deck, and leaped to the ground.

"Head for the outcropping," McMurphy shouted, pointed past the tail of the Airbus. "We'll regroup there."

Parker withdrew from the cowl of the chopper. She stared at Tara, noticing for the first time the katana sword strapped to her back. "A sword?"

"What?" McMurphy asked. "You thought we called her Blades for no reason? Move!"

He pushed the redhead past him and dropped to one knee under the tail section of the Airbus. He fired his carbine into the dark hillside, not much concerned with hitting anything. His intention was to keep the mercenaries pinned down, providing cover for Tara and Parker as they made their way to the rock outcropping.

Once in position, they returned the favor, giving McMurphy a chance to dart across the open beach to their location without getting shot. Settled in, now it was time to pinpoint their offense. McMurphy peeked over the rocks, trying to locate their enemies' positions from their muzzle fire.

Before he could get a shot off, he heard the familiar thump of a LAW rocket launcher.

"Oh, hell no!"

He saw the red-hot flare of backfire from the weapon. He groaned, watching in horror as a smokey contrail laced straight toward the Airbus' open crew cabin door.

"Aw! No, no, no, no."

A second passed in silence. Long enough for him to begin to hope....

But nope....

The Airbus exploded.

A powerful blast of fire and smoke blew out from the open cabin doors. Black smoke roiled skyward. Orange and red flames licked out from the doors. Another second later, a second explosion rocked the chopper. The fuel tank exploded. The cockpit glass blew out, sending sparkling silver shards everywhere. Now flames licked from those openings as well.

"Oh, man. Now that was completely uncalled for." McMurphy wiped rain from his face. His red hair plastered across his forehead. "You two. You've gotta promise me you'll tell Lizzie that wasn't my fault."

CHAPTER THIRTY-SEVEN

Versteek Island
Isles of Shoals

THE EXPLOSION ROCKED THE house to its foundation. The artwork on the walls rattled. The lights flickered and then went out. In the dark, something crashed to the floor. A second, smaller explosion cracked the large glass panes in the sliding wall panels.

Clutching Kayla's hand, Bannon ducked to the right. He scooped the sword case off the floor and pulled Kayla toward the stone fireplace. They ran, crouched, staying below a pair of brown leather sofas.

Two shots rang out. The darkness flared with muzzle fire.

From the flashes, Bannon saw Jade. She stood near the archway to the foyer, her back pressed against the wall. She held her gun out in a two-handed grip.

He hadn't spotted van Wyk, but heard him shout. "Get the sword! Get the case."

Bannon and Kayla stayed low behind the sofas. They soldier-crawled over to the hearth. Bannon grabbed an iron poker and passed Kayla a pair of long-handled fireplace tongs. He weighed his poker. Wrought iron. Heavy.

Rattling the remaining tools, he drew more gunfire from Jade. Bullets chipped off the stone mantle. Tinged off the fireplace tools.

Two more shots. Bannon recognized Jade's pistol as a Vektor SP1. A close copy of the Beretta M92. It fired 9mm rounds. Had a fifteen-shot magazine capacity. With one in the chamber, she had eleven rounds left.

Bannon grabbed the wrought iron shovel. This time quietly, before tossing it across the room.

Jade fired twice at the noise. Bannon counted down. Then there were nine.

"The case, Daughter," van Wyk called. "Get the damn case!"

Jade remained near the wide archway.

In the pale, ethereal blue haze of outside light, using hand signals, Bannon instructed Kayla to sneak around to the right. Circle the room, but stay low and stay close to the wall.

Once she moved out, Bannon drew more gunfire by grabbing the long-handled broom and knocking the iron catty to the stone hearth. The metal rang against the stone.

Jade squeezed off two more shots. More bullets sparked and chipped the stone hearth.

By then, Bannon was halfway across the room. But then, caught like a deer in headlights, a flash of lightning gave him away. It flashed through the open retractable wall out to the portico.

Jade lined up the shot.

A kill shot, Bannon froze with nowhere to go.

But more explosions from outside, from the dock area, flared orange in the room as Kayla rose up next to Jade. The tongs raised over her head. She swung them down, smashing the long, wrought iron tool across Jade's arms.

Bannon dove for cover under the baby grand piano.

Jade's shot went low, dug into the wooden floor. She cried out, dropping her gun.

Kayla swung the tongs again. This time upward between Jade's legs. A painful blow, whether for a man or a woman.

Jade cursed and went down on her knees. A third swing of the tongs struck a glancing blow across the back of the dark-skinned woman's shoulders. Or her head. Bannon couldn't be sure.

Either way, Jade collapsed to the floor, out of the game.

Another flash of lightning, this time accompanied by rapid machine gunfire, revealed van Wyk still in the foyer. An expression of anger and indecision on his face. Bannon wondered what troubled him more. Abandoning his daughter or giving up on the Honjō sword.

Bannon charged after him, awkwardly carrying the sword case in one hand and the poker in the other.

Kayla grabbed Jade's dropped gun and followed after Bannon.

Bannon reached the foyer first.

Illuminated by the candles in the wall sconces, they glowed eerily in the dark, wood-paneled entry. The front doors were still open. Rain and wind lashed past the opening, whipping the candle flames into a frenzy.

"Give it up, van Wyk," Bannon said. "It's over."

"You'll never get off Versteek alive. None of you will."

Van Wyk grabbed the sword held by the suit of armor. He wrenched it from the faux knight's grasp. A planted weapon. Held in plain sight.

Bannon was almost impressed.

Van Wyk raised the sword, ready to swing.

In the hallway between the foyer and the gathering room, Kayla shouted, "Put it down." She had Jade's gun aimed at van Wyk. "It's over."

But Jade charged out from the gathering room. She tackled Kayla. Her face was covered in sticky blood from a deep wound across her forehead. They hit the far wall, shaking the house. Both women grunted and collapsed into a swinging, punching pile on the floor. The gun went off.

Bannon shouted, "Kayla!"

"Worry about yourself, Bannon." Van Wyk rushed forward. He swung his sword.

Bannon held the case up, deflecting the blow.

Kayla shoved Jade off her.

The dark-skinned woman rolled and came up on her feet, crouched.

Kayla lashed out her foot, kicking the woman in the knee. She was rewarded with a loud grunt of pain. Kayla scrambled to her feet. She held the gun on Jade.

The woman, on her hands and knees, panted. Jade's one eye was covered in blood. She snarled like an animal.

"Don't," Kayla shouted.

But she did. Jade leaped off the floor and lunged for the gun.

Kayla pulled the trigger but only got a hollow click. Empty? Or a misfire?

Jade flinched, slow to realize what had happened. When she did, she turned and ran.

Kayla glanced at Bannon.

Bannon swung his poker at van Wyk.

Van Wyk stepped back. With his sword, he knocked the poker away.

"Go!" Bannon shouted. "I've got this."

"You're sure?"

"Yeah," Bannon huffed. "Piece of cake."

Kayla charged down the hall toward the side door Jade had run through. She smashed into it before it closed.

"You're a fool, Bannon," van Wyk said. "I'll have that sword and your life."

Bannon swung the poker and missed.

Van Wyk lunged with the knight's sword. Bannon arched his back, avoiding getting skewered.

He swung the case down across van Wyk's back.

Van Wyk stumbled forward, past Bannon.

Bannon twisted around. He faced his enemy again. He swung the poker at van Wyk's knee. But missed.

The awkward swing put him off balance. Before Bannon could shift his position, van Wyk's sword sliced through the outer part of his upper arm. Van Wyk brought the sword down. The blade cut through Bannon's calf.

He cried out and went down on one knee.

Van Wyk punched the pommel of the sword into Bannon's temple.

Bannon dropped his poker but still clutched the case. His vision blurred. He saw stars as he went down on his other knee.

With his opponent on his hands and knees, van Wyk placed the sword's blade to his captive's neck. Bannon felt the razor's edge bite into his flesh, slice through his skin.

Bannon still held the sword case in one hand. "What about the bomb?"

Van Wyk grinned. "I'll figure something out."

CHAPTER THIRTY-EIGHT

McMURPHY, PARKER, AND TARA were pinned down behind a boulder at the edge of the beach. They faced a well-armed, entrenched enemy that held the higher ground. He held a pair of binoculars to his eyes and scanned the dark, craggy hillside. There were a lot of crevices and folds to search. Plenty of shadowy, protective places for the enemy to lay low, giving them superior cover and concealment. The tactical advantage. A situation that was less than ideal.

On the beach, the helicopter burned bright. Black, oily smoke billowed in a column bent by the relenting wind. The flames licked high around the blackened metal, defiant of the heavy downpour of rain. The hot metal sizzled.

Each time they tried to move, they were brushed back by gunfire.

"How many?" Parker asked.

"I count twelve for sure," McMurphy said. "Maybe— probably—more."

"Any suggestions?"

McMurphy lowered the binoculars. "We stay put and wait, Red."

"Wait?" Parker asked. "Wait for what?"

McMurphy pointed. "That."

He handed the binoculars to Parker.

Through them, she saw what he had spotted.

With more stealth than Parker had thought humanly possible, Tara snuck through the nooks, crawled over the crannies of the hillside, unseen and unheard, until she appeared behind an unsuspecting mercenary crouched behind a rock outcropping. He had a rifle aimed at McMurphy's and Parker's position.

"Where the... How'd she.... I didn't even notice she was gone."

McMurphy smiled. "That's Blades for ya."

Tara slinked down the slope, then rose up behind the man. Her movements were fluid, like water. She slit the man's throat with a double-bladed, handheld knife the likes Parker had only ever seen in museums.

"That's not a...."

"A haladie. Yup," McMurphy confirmed. "Ancient Indian weapon used by the Rajput clan. That one's made from high-carbon Damascus steel. The blades are eight-and-a-half inches long. Good for stabbing and slicing. Dicing, too, I'd guess. It's one of Blades' favorites."

Parker watched through the binoculars as Tara moved on.

She melted back into the dark folds of the incline like a chameleon, only to reappear above her next target. She drew her katana from her back and drove it downward. A two-handed strike. She plunged it through the base of the unsuspecting man's neck, down between his shoulder blades.

"So, that's what she brings to the team," Parker observed. "She's kinda scary."

"Yup. Just be glad she's on our side."

TARA LAID HER NEXT dead adversary gently to the ground. A trail of blood trickled from his mouth. The man wasn't more than twenty years old. Tara put that out of her mind while she crouched over him to survey the path upward. McMurphy and Parker plinked bullets into the hillside, drawing fire. A calculated strategy, revealing her adversaries' positions by movement and muzzle fire and masking her advance.

She identified her next target. Moving out, she rolled over a rain-slicked boulder, found a gully between the rocky folds, scurried, and climbed farther up the rocky hillside.

MINUTES BEFORE, ON THE opposite side of the island, Ng, Ellis, and Connell emerged from the sea and climbed the shoal above where the ocean waves crashed against the jutting boulders and striated rocks. They removed their rebreathers and checked their weapons, specifically their Mk.18 COBR rifles. The close-quartered weapon was the Coast Guard's MSRT's preferred replacement to the Colt M4 rifle with its unwieldy fourteen-and-a-half-inch barrel.

Ng surveyed the cliff face above them. A bit of a misnomer, she thought. The bedding planes of the stratified rock layers had formed in such a way they gave the team climbable ledges to use as hand and footholds. While a strenuous ascend, they would not need climbing equipment.

"We should move out," Ng said. "I want to be on the ridge, ready for the Chief's signal."

"It would be nice knowing what it'll be," Ellis said.

"You know, McMurphy," she said. "It won't be subtle. I doubt we'll miss it."

"He was rather vague about hostiles, too."

"Can only give us what he knows," she said. "We don't know how many, but we know we can expect resistance. From the tussles they'd had already, we know they're highly trained and probably well-equipped." She glanced at Connell, including her newest member in the conversation. "We go in expecting the worst. Prepared to deal with what we encounter."

"Semper Paratus."

Always ready. The Coast Guard's motto. Connell was former Marine. Five years, and he'd carried that gung-ho attitude over with him to the Coasties. She liked that about him. Ellis, the more seasoned of the two and perhaps a bit more world-weary, groaned. "If you *oorah,* I'm tossing you back into the ocean."

Ng laughed. "Let's move out. I want to be ready for McMurphy's signal."

Ellis groused good-naturedly. "Whatever it's gonna be."

They climbed.

Leading her team, Ng reached the summit first. She lay low, a dozen feet below the crest. Rain lashed at her. Wind blasted into her face. It was like being in the shower with all your clothes on.

The others gathered around her. "I'm going up to take a look around."

From flying in, they knew there was a main house on the main plateau to their left. The lighthouse was further north on the island's headland. So far, everything appeared quiet. She reached the ridge and stayed low, waiting for the lighthouse beam to sweep across the island before she poked her head above the ridge.

Ng again wiped rain from her face and blinked.

From her position, she had her first full view of the island. The main house dominated the flat mesa. It overlooked a beach inlet with a dock. She saw two boats. One in a cradle out of the water. The other, a speedboat, lashed to the dock, getting buffeted by the storm and thrashing sea. Beside the house, closer to her position, she spotted two small buildings tucked in the valley between the plateaus. Further down the ridge they were perched on was a third building, built into the sloping, rocky face above the beach.

She caught a flash of light in the night sky over the inlet. The darkness and sheets of rain were so thick and heavy she hadn't noticed the matte-black Airbus looming over the cove.

She caught sight of a missile's contrail seconds before the valley between the plateaus exploded in a thundering, blinding fireball. Shocked by the unexpectedness of it, Ng covered her ears and scrambled a few feet down the rock facing, sliding back to Ellis and Connell.

Bricks, rocks, and other debris rained down on the hillside, pelting them. A fiery glow illuminated the valley between the mesas. Thick black smoke curled up into the air.

Ng grinned at her people. "Who wants to guess that was our signal?"

PARKER LOST SIGHT OF Tara after counting four kills. She handed the binoculars back to McMurphy. "Now what?"

McMurphy put the binoculars to his eyes. "We wait."

"More waiting." Incredulous, she said, "I thought you were a man of action."

McMurphy swept the binoculars across the terrain. "I'm a man not into dying. There's still more than a half dozen weapons aimed right at us."

"We follow Tara," Parker said, waving a hand. "She's clearing a path for us." A bullet pinged off a rock behind her. "Yowzah. That was close."

"Keep your head down, Red," McMurphy said. "We're not following her 'cause we don't have to."

He handed her back the binoculars. "Top of the ridge. To the left."

Parker panned the terrain, following his instructions.

Above the structure built into the hillside, now aglow in the burning hot, bright aftermath of the generator buildings exploding, she saw three dark figures.

"Oh, right," Parker said. "The MSRT team."

"Time to rock this party into high gear."

TARA SNUCK UP ON a particularly well-concealed mercenary. She lay low across the cold, wet rocks above him, ignoring the rain pelting her face. She debated how best to deal with him. Katana or haladie?

She drew the double-bladed knife, preferring it for the close quarters between the folds of rock where the mercenary lay. He sighted up a shot through his weapon's scope.

The ease with which she was taking them out stirred a pang of guilt. What was that? Utilizing her superior skill against them. Was it being unfair? Unsporting of her?

She shook the nonsensical thought away.

They'd kidnapped and sealed women in cargo containers in an attempt to kill them. Killing one. They trafficked them to other countries. Sold them into slavery. Forced them into a life of prostitution, drugs, and despair. If not these men in particular, men like them. Men they chose to work for, like Bernardor van Wyk.

Then there was Simon Angula and Darren Hornsby.

And the many attempts on their lives.

No. Fairness or sportsmanship didn't enter into it at all.

While these were merely hired mercenaries, they deserved no sympathy, no mercy, from her. No. This was war.

And she would act accordingly.

Tara began to slide down the face of a boulder. The granite was slick with rain. Her foot slipped where a knob of granite she'd chosen for a foothold caved off. The rumble of cascading rocks alerted the shooter to her presence less than a foot away. He spun, aiming his rifle, and fired. She scrambled up the boulder, flipped, and leaped to the crevice floor. She twisted her ankle on the landing. Not badly, but it was painful.

The shooter was too close to line up a second shot. He swung the rifle like a club.

Tara blocked the attack with her upper arm. A shocking pain radiated down to her fingers. The fold between the granite was too narrow to draw her katana. She opted for her haladie, but before she could use it, the shooter stepped back. Giving himself enough room, he raised the rifle, aimed it at Tara's chest.

She sucked in a breath.

The crack of a rifle shot split the air. The shooter stared at Tara. His eyes went wide. A surprised expression. Blood leaked from a newly formed hole in his forehead. As he fell to the ground, Tara glanced up the hillside.

The MSRT team was traversing down the slope. Ng's carbine still aimed where the shooter had stood. Tara waved and sheathed her haladie. The need for stealth was gone. Tara unholstered her Glock.

Ng's team continued descending the rocky slope, firing at the encroached mercenaries from behind, picking the soldiers off one by one.

McMurphy, with Parker joining him, shot up the slope, pinning the enemy forces down, providing cover for the MSRT team and Tara, now decimating their ranks, quickly turning the tables on van Wyk's private band of mercenaries.

"Now we can move." McMurphy patted Parker's shoulder and waved for her to follow him. "Stay low and close to the rocks."

"Where are we going?"

McMurphy pointed toward the zigzag pattern of weather-beaten stairs and landings that traversed the hillside upward to the main house.

They reached the base of the stairs without harassment. They crouched around a railing post. Not much cover, but the mercenaries were too busy defending themselves—or trying to—against the cool and efficient advances of the MSRT team and Tara.

Satisfied the enemy forces were otherwise occupied, McMurphy started up the stairs that led to the main house. "Come on."

They stayed low, ascending quickly. Off and on, he and Parker popped off an occasional shot to brush back a merc, aiding Tara and the MSRT team when they found themselves in a tight spot.

About halfway up the stairs, McMurphy froze. "Crap."

Parker came up behind him. "What?"

At the top of the stairs, a figure ran across the uppermost horizontal platform. Jade.

A second figure chased her, close on her heels. It took McMurphy a minute to realize it was Kayla. She threw a flying tackle and brought Jade down hard on the rough gray landing near the uppermost flight of stairs. From down below and over the howling wind, McMurphy heard them grunt.

McMurphy charged up the stairs. "We've gotta get up there."

CHAPTER THIRTY-NINE

KAYLA RACED THROUGH THE dark corridor. It grew darker as the door swung closed, cutting off what little light the outside night provided. She didn't believe Jade had any other weapons on her, but when she reached the door, she eased it open slowly. Judiciously, she peeked around the jamb. She caught sight of Jade leaping down the first flight of stairs to the boardwalk that ran under the pool.

Kayla charged after her.

The rain soaked her sweatshirt and pants almost immediately, weighing them down. The lashing rain plastered her wet hair across her face before she reached the top step.

Jade had a head start but was in bare feet. The weather-warped boards would be hard on her feet. Splinters would slow her down. Silently, Kayla was grateful for the pair of slippers the van Wyks' had provided her with. She charged full speed across the straightaway. Her need to stop the woman was all-encompassing.

A sprinter on her high school track team, Kayla gained on Jade quickly. Lightning flashed across the sky. A rumble of thunder followed. Jade had nearly reached the next flight of stairs. Kayla had closed the distance between them to within an arm's reach.

She leaped.

Kayla crashed into Jade's back. With one hand, she grasped her shoulder and wrapped her arm around the woman's waist. Her momentum knocked Jade forward with a grunt. She fell face-front to the landing below, Kayla on top of her.

Jade let out a woof, the breath knocked from her chest. "Get off of me!"

She grabbed for the edge of the landing, tried to pull herself out from under Kayla, twisting around at the same time. Her face had raked the splintered wood. Her face was freshly bloodied. Her forehead wound had begun to bleed again, too.

Kayla winced. That must hurt.

She got to her knees and threw a left-handed punch, striking Jade's jaw. The dark-skinned woman's head snapped to one side, but she got her foot up between them. She kicked out.

Kayla took the kick in the ribs. The blow threw her back. With her breath knocked out of her, Kayla wheezed. She crashed into the railing behind her, sending an excruciatingly sharp pain across her back.

Jade tried to scramble away from her, crawling for the next flight of stairs.

Not about to let that happen, Kayla latched onto her foot and yanked her back.

Jade grunted, twisted, and kicked out again.

The woman's leg, slick with rain and blood, was too slippery to hold onto.

Kayla tried to get a better grasp, but Jade thrashed her feet, kicking wildly. Her heel hit Kayla's wrist, snapping her hold. A second thrust of Jade's bare feet sent Kayla reeling into the landing's corner.

Jade scrambled to her feet.

Kayla launched herself off the boards. She dove at the woman, wrapped her arms around Jade's legs, tangling her up. At the edge of the landing, Jade pinwheeled her arms, falling backward.

Kayla scrambled after her, clawing to maintain her grip on Jade's legs as the woman fell back.

Jade cried out. She hit the next landing down flat on her back. Her head hit the boards with a sickening crunch. Kayla had again landed on top of her.

The body under her remained motionless.

Jade stared up at the sky, rain pelting her face. Her eyes remained open. Unblinking. A thick pool of blood spread across the boards under her head. Mixed with the rain, it flowed down the steps and through the gaps between the weather-beaten boards. The woman's neck was at an odd angle.

There was no doubt. Jade van Wyk was dead.

Kayla pushed off her and sat on the lower edge of the steps. She sighed heavily, trying to fill her lungs with air.

McMURPHY HAD GOTTEN ABOUT halfway up the traversing staircase when he saw the two women crash down on the next landing. In the rain, Kayla's sweatpants and sweatshirt were dark and soaked through. He blew out a held breath, seeing Kayla scramble to a sitting position at the top of the stairs.

What he'd missed was the large hulking form charging at him out of the dark from his left.

Parker cried out a warning, but it was too late.

From a crevice he'd been ensconced in, Mzobe leaped over the railing with the surprising grace of a man a third his size. His heavy boots thudded on the boards before the man bulldozed McMurphy across the narrow stairs. The big Irishman slammed into the railing behind him, pinned by the weight and momentum of an enraged Mzobe. The railing cracked. Better that than his spine, McMurphy thought.

His hands wet, McMurphy lost his grip on his Glock. The pistol spun into the air before cascading down the rocky slope under the flight of stairs they were on.

McMurphy double-fisted his hands and slammed them down on Mzobe's back. The large bald man drew back one hand and drove a solid punch into McMurphy's ribs. McMurphy felt one crack.

He planted a foot on the lower rail behind him and pushed off with a deep growl. Mzobe stepped back but couldn't stand against McMurphy's brute force drive. Mzobe hit the post behind him and cried out.

Turnabout's fair play, McMurphy thought.

He put a hand over Mzobe's face and pushed his head back, arching his back over the post.

He drove a fist into the big man's stomach, doubling him over. A second punch into his jaw and Mzobe spit out a bloody tooth.

But he blocked McMurphy's next punch and backhanded a fist across the pilot's jaw, spinning him to the side. Dizzy, McMurphy stumbled down to one knee. Mzobe grabbed him by the shoulder but then froze.

McMurphy heard a sickening crunch. He couldn't figure out what caused it until Mzobe turned. The back of his bald head was bloody.

Two steps below them, Parker stood, grasping a heavy piece of driftwood.

Mzobe snarled at the DHS agent.

The distraction bought McMurphy the time he needed to get his senses about him. He grabbed Mzobe by the back of his neck. He pummeled several punches into the man's kidneys, dropping him to his knees.

Parker drew back the piece of driftwood, looking like a major league baseball slugger. She swung. The driftwood connected with Mzobe's jaw. Blood and spittle and more teeth spewed from the big man's mouth. He lunged to the side, grasping for the railings the way a defeated wrestler clung to the ropes in a ring and tried to pull himself up.

Parker swung her board again, cracking it across the large man's skull, dropping him to the landing. Out cold.

Kayla made her way down the steps, unsteady and clutching at the railings.

McMurphy caught her as she stumbled off the last step into his arms. "Easy, girl. I've got you."

"Are you okay?"

Kayla nodded, her face bloody and wet. "Will be. You guys?"

McMurphy looking down at Mzobe's prone, unmoving body. "Better'n 'im. Thanks to Parker."

"Anytime, Red," she said with a wide smile, fist-bumping McMurphy.

Kayla regained her footing. "Blades?"

McMurphy jutted his chin toward her and the MSRT team, taking out the last of the mercenaries. "Mopping up. Where's Brice?"

Kayla looked up the incline to the house. "Up there. With van Wyk."

CHAPTER FORTY

BANNON WINCED. THE RAZOR-SHARP steel blade bit deep into the skin. Van Wyk drew the sword upward. Bannon felt a trickle of blood flow down his neck. He flexed his arms and pushed off the carpeted floor, throwing his body against van Wyk's legs.

A weak effort.

Not enough to knock van Wyk off his feet, but he did stumble back, off balance. Bannon clutched the wooden case to his chest and rolled in the opposite direction. Putting distance between himself and his adversary. He bounced up against the antique desk, cutting short his escape.

Van Wyk lunged with a stabbing blow.

Bannon deflected it with a swing of the case. Again, putting van Wyk in an awkward stance. He then quickly swung the case in the opposite direction, smashing it into van Wyk's knee, buckling it.

Bannon scrambled away. Breathless, sore, and tired.

By bringing van Wyk to his knees, Bannon could scramble away. He opened the case with sharp, loud snaps of the latches.

Van Wyk watched in horror. "You wouldn't?"

"If I'm gonna die," Bannon said. "I'm not going alone."

Bannon had the outer lid open, revealing the glass-encased sword.

Their battle had been fought by flickering candle light. Now, the red blinking light inside the case flared like a beacon of doom. Bannon punched through the glass, ignoring the painful cuts to his hand. He seized the hilt of the Honjō Masamune sword.

"But," van Wyk sputtered, his mouth agape, "the bomb?"

Bannon rose to his feet. He held the legendary perfect sword in his bloody hand.

"It's amazing," he said, "what you can do with a block of molding clay, some wires, and a blinking light. Pretty convincing, wouldn't you say?"

"A bluff?"

"You're pretty slow on the uptake, aren't you, mister global-thinker? I lied. Plain and simple."

Van Wyk tightened his grasp on his sword. "Bastard."

The two faced off like ancient samurai warriors.

Van Wyk lunged with a two-fisted swing. Bannon stepped to the side and swung his sword down, blocking the strike. The clang of metal echoed in the chamber. It reverberated up Bannon's arm. Van Wyk pulled back. He raised his sword. Bannon swung a choppy blow from the right. Van Wyk easily blocked it.

Bannon's arm throbbed from the earlier cut he took to his bicep. The blood from his wounded hand coated the sword's handle, making it slick. Slippery to hold.

"There's no escape for you, van Wyk. Take the loss."

Another clash of swords. Bannon pushed van Wyk back a step. "There's always a way out."

Two more swipes and blocks. Metal-on-metal clanging. Bannon had taken fencing lessons years ago but hadn't taken it beyond a beginner's level. He had played an extra in a low-budget pirate movie once. Part of an undercover operation. He'd spent three days training with a stuntman for a swordfight scene. His character lost. The scene was cut from the final production. Thus, ending his short-lived acting career, but he remembered those lessons as he clumsily parred and blocked. Swept, thrust, and he blocked again.

"Even if you were to escape here," Bannon said, avoiding a van Wyk lunge. "There's no place you can hide. You heard the explosions. The gunfire. Your boats are gone. My team's dealt with your private army. They're either all captured or dead by now."

Van Wyk got a stab passed Bannon's defense. The tip of his sword cut through Bannon's pants, but barely nicked the skin.

"Your American confidence is tiresome, Bannon. Twenty-five trained mercenaries don't go down that easily, Commander. Not against three people."

"And a deployable securities force," Bannon said. "It helps to have friends."

Van Wyk paled at the news but shook it off. "Still, I bet on my people."

He lunged.

Bannon sidestepped. "With your life? Your daughter's life?"

He swung the Honjō sword in an upward thrust. The blade impaled van Wyk through the stomach. Bannon shoved hard, driving it all the way up to the hilt. The blade sliced through skin, tissue, and organs, then pierced van Wyk's back.

Van Wyk's eyes went wide. Blood bubbled from his mouth.

Bannon held onto him, chest to chest. He twisted the perfect sword.

Van Wyk gasped.

Bannon pulled him even closer. In van Wyk's ear, he said, "You got it wrong, van Wyk. All of it. And now, you're done."

Bannon twisted the sword again.

Van Wyk gurgled, spitting up more blood.

Bannon pushed him away and yanked the Honjō Masamune from the man's bloody body.

Van Wyk staggered back a step, clutched at the blood flowing freely from his stomach wound. He staggered, grasped for the table, scrambled to hold onto it, leaving streaky, bloody marks across the wood before he fell. He was dead before he hit the floor.

Bannon spun, hearing a commotion in the corridor behind him.

He turned, holding the Honjō sword at the ready. The blade was covered in rich, red blood. Droplets fell from the tip to the Oriental carpet under his feet.

McMurphy barreled into the foyer. Tara, Kayla, and Parker crowded in behind him. They stood, opened-mouthed, looking at Bannon standing over the bloody body of van Wyk, the dripping sword in his hand.

"About time you all showed up."

Parker stared. Her eyes were wide in horror. "Oh, lordy! Please don't tell me you used the Honjō sword to kill him?"

"I—"

She raised her hand and closed her eyes. "Shush. Shush. I can't believe you used the Honjō."

"Would you prefer he killed me?"

She didn't answer.

"Well?" Bannon asked.

Angry, Parker furrowed her brow. "Give me a minute. I'm noodling on it."

CHAPTER FORTY-ONE

SIX HOURS LATER, THE storm offered its first signs of letting up. Though dawn was still a few hours away, the ominous black clouds had begun to lighten to a still swollen, dark gray. The driving rain had lessened to a steady downpour. The winds had died down to a fairly consistent twenty miles per hour. The buffeting gusts were fewer and farther apart.

Bannon stood on the portico, sheltered from the rain by the overhang.

Lieutenant Ng came up behind him.

"We've secured the prisoners in the guesthouse," she said. "The lower level's a bunkroom with cots. Ellis and Connell are guarding them. Connell's patched up the wounded as best he could."

Bannon squeezed his hand, wrapped in a bandage. His other cuts had been treated by Connell as well, but only after the trained medic had taken care of Kayla, Tara, and McMurphy. Each had only suffered minor cuts, scrapes, and bruises.

"Good, but don't make 'em too comfortable."

"Understood, sir."

"How many?"

"Seven. Five wounded. And eighteen dead."

Bannon nodded. He'd ordered Mzobe, Jade, and van Wyk's bodies moved to a walk-in freezer they found in the gourmet kitchen. The other bodies would remain where they lay until the *Lightfoot* arrived in the morning with a team to deal with them.

"There's also house staff. Three women, two men, and two young teenagers. A boy and a girl. They're only sixteen."

"Where are they now?"

"In the guesthouse as well," she said. "With Ellis and Connell, but up on the main floor, away from the prisoners."

"Probably trafficked victims. But keep an eye on them. You never know where their loyalties might lay. Great job, Charlotte. You and your team."

Ng smiled. "Put us on speed dial, sir. We're always ready."

"Make sure you all get something to eat. And drink. And, Lieutenant, I'm not a stickler for regulations if you catch my drift."

"Yes, sir. Like the ad said, we'll drink responsibly."

His satellite phone rang in his pocket. Bannon took it out and checked the screen. He held it up. "The boss. Got to take this. Excuse me."

"Of course." Ng left to take care of her people.

"General," Bannon said, answering the phone. "How are you?"

"Shouldn't that be my question to you?"

He smiled and crossed the portico. From behind the bar, he retrieved a beer from the icebox, popped off the top and took a long sip.

"The casualty list is high but one-sided. For us, a few cuts and scrapes and a twisted ankle. Otherwise, we're all in one piece. The van Wyks, Mzobe, and most of their private army are dead. Ng and her people are guarding the few survivors we've got from that lot and a handful of house staff van Wyk had. They're being looked after as well."

"The one survivor from the hit squad sent after you and John in the harbor, when we told him van Wyk was done for, he suddenly knew English very well and demanded a lawyer."

"Dangle the right deal," Bannon said. "He'll talk. If you were facing five life sentences, wouldn't you?"

"That's what the legal eagles are working on now."

Bannon left the portico. He crossed through the gathering room. McMurphy had built a roaring fire in the stone fireplace. The wood-paneled room, with its timber ceiling and heavy leather furniture, had a cozy feel despite its overly masculine trappings. Akin to a hunting lodge in the mountains. They'd yet to restore main power, but the hum of smaller, portable generators provided electricity to sections of the guesthouse and the north wing of the main house.

"This house staff. Are they all right? Have they been abused?"

"It doesn't appear so. Surely, they were employed against their will, trafficked. Like the others."

Bannon entered a wing off to the right, where Kayla sat at a massive mahogany desk. Her focus was on a laptop computer screen. Stacks of papers and files covered the work surface of the desk. A printer in the corner whirled, spitting out page after page of what looked to Bannon to be ledger spreadsheets.

Tara had a large filing cabinet open. She poured through hanging folders, extracting files and placing them on a table under an ornate lamp with a multicolored, stained-glass shade.

"Kayla and Blades have found a treasure trove of financial and banking documents, company records—"

Kayla glanced up. Her skin was awash in blue from the glow of the computer screen. Her scrapes were treated and looked less ugly. Her blackened eye was still a mess but would heal. She mouthed, *Grayson?*

Bannon nodded.

"Tell her I've uploaded dozens of records to her office. Of most importance, there's a ship preparing to leave Namibia the day after tomorrow. If these files are correct, there'll be more women onboard. Bound for here. I've forwarded the registry and other shipping information."

Bannon relayed the information. "She's got it and is putting a team on it right now."

Bannon gave Kayla a wink. Good work.

"We found the stolen hard drive from the dry cleaner," Tara said. "The video is a complete recording of Jade and Mzobe's massacre of Kwon and his people. There's no question of their guilt. Dozens of other records document her full involvement in every aspect of van Wyk's illegal operations."

"Nicely done." He patted Tara's shoulder before leaving the room.

In the corridor, he found Parker examining a large, irregularly cut yellow stone under a display glass. The gem had an interesting green glow to it. Excited, she said, "Brice, have you any idea what this is?"

Bannon frowned and shook his head.

"It's the Florentine Diamond. Can you believe that?"

Bannon's expression conveyed his continued ignorance.

"A crown jewel. Taken by Emperor Charles I of Austria into exile when his empire fell after World War I. It was stolen sometime after that. In 1918, it was reportedly seen in South America, then later brought to the United States. It was believed to have been recut, butchered, basically, and resold. Do you know what this means?"

Bannon guessed. "It wasn't. And it's very valuable?"

Parker sighed. "A hundred years ago, it was thought to be worth three-quarters of a million dollars."

Bannon whistled. "That's valuable."

Over the phone, Grayson asked, "What of the Honjō Masamune sword?"

"The Secretary wants to know the status of the Honjō sword?"

Parker's features darkened. Became as scarlet as her mane of red hair. A crimson storm of anger. "Once we get it cleaned up—"

"Did she say 'cleaned up?'" Grayson asked. "What the hell did you do, Brice?"

Bannon ignored the question and signaled for Parker to continue.

"I've got several reputable appraisers on standby. It'll be examined thoroughly once we return to the mainland. If the sword is, in fact, the Honjō Masamune, and it's undamaged," again she gave Bannon the evil eye, "we'll make arrangements to return it to the Japanese people. Among much fanfare, I would presume."

Bannon passed along the information.

"What did she mean 'if undamaged?'" Grayson insisted.

"The sword's in good hands, General. Being well taken care of."

Parker still glowered at him.

Bannon returned to the gathering room, then strolled out to the portico again. The rain had let up even more. The steel gray clouds had started to part over the horizon, dissipating in ribbons across a brighter but still purple sky. Promising a clear red dawn.

Grayson sighed, revealing her exasperation with Bannon. A state she often found herself in when dealing with him and his team. Speaking of which, "And John. How's he?"

Bannon glanced at McMurphy. He'd found a stashed chaise lounge and set it up under the overhang. He stared out into the rain. With his feet up and his boots off, he had a beer bottle in his hand. Two empties were already on the side table next to him.

"John?" Bannon asked. To McMurphy, he said, "The General wants to know how you're doing?"

McMurphy opened his half-closed eyes and raised his bottle. "Living the dream, Lizzie."

"He's in seventh heaven drinking a Westies 12."

"A what?"

"A Westvleteren 12. It's some kind of rare Belgian Quadruple beer brewed by Trappist monks in Vleteren, Belgium. I only know that because Skyjack told me. Twice."

"I hope he's enjoying it."

McMurphy nodded, closed his eyes, and settled his head back down.

"And the Airbus?" she asked. "I trust it's in pristine condition."

"The helicopter, General?" Bannon asked.

McMurphy sat bolt upright. His eyes popped open wide. He shook his head violently and made a frantic cutting motion across his throat. Bannon glanced out over the infinity pool to the beach below. The storm had put the fire out. The chopper sat where it had landed, a blackened husk of metal and melted glass and parts. The rotor blades drooped sadly. The cowl had a sort of sad, weeping, frowny bend to it.

"It's… well, it's…. "

McMurphy mouthed; *No. No. No.*

Bannon had trouble holding back his laughter. "I'll let Skyjack explain. When he sees you."

McMurphy threw his arms up in disbelief. Mouthing: *Really, dude?*

"Put him on the phone," Grayson demanded. "Now!"

Bannon frowned and stepped back inside the house. "General, there's something else. Something more important we need to talk about right now… "

CHAPTER FORTY-TWO

BANNON TOOK HIS PHONE call into the kitchen. Other than in a restaurant, Bannon had never seen as large or as magnificent a kitchen as this one. It had a commercial gas range with wrought iron grates, two double ovens, an open-face brick pizza oven, two oversized stainless-steel refrigerators, rich cherry wood cabinets, and granite countertops, with inlaid lighting and more pots and pans hanging from racks than an Army chef could ever use in a lifetime feeding a battalion of soldiers.

He moved past all that to the full-size, walk-in freezer. He pulled the heavy latch, opening the door. A cold cloud of air billowed out. He left the door standing open and went inside.

The sound of the nearby generator used to power the unit was loud, causing the floor to hum.

Still on the call, Grayson said, "I'm in the Oval Office with the President now, Brice."

As he'd walked through van Wyk's island getaway, she'd made her way through the White House.

"You two alone?" he asked.

"You're on speaker phone, son. Just us." President David Kingsley owed his life to Bannon, and both men knew it. It had earned Bannon some leeway with the man and a certain level of trust. An earned faith Bannon was careful not to abuse. That said, he was also happy to use it as needed to cut through the infamous bureaucracy that was the federal government.

"When was the last time the office was swept for bugs?"

"Last night. As it is every morning and night, Brice," Grayson said. "What is going on?"

Still, Bannon was cautious.

Over the past week, it had become increasingly clear the chain of command had been compromised. There was a mole, or moles, in very highly placed positions. How high up and how many, he couldn't say. But all the way up to the Oval Office wasn't an unrealistic assumption. Nor was it unreasonable to assume such highly placed assets could be in charge of the White House security sweeps. They could falsely report untrue findings. Or plant bugs of their own.

Bannon implicitly trusted Grayson. They'd known each other, worked with each other, for over a decade. But he wasn't going to take any chances. As for Kingsley. What choice did he have? He was the President, after all.

The man had also almost been killed a few months ago at Tiamat Bluff when a hit squad abducted him and Grayson with the express purpose of assassinating them. So, he had that in his favor.

Bannon did trust the security of the sat phone connection he used. The encryption software had been installed and regularly monitored and updated by Kayla Clarke. "I'm going to send you a photo. Do not discuss it. Delete the picture immediately after you've viewed it."

"Understood."

Inside the freezer, Ng and her team had cleared off space on three shelves. There they'd laid out the bodies of Bernardor van Wyk, Jade, and Mzobe. Each was wrapped in plastic tarps they'd found in an equipment shed down at the dock.

Bannon unwrapped the plastic around van Wyk and spread the lapels of his smoking jacket. Underneath, he had on a black t-shirt. Bannon had already sliced through that. He spread the bloody material and snapped a picture of the dead man's chest. The pectoral over his heart. He uploaded it to Grayson's phone.

While he waited, he draped the plastic tarp over the body and face, covering him up completely once more. Bannon left the freezer and shut the door. In the kitchen, he shivered. From the cold in the refrigerator, assuredly, but it felt like a ghost had stepped through his body.

Bannon asked, "Got it?"

A moment passed.

"Yes, we have it. I've just deleted it."

Bannon looked at the image of the man's chest on his phone.

Tattooed into van Wyk's upper chest was a dragon surrounded by seaweed and waves. An intricate, dramatic, highly detailed work of art. Bannon had seen this tattoo before. He'd discovered it on Chase Lang's right wrist. The man who had led the death squad that tried to kill Grayson and Kingsley while they visited Tiamat Bluff.

During the siege of the experimental prototype city under the sea, Bannon and his people had learned of the existence of what was shaping up to be a vast, possibly worldwide, deep-state conspiracy called Leviathan. Their goals, purpose, and how widespread this cabal—if that's what it was—might be was all still a mystery.

"You understand it's significance."

"We do," President Kingsley said.

Bannon deleted the photo from his phone, the same as he'd instructed Grayson to do.

"In his final moments, van Wyk spoke in terms of global thinking. He pontificated on the idea that funding, the financial gains of his operations, his human and drug trafficking rings, his taking over the criminal syndicate here in the Northeast. All of that was but a means to a goal. Not the endgame."

"Brice," Grayson said. "Something's happened here. You and your team need to get to Washington. As soon as possible."

EPILOGUE

Maritime Museum & Gift Shop
Kittery, M.A.

ONE WEEK LATER, PARKER Quinn stepped out of the government car. Behind a big pair of sunglasses, she glanced up at the sign over the museum door. She wore her hair big and bouncy, a riot of bright red follicles. Her Anne Taylor suit too warm for the sticky, humid day.

After leaving Versteek Island via the early morning arrival of the *Lightfoot*, Parker bid her goodbyes to Bannon and his team. A finer lot of operatives than she'd ever had the privilege to work with. She told them that. And got an honest-to-goodness hug from Skyjack McMurphy.

Yet, he still refused to tell her how he'd earned his peculiar nickname.

"Maybe next time," he said.

Though she was worn slap out, the rest of the week was spent working with appraisers—government and otherwise—to authenticate the recovered Truman swords and the Honjō Masamune. Neither had been verified or confirmed yet, though Parker was confident they would be soon. She'd also led a team of investigators, armed with federal search warrants, on a raid of Peter Jorgen's home. His expression upon seeing her with the federal SWAT and forensics teams had been priceless. Snapping cuffs on him had also been more satisfying than she'd have thought.

Now, she smiled at the memory, cradling an item in a small, black velvet bag cinched with gold braided tassels. Stepping through the old museum's front door, she removed her oversized sunglasses. The old ship's bell overhead rang. She drank in the rich, teak oil scent that filled the main showroom.

Thaddeus Michael Perry looked up from his place behind the sales counter. His ancient face broke into a wide grin. His deep blue eyes sparkled with delight. "Now, ain't this a wonderful surprise."

"How do, Thaddeus," she said.

"Rumor is you and Brice did it," he said. "You two found the Honjō Masamune."

She smiled. "We did. There's still work to be done, but I'm confident the perfect sword will be returned home to Japan and to the Japanese people where it belongs."

She placed the black velvet bag on the sales counter.

"What's this?" Perry asked.

Rather than answering, she glanced at the old wine barrel.

Perry smiled. "Go ahead. Ever hear of Kate the Great?"

Parker removed the barrel lid and stared down at the dark beer bottles sticking out of a sea of ice. She extracted two.

"It's a Russian imperial stout. Brewed by the Portsmouth Brewery. The first and oldest brewpub in New Hampshire."

He waved for her to pass the beers to him, using a 1950s bar blade to pop off the caps. "Some say it's the best and most sought-after beer in America."

Parker took a heavy pull and smiled. "Ah. Yup. That's a good one."

The old man drank but couldn't keep his eyes off the black bag, like a little kid eyeing a present under the tree on Christmas morning.

"Go on. Open it."

Perry's aged and weathered hands pulled the tassels and opened the bag. His hands were remarkably steady for a man of his years. He shook out the item and nearly gasped at the clasp knife now in his hand.

Not much different than modern-day folding knives, the clasp knife had a hinged blade that folded into a slot in the handle so that it could be safely carried in a pocket or hidden out of sight in a fisted hand. This one was made of rusted steel and wood. Unremarkable in every way except that it was old.

When she had first visited Thaddeus with Bannon and McMurphy, his interest in Jorgen piqued her curiosity. She'd returned to the shop to talk to the old man about it further under the guise of having left her cell phone behind.

She asked Perry straight up. "What's your interest in Jorgen? It's something personal, isn't it?"

He confessed. Jorgen had an item, the clasp knife, in his collection. An item Perry once possessed. Stolen by Jorgen. All of Perry's efforts to get it back had been for naught.

"What's its significance, Thaddeus?"

"It was recovered from a shipwreck off the coast of Cape Cod nearly forty years ago. A British collier called the *General James Carden*. Sunk in 1785. I was working with a salvage team that discovered the wreck. We brought up a treasure trove of relics from it. Just five miles out from Providence Town. Among the recovered items was this knife."

Parker frowned. "It doesn't seem particularly valuable."

"It's not," Perry admitted. "Not to anyone but me. Which was why Jorgen wouldn't give it up. He and I... I didn't tell you and Brice before. Jorgen and I had history, even beyond," he heaved the clasp knife, "this."

Parker got that. She had a few adversaries in her rogue's gallery as well.

"But the knife?"

"It belonged to the captain," Perry said. "Gabriel Thaddeus Perry. My great-great-great-something grandfather."

He wiped a tear from his cheek, squeezing the clasp knife tightly in his hand. "I am forever grateful to you for this, Parker. Thank you."

She smiled. This was why she did what she did. The warm fuzzies she got when reuniting lost and stolen artifacts with their rightful owners. The gratitude, the emotional connection people had with certain items, the bonds with history, sometimes, as in Perry's case, was often deeply personal. It filled her with a fulfilling, giddy satisfaction.

Parker tapped her beer bottle to his. "My genuine pleasure."

Perry raised his beer and toasted Parker, stealing a line from Casablanca. "I think this could be the start of a beautiful relationship, Parker Quinn."

\#

AUTHOR'S NOTES

The Isles of Shoals is an actual archipelago of islands straddling the borders of New Hampshire and Maine in the Gulf of Maine. In the real world, the Isles are comprised of only nine islands, not ten.

Versteek Island is a wholly constructed product of my imagination.

As of this writing, and to my knowledge, there are no year-round residents living on any of the islands. Certainly, none like the fictional Bernardor van Wyk of the fictional Versteek Island.

At least, I hope not.

I do hope you enjoyed *Crimson Storm.*

David DeLee

Thank you for purchasing this book. We hope you enjoyed it.

If you'd like to stay informed about new releases, special events, and exclusive content only available to subscribers, sign up to get David DeLee's newsletter

https://www.subscribepage.com/daviddelee

And don't forget to check out David DeLee's other pulse-pounding crime thriller series.

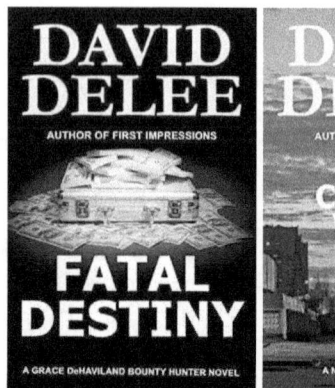

ALSO BY DAVID DELEE

Brice Bannon Seacoast Adventures
Crimson Storm
Siege at Tiamat Bluff
The Yakuza Gambit
Strike of the Stingray
The Oceanic Princess
Facing the Storm

Nick Lafferty Crime Thrillers
Cold Cases
Out of the Game
Crystal White

Flynn & Levy Police Thrillers
Between Truth and Lies
While the City Burns
Moral Misconduct

Grace deHaviland Bounty Hunter Series
Too Far
Stare at the Moon
Takedown
With Intent to Deceive
Pin Money
Fatal Destiny
Runners

ABOUT THE AUTHOR

David DeLee is the award-winning author of the Grace
deHaviland Bounty Hunter series. In addition to the novels,
he's written many short stories featuring Grace, most notably
Bling, Bling, which appeared in the anthology *The Rich and
the Dead,* edited by Nelson DeMille.

David's other work includes his Nick Lafferty thrillers. The
first-in-the-series, *Crystal White.* SUSPENSE MAGAZINE
called "...a dark portrayal of the evil that men—and
women—can do." He's also written the Flynn & Levy police
procedurals and the Brice Bannon Seacoast Adventures, the
latest being *Crimson Storm.*

A member of the Mystery Writers of America and
the International Thriller Writers Organization and a
former licensed private investigator, David also holds a
Master's Degree in Criminal Justice. He makes his home
in New Hampshire.

For more information, join David's newsletter:
https://www.subscribepage.com/daviddelee

Dark Road
PUBLISHING